The
Honey
Village Diaries

Kate Forster is the bestselling author of *Starting Over at Acorn Cottage*, *The Perfect Retreat*, *Finding Love at Mermaid Terrace* and many more books that she would want to read herself, so she wrote them. When not writing, Kate loves hanging out with family, friends, and her dogs. A dedicated houseplant lover, Kate also enjoys outdoor gardening and is the founder and moderator of one of the largest online women's writing support groups on Facebook.

The Honeystone Village Diaries

Kate Forster

ORION

First published in Great Britain in 2024 by Orion Fiction
an imprint of The Orion Publishing Group Ltd
Carmelite House, 50 Victoria Embankment
London EC4Y ODZ

An Hachette UK Company

1 3 5 7 9 10 8 6 4 2

A CIP catalogue record for this book is
available from the British Library.

ISBN (Paperback) 978 1 3987 1785 5
ISBN (eBook) 978 1 3987 1786 2

Typeset at The Spartan Press Ltd,
Lymington, Hants

Printed and bound in Great Britain by Clays Ltd,
Elcograf S.p.A.

www.orionbooks.co.uk

To my Funts – Rah and J.
Thank you for the best group chat, dinners, music recs, film recs, TV recs, brunches, fashion critiques, award show tea, memes, and love. Lucky me to have you two!

I

Anthea

The people of the small village of Honeystone should have known that change was coming when a once in a lifetime wind blew through their streets in early March, causing chaos and conversation for at least two weeks.

The event was even shown on the local news, where weather experts proclaimed it as a mini tornado, previously unheard of for the area.

Thankfully, evidence of the uncommon event was provided to the local news station by Barry Mundy's dashboard camera from his beloved Audi. This remarkable footage showed the vortex that carried Jenn Carruthers's clothes horse, still pegged with her unmentionables, and the recycling bins from the church hall, filled with empty wine bottles that shattered on the road. No one in Honeystone has yet owned up to hiding their wine bottle collection in the church hall bins but since the tornado, the bins were no longer used for hiding their sins.

Selling the video footage was the smartest thing Barry Mundy had done in the last ten years. After selling the footage to the news station, he promptly bought new seat covers for his Audi and a new tennis racket for his upcoming tennis party. It was a party he had yet to receive any RSVPs for, but this story isn't completely about Barry's tennis party.

This story starts with Spindle Hall. The old house in the valley, once a grand country pile, had been empty – aside from a flock of pigeons living in the roof – for fifty-five years. This was the same number of years its new owner, Anthea McGregor, had turned around the sun. If this was of any importance, no one could tell the residents of Honeystone because the wise women in the area had been burned centuries ago. The only harbingers of change were the unusual wind and new signs on the fence telling people to stay out of the grounds of Spindle Hall.

There was a drawing done of the wind arriving at the village the day before it arrived, but that was done by a small child named Clover Hinch who people dismissed because she was a child, and everyone knows that grown-ups don't listen to children enough. If they had noticed her drawing in her notebook, they would have seen the bottles flying through the air along with a pair of M&S cotton knickers and a single sock.

The signs around Spindle Hall were not welcomed by the locals, as the grounds had been used by the villagers for half a century as a place to walk their dogs and to collect chestnuts from the trees, grown from the seeds of the seeds of the Romans eons before.

Now there were ugly coloured signs in neon colours that read – **Keep Out.**

Jenn Carruthers had taken photos of the angry-looking signs and sent them to the village WhatsApp group with an angry face emoji to show her feelings about the matter.

Barry Mundy said he would take it up with the council and to stay tuned. No one wanted to tune into anything Barry was broadcasting but Jenn sent him a thumbs up emoji just to let him know his message had been received.

And now, exactly one month after the wind came through

the village, on the first Tuesday in April, the large oak door of Spindle Hall, carved with three hares in a circle, was flung open by Anthea McGregor herself, who was breathing in the country air and filled with hope after eighteen months of despair.

Anthea had arrived at Spindle Hall bringing with her potions and tinctures and a reputation and bank balance as the most successful perfumer in England, and an assumption that the villagers of Honeystone would leave her alone.

But change doesn't come alone, and with Anthea came plans for Spindle Hall, its grounds and an ambition that Honeystone hadn't seen the likes of since Barry ran for Mayor, which was a bit misleading as it was a token role, mostly for tourism reasons, and Barry didn't want tourists. He liked Honeystone exactly as it was, claiming tourists would bring in all sorts of issues, from crime to the black plague. Imagine his consternation when the final vote went to Robert Grayling who owned The Hare and Thistle, the three-hundred-year-old pub positioned slap bang in the middle of the small village.

Barry took the news of his defeat as well as Jenn Carruthers took to seeing her knickers on the news. There was a tantrum, a letter to the *Honeystone Herald*, and a petition left at the doctor's surgery asking for a recount. The only person who signed it was Dora, his wife, and by the looks of the shaky signature, it wouldn't have been unreasonable to assume it was signed under duress.

But back to Honeystone, which people might have said was slow on the uptake of anything. They were the last to get fibre optic cable and the new bus route from Cirencester, and while it looked like time had stopped with the centuries old honey-walled houses that gave the village its name, the narrow streets and the small stream that ran through the village with a bridge that took one car at a time across the flowing water, it wasn't a complete backwater. It simply needed time to adjust to new ideas.

It was situated outside of the Cotswolds by a mere mile, and purists over the years had insisted Honeystone was hard done by in the original cartography of the area. But many of the villagers were glad to not be included in travels of the tourists on the large air-conditioned coaches that stopped for photos at the Castle Combe bridge, dreaming of being the newest members of the Crawley family from *Downton Abbey*.

They didn't mind Honeystone being looked over by the interlopers who wore bumbags and sneakers and asked if there was dairy-free clotted cream at Mabel's Table, the small tea rooms that only opened on the weekends, where the scones were the size of saucers and the height of teapots according to the guidebook she had picked up at the pub (written by Jenn Carruthers with illustrations by Dora Mundy).

It was exactly these reasons why Anthea had chosen Honeystone as the place for her next dream. On her first trip to Honeystone, she had said to her business team – two English pointers, Rupert and Taggie – that it would be perfect for her plans. She had tea at Mabel's Table and felt comforted by the lack of interested in her.

On her second trip to Honeystone, she had noticed the small doctor's surgery, with a vacant sign on the front with **Doctor Wanted** written on it in a stern-looking font.

There was a church hall but no church, as it had burned down twenty years before according to the small guidebook.

The third time she came to Honeystone, she had stopped at a small grocery shop called Biddy's Bits and Bites. The sign read that the store sold organic wine and when she peered through the window, she could see cane baskets and expensive chocolates and nougats with edible flowers on top and a lack of customers but it was always closed with a sign in the window reading *Back Soon.*

Anthea had decided Honeystone was the perfect place to recover from two years of illness and find out who she really was without her gift, and Spindle Hall was a fine old house to hide in. She didn't want to meet anyone, become friends with anyone, do anything to become a part of the community of Honeystone. She would be more than happy sitting in her house in the valley, plotting and planning the potions she would create that would bring her ex-husband to his knees.

Peony

Peony Grayling assumed she had been robbed when she first arrived home to the flat in Islington that she shared with her boyfriend of ten years, Fergus.

The door slammed behind her as Peony hefted the bags of shopping through the door.

'Any help?' she called out as she walked into the small kitchen. She was planning on making beef bourguignon and then crêpes for dessert, with a little array of toppings including her favourite lemon and sugar and Fergus's favourite of Nutella and banana. Peony had a gift for knowing what food people needed to get through the worst and the best of life.

There was her wonderful chicken Marbella filled with garlic and red wine vinegar and oregano and bay leaves that she made for people who were moving into a new home, or for those friends who needed a little bit of nurturing. If Peony had bothered to look into why the food resonated so, she would have learned that ingredients in the dish all had a meaning. Everything has a meaning in life but Peony cooked without knowing that bay leaves were once used for protection, salt for purification, vinegar for health, plums for love and apricot for reviving the spirit.

That the Egyptians used pumpkins as a symbol of good luck and fortune, and the Greeks as a symbol of fertility, was lost on Peony yet she always made her delicious pumpkin soup for friends who were trying to become pregnant, served with her beautiful olive focaccia with extra salt on top.

But Peony didn't know anything about such malarkey, she just did what her soul told her to do, and sometimes that's more than enough knowledge to have. It was simply a shame that Peony didn't listen to her soul in other areas of her life.

In the kitchen the cupboards were open and she saw a few plates and cups on the bench.

'Ferge?' She called again, putting the bags on the floor.

There was no answer as she walked to the living room and saw the PlayStation was gone, and the stereo, and the *Kill Bill* poster above their sofa.

'Oh no,' she said aloud and she pulled her phone from the pocket of her coat and dialled Fergus's number.

She went to the bedroom, where the door was ajar. She kicked the door open, her throat in her stomach and made what she hoped was a threatening karate pose.

The bedroom was empty, but the wardrobe's door was open.

She looked and saw Fergus's shirts were gone, along with his shoes.

'Peony?' She heard Fergus's voice on the end of the phone.

'We've been robbed,' she said. 'They took all your underwear, that's so odd, like a reverse snowdropper – that's the name for a man who steals women's underwear. What do

6

they call a man or a woman who steals male underwear? Brown dropper?'

She laughed at her own joke, despite a gnawing feeling this wasn't a normal robbery.

She had pulled open his bedside table and saw his cufflinks and old watch were gone and left were an old condom wrapper and some coins.

'Fergus?' She walked to the wardrobe and saw the empty hangers.

'Peony,' he said again and she sat on the edge of the bed.

'We haven't been robbed?' she asked.

'No.'

There was silence.

'Peony,' he said again.

'Stop saying my name and tell me what you've done.'

'I've left,' he said.

'You've gone?' Her stomach rolled and bile was in her throat.

'It was time, we both knew it,' he said in his thick Scottish accent. It was at its most smooth when he was trying to convince Peony of anything.

'No, we didn't know it. Why didn't you talk to me?'

'Peony, you know you're terrible at endings.'

He always did this.

'Don't make this about my failings, Fergus.' God, she hated it when he turned it around on her.

'I was going to leave you anyway,' she said and felt petty but better for being honest.

'You weren't, Peony, you just asked a lot of people and didn't do anything about it, like you always do. I know because the man at the off-licence asked if you'd gone yet, and Gerald at the football club told me you had asked his wife what to do when you were watching me play a game for feck's sake. You knew what you had to do and you couldn't do it. Neither of us could for a long time, until now.'

Peony was silent. If there was one thing in life that Peony knew it was that you needed to make the change in your life before life made the change for you. Because if you didn't make your own move then the outcome was brutal, unflinchingly cruel and often, with a sense of humour that would make you shake your head in ten years and say, I should have known.

Peony knew what she had to do except she was avoiding the issue, the discomfort of change, like wearing too tight pants during a job interview, knowing you had to go a size up but feeling uneasy at the new number on the label. Denial wasn't just a river in Egypt.

Peony had seen it in the hospital where she worked as a social worker. The man who knew he hated the job he was in, talking about leaving for the past ten years and then one day being diagnosed with a cancer that was probably preventable if he had listened to his body and been kinder to himself.

The woman who put off having a baby even though her arms ached to hold a child until it was too late and her eggs were no longer viable and her hopes dashed after expensive and failed fertility treatment.

Peony knew all this and yet she couldn't make the move. She dithered and went back and forth in her decision, even asking strangers their opinion of her options, including a lady in the brown raincoat in Asda who was only checking to see if the avocados were ripe and didn't want to have to advise a stranger on her future. She was simply looking for a nice avocado.

So while Peony was still collating the data and opinions from her random vox pop surveys, the decision had been made for her. And this is where we find Peony on the worst day of her life so far in her thirty-four years.

'I had to be brave enough for both of us,' he said.

She rolled her eyes. 'You're not a live organ donor, Fergus, come down off the cross.' The line went dead. He had hung up on her.

She opened the drawer in his bedside table and saw an empty condom wrapper. They never used condoms.

Who had he cheated on her with? Probably Roxy from the football club. She was always hanging around and asking him to say things in his Glaswegian accent, which he dialled up for her benefit. Roxy with the big boobs and hair extensions. Fergus was such a cliché, she thought. She squeezed her eyes tightly, trying to make tears fall but nothing came out. She tried again, thinking about the good times but they were so long ago, vague, like ideas more than memories.

Maybe this was shock, she thought. This was why she couldn't feel anything.

And why wouldn't he choose Roxy over her. Peony with her dishwater blonde hair, thin from straightening it too much in her twenties.

Peony had no place to go, and no money and no prospects. She felt like a supporting character in an Austen book, but it was worse for her, because she didn't have a chance of marrying for convenience. She was alone on a shitty social worker wage, in a city where the price of everything was going up, while her wage wasn't, and she hated her job. She was burned out and on her last nerve.

There was only one place she could go.

For the record, the lady in the brown raincoat had told her in no uncertain terms, if you're not married after ten years it's bad luck to marry. 'No point,' she had said, 'everyone knows that.' Peony hadn't known that but she did now.

Izzy

The power of planting a seed and watching it grow and unfurl into a healthy plant never failed to amaze Izzy Hinch, which was a hard task because Izzy was born under a balsamic moon and thus, she was slightly vinegary for a woman of twenty-five. Izzy hated more than she liked. She suffered no fools, and the only thing she truly loved was her niece, Clover June, and her garden at the house on her parents' orchard, named Raspberry Hill Farm although it primarily grew apples. Nothing made much sense in Honeystone so no one bothered to correct it, but Izzy capitulated to the house's moniker and had large areas of raspberry canes growing. Her niece Clover would pick and eat them, her hands and mouth stained with the crimson juice while claiming to Izzy she hadn't taken a single one from the canes.

Everything seemed easier when Izzy was in the garden. She would rise in the morning before Clover woke, and she would slip into her gardening clogs, taking her strong cup of tea out into the garden, surveying the beds and the growth and any damage from animals or slugs overnight.

There was nothing quite so satisfying as growing your own food, Izzy would say to anyone who would listen, and eating something that you grew, well that came with a sense of freedom that was hard to explain and also a sense of smugness that if the apocalypse came, Izzy would be prepared to feed her brother and her niece and anyone else that she thought was worthy of survival in Honeystone.

To date, the list of survivors who would receive cabbages and tomatoes from Izzy's garden was small but Izzy had not yet learned that forgiveness was as liberating to a person as growing food from tiny seeds is.

After a day in the garden, Izzy would stand under a hot shower and let it wash the dirt from her and she would think about how everything made sense in the garden. The scent of the tomato leaves on her hand in the summer and the scent of woodfire from burning the leaves in winter were her anchors in a world where everything seemed a little unknown outside of Honeystone.

And yet, she hated Honeystone and its smallness. The everydayness of the same routines, the same people, the same shops, nothing ever happened in Honeystone. Even when the strange wind came through, the only thing that had happened to Raspberry Hill Farm was the roof of the potting shed lifted up and dropped down again.

Thankfully her garden had remained untouched. There were six raised beds filled with vegetables and herbs, beautifully planted with flowers for pollinators and everything with a companion plant to support the other. And while Izzy didn't have any friends in the village, or nearby, she found friends in the garden. The lace-winged bugs that ate the thrip on the roses, the damsel bugs that ate the destructive caterpillars on her lettuces and the elegant praying mantis, who coolly and calmly ate the crickets and moths like a garden ninja.

Nothing in the garden asked her about what she wanted to do next with her life, like people did with their nosy questions. Had she thought about travelling? Had she considered finishing her university degree? Had she thought about what she would do when Clover was at a mainstream school every day? What then? But Izzy didn't know what she wanted to do in life other than be in the garden and care for Clover.

The sense of comfort Izzy had when she was holding Clover, explaining to her how the tiny buds would turn into peppers or tomatoes, when she showed her the bee looking like it had slippers made of pollen, and when she put her hands into the earth and excused herself to the worms that wriggled away, that's when Izzy felt important and special.

This particular morning, her brother Connor was outside drinking tea when Izzy opened the kitchen door as the sun was rising. He was tall and had messy curly hair that he didn't like to cut often as he said it was a waste of time and money. His face was tired and he was wearing his usual garden outfit of blue work trousers, boots, a warm cream jumper that Clary had knitted him and a gilet with many pockets in it to store his knives, string, grafting tape and mints. Connor always had a mint in his mouth when he was working, and when he wasn't, he was sipping on a cup of tea or a cider after work.

'You're up earlier than usual,' he said.

'Couldn't sleep,' she answered. She went inside and poured herself a mug of tea from the pot that Connor had brewed.

'Why couldn't you sleep?' Connor was back inside now, leaning against the bench.

Izzy didn't answer the question. 'Do you think the school will cope with the wheelchair if she needs it?'

'Yes, they have already said they will, and she's becoming stronger so she won't need it as often, the physiotherapist said.'

Izzy sniffed her disdain.

'I don't like that new physio,' she said.

'That's because she's encouraging Clover to be more independent. I know you want to protect her forever but at some stage you have to untie the stake and let her strengthen on her own. A few little gusts of wind might knock her over a bit but we won't let her uproot, you know that, don't you?'

It wasn't lost on Izzy that Connor wrapped Clover's

evolution in a garden metaphor but she didn't dislike it. It made sense. For the past seven years Connor and Izzy had stood on either side of Clover, propping her up until she was ready to stand on her own. And she was now ready.

But Izzy was struggling to truly relax into the idea of Clover's independence, even though she knew that Clover would never thrive while she held onto her so tightly.

'I heard there's more wind coming,' she said, changing the subject. If allowed, she could catastrophise all the things that could go wrong for Clover over the next eighty years of her life, but she knew Connor didn't want to hear it. Was she the only one that worried about Clover the way she did?

'It's OK, I've secured the roof of the potting shed. It was so odd when that wind came through last time. The roof of the shed actually went up and down, as though it was tipping its hat in a greeting to something.' He laughed and Izzy smiled to humour him but something made her turn to look out of the kitchen window towards Spindle Hall.

The old house overlooked their farm, their land merged at the stone fence, the titles were unclear as to where it started and finished but there had never been an issue between the Hinch family and the former Dow family of Spindle Hall. But they were long gone and Spindle Hall had been left vacant from before Izzy was born.

Taking the small pair of binoculars, she had on the windowsill to spot birds in the garden and identify them with Clover, she looked at the house and saw the front door was open.

Surely it wasn't trespassers. She put her hand up to her eyes, to block out the sun and to get a clearer view.

There was a truck now, a large one, that looked more like a construction truck than a moving van.

'There's movement up at Spindle Hall,' she said to Connor.

'OK, Mrs Curtain Twitcher, you better let the Honeystone WhatsApp chat know.' Connor laughed at her.

Izzy turned to her brother. 'Aren't you even a bit interested in knowing who is at the house? There are trucks and everything.'

He laughed at her. 'Not really, if they want to know who we are, they will come and find out.'

'But there seems to be lots of movement,' she said.

Connor put some tea in his Thermos and Izzy went back to looking through the lenses at Spindle Hall.

'You are no better than Jenn Carruthers, and yet you claim to hate it here and still you want to know what's going on.'

Connor was right about her being nosy but there was something else.

Change was in the air and it was coming from Spindle Hall. Or was it coming from her? Izzy couldn't put her finger on it but it wasn't Clover, it wasn't the garden and it wasn't Connor. Change was here and whatever was happening, she knew it couldn't be undone.

After Connor went to the orchard to check on his beloved apples, and Clover was up and had eaten breakfast and had done her physiotherapy exercises, Izzy went outside and cut some artichokes, put them in the basket and then sent a text to Connor.

She walked into the house where Clover was sitting in front of the television, watching Nigella Lawson and drawing. What other seven-year-old wanted to watch Nigella? But then Clover wasn't like other children.

'What are you drawing today?' asked Izzy. 'You still drawing roses? That's all I saw you working on last week. The big fat ones, I liked them a lot.'

Clover looked up at her aunt. 'The roses have gone from my mind now, now I'm drawing Eggmerelda, she's up on the roof,' she said.

'How did she get up there?' asked Izzy. 'Remember Eggmerelda doesn't fly and she only has one wing.' Izzy reminded her. 'But she's our best egg layer.'

'You told me when I was using my new walker that we can all do amazing things, why can't Eggmerelda do amazing things?'

Izzy laughed, 'She can, she lays eggs, now come on Nigella, we're going into the village.' She bent over and fixed the splints onto Clover's legs.

'To see Rob?' Clover asked as she spotted the artichokes in the basket. 'Nigella does a linguine with artichoke. Maybe the pub can do that for lunch?' Clover offered.

'Maybe,' Izzy said, as she resisted the urge to pull Clover to her feet, and waited for Clover to get up alone, as the occupational therapist had taught them.

'Ready?' Izzy asked her niece.

'Yep,' Clover said as she walked out of the house and towards the car, her face a picture of concentration; her glasses were on the end of her nose as she took the steps slowly. She looked like an old lady except for the baby doll under her arm, her hot pink dress and neon yellow trainers.

'I can show Rob my new trainers and how I walk in them.' Clover said as Izzy helped her into the car and pulled the seatbelt tight around her little thin frame.

No one understands or forgives a mother who leaves a child, although men do it every day. Clover's mother, Mel, left when Clover was still in the hospital and never came back, leaving her like a forgotten package at the post office.

Every step Clover made, every success, no matter how small, should have been celebrated by the woman who birthed her, instead Mel had gone into the world without a backwards glance at her child. And no one would tell them where she was, not even her parents who refused to answer Connor's calls or open the door to him, who returned the photos and cards until he stopped sending them. Izzy could never understand it but then again, Izzy didn't understand anything people did, especially those who hurt the ones they loved.

That's why Izzy had decided she would never fall in love. There was too much at stake and the only stakes she wanted were in her garden, not in her heart.

Dora

The winds had upset Dora Mundy but not in the way you might expect. Dora had actually hoped the winds would lift her up from Honeystone and deliver her to another village, along with Jenn Carruthers's unmentionables, and Dora would have a new name, her own bank account and a life as cosy and as simple as possible.

In her imaginary life, Dora would draw every day, and have cats and a windowsill where she could cool the bread she had baked and that looked out over a lovely vegetable garden. She has seen Izzy Hinch's garden which was a chaotic yet ordered tumble of flowers and produce all mixed together and that was what she saw when she imagined her own garden. Dora would have been the mother of a daughter who she loved and who loved her in return and she would make them paper dolls with all sorts of funny outfits that she would draw and paint herself, and they would eat jam sandwiches for lunch and plan parties for just the two of them.

But instead, her view from the kitchen window looked out over the garage where Barry parked his prized Audi. There was no bread being baked as Barry was very anti carbohydrates and also allergic to cats. As for children, Barry had never wanted them, even though he told her when they first went out that he was open to having them.

And over the years, he'd told her it was never the right time, until one day it was too late. Tests showed that Dora's eggs were scrambled and Barry refused to even consider medical help to get pregnant. And that's when Dora started to drink.

Today was Thursday and Dora arrived at The Hare and Thistle for her shift, aware that lunch wouldn't be served that day, not since the cook had run away with some equipment, leaving the pub in the lurch, food-wise.

The cook wasn't any good, his vegetable soup was almost a punishment, Dora had thought after she had tried some one winter, but Dora wondered if Robert would be able to keep the pub open without serving food.

She opened the downstairs door with her key and turned on the lights. Robert was probably upstairs, doing his word puzzles, she thought as she set up the bar for the day. Lunch would usually be served in the next hour, but now it was just drinks and a packet of crisps available.

Her phone chimed in her pocket and she looked at it and saw a message from Barry.

It was only ever Barry who called or texted her.

You at work?

Yes. She typed back.

There was a pause in the exchange and she waited. She was never sure if she should continue a text conversation with him as he was often dismissive, telling her he was busy or then telling her off for not replying. She never knew where she was with him.

Can you clean at the surgery after your shift. Everything is there.

She noticed he didn't leave a question mark with his question, so it wasn't a question, it was a command.

If she wasn't such a coward she would have texted back, clean it yourself, I have a shift at the pub, you aren't doing anything since you were let go from the accounting firm in Gloucester. He wasn't even an accountant, even though he told everyone he was, he was a finance administrator and not a very good one at that, judging from their precarious financial state.

But she didn't because it wasn't worth the drama it would create. Instead, she typed back that she would, and then slipped a cheap bottle of house wine from the fridge into her tote bag. Robert would never notice and she would drink it while she cleaned the surgery for the new doctor who was coming to Honeystone.

No doubt he would be like the last doctor, pathetic, under Barry's thumb again, telling him everything about everyone in the village. Not that she blamed him. Barry had that ability to make you feel like you were his best friend and then he turned on you, using your secrets as a weapon.

Dora hooked up the kegs and wiped down the bar and then went outside and put out the chalkboard sign stating the pub was open for business.

It would be slow, particularly now there wasn't a lunch on but still, it was better than being at home while Barry huffed about the house. He was planning a tennis party and since they didn't have the money they used to, Barry was insisting he would do it all himself, which really meant Dora would do it all.

Dora leaned against the counter and wondered what would have happened if the wind had swept her away, like a boat out to sea, no idea where she was going but hopeful that the destination was better than the starting point.

2

Peony

Old Ed, who came to the pub in Honeystone once a week for two ales and a steak pie always said that the wind on the hill at his farm was so strong, that if you weren't careful, it would blow the milk right out of your tea.

Peony thought about this saying as she steadied her car driving towards the village. The spring winds seemed to be exceptionally strong, the trees bending to the gusts as she drove down the narrow roads as Peony wondered why she hadn't left for Honeystone a year ago. A year ago, she knew it was all going to the dogs and yet she stayed. She stayed because of many reasons but above all, she stayed because she was loyal. Once, when she was younger and in love for the first time in her life, she had thought she would stay with that boy forever, but he pushed her away at the worst time in his life and even though she wanted to stay with him, she couldn't. There was no way she was leaving Fergus unless he left first, it was the principle, she told herself, even though the principle made her sad and depressed and slightly anxious.

What Peony hadn't learned yet, even now after coming home to an empty flat and her imagined future blown up, was that coming to a decision in your life was you finally understanding that you knew what you were going to do all along. It was inevitable that she and Fergus would end, perhaps she had known from the moment they began that it wasn't forever but still she'd stayed, despite her internal compass telling her to head another way. When had she stopped listening to herself? When was her heart broken for the first time? When her mum died? When she pretended she was asleep when Fergus came home late from the pub, smelling of another woman's perfume?

The problem was that Peony had always denied the inner knowledge she had about herself and what she knew she had to do. She had read the quotes that said use the good china now, wear the fancy dress to the local chippy, live in the now, but somehow she was unable to put the knowledge into action. Most days Peony felt like she was standing at a bus stop waiting for a bus to take her somewhere but the right bus never came along, so she was waiting for something she wasn't sure was ever going to come.

She and Fergus were over a long time ago but Peony had refused to acknowledge the fact, she ignored the signs, the hairs on the back of her neck, the suspicion he wasn't where he said he was, the furtive calls from another room. And like anything that is ignored, it tends to fester, go mouldy or die, until there is nothing left but the outline of something that once was.

Of course, good things have been left from mould forming, like penicillin but that was a happy accident and the day that Peony left London for Honeystone she hoped was the start of her own happy accident, or at least the trip would act as a type of spiritual penicillin, curing her of her heartache.

The truth was she missed Honeystone more than she would admit. The urge to leave the village as a teenager, telling her father he was backwards for wanting to live in the country and how slow and boring life was now made her cheeks flush with embarrassment at how wrong she had been.

The old saying, you end up where you started, had been ringing in her head for a number of years and she had tried to drown it out with wine, dancing, work, book clubs, trips to Greece and Spain, redecorating the flat, yoga, Pilates, meditation, drinking a lot of water, taking turmeric and whatever else was being recommended at the time but the call of the village was becoming louder.

And it wasn't as though she'd had a plan to head back but life had kicked her in the behind and now, she found herself on the M4, wondering what she would do when she arrived in Honeystone not knowing that Honeystone already had plans for Peony Grayling.

For years Peony had tried to stay away from Honeystone but here she was, driving into the village and seeing everything remain the same from the outside but she wondered what was happening behind the century old walls.

Mabel's Table looked to have a few inside, as she drove past the old building. Her dad had said a new couple had taken over earlier in the year and it was becoming well known for large scones and excellent jams made with local fruit.

She wondered if the fruit was coming from the Hinch's orchard and then pushed the Hinch family from her mind. She had enough in her head without adding unpleasant memories.

Biddy's Bits and Bites was still closed, she noticed. Whatever happened to Biddy? She wondered. One day she was selling handmade nougat with flower petals in it and the next day she was gone with only a sign on the door reading *Back Soon*.

But that wasn't the mystery for Peony to solve and Biddy had always been very private. Perhaps there wasn't enough money in nougat to keep the shop open, Peony thought as she came around the main street and towards the pub.

The first thing Peony noticed was that the pub looked tired. The stone needed a clean, which was an expensive process for a building as old as The Hare and Thistle. The window frames could do with a lick of paint and for the first time in as long as Peony could remember, there was nothing in the hanging baskets that swung happily in the spring and summer, usually filled with bright blooms.

'I understand how you feel,' Peony said as she pulled into the carpark at the front. She was also empty of bright blooming feeling and right now, after not showering in London after leaving in a rush, she needed more than a steam clean and lick of paint. She felt like she needed to be run through a car wash, strapped to the top of her car.

She opened the car door and looked up and down the street and then peered through the pub window.

If she was someone who was easily spooked, she would have assumed that something bad had happened. The village was quieter than usual. Not a single car had passed her since she arrived and the darkness of the interior of the pub was foreboding but Peony didn't pay attention to the signs. Instead, she pulled her phone from her back pocket and dialled the number of the person who would have all the answers as to what was happening in Honeystone and most of all, why the pub wasn't open for lunch.

Robert

Robert had no idea Peony was on her way home. His world in Honeystone was very small and as he was nearer to sixty than he liked to acknowledge, he kept his days easy.

Robert Grayling was a man of simplicity. He liked his routine but wasn't wedded to it. He could take care of himself, had been caring for himself and Peony since his wife, Christina, died when Peony was twelve. Cancer, misdiagnosed by the idiot doctor across the road, who refused to admit he buggered up the tests, so Rob took Peony to a doctor in the next village after that.

Robert was a handsome man, but had no idea, which made him even more handsome, with his thick greying hair and bright blue eyes. He was tall but not absurdly so and kept himself neat and tidy and ironed his own shirts every Sunday while he watched the news. He hadn't dated anyone after Christina died, because he had Peony to care for and he simply couldn't be bothered trying to find something as remarkable as what he'd had with Christina.

On this particular Tuesday, he was busy doing a Wordle and drinking a very strong coffee and avoiding thinking about how he would find a new cook when he saw his daughter's name come up on the phone screen.

'Hello Sweets,' he answered. 'Five letter word, ends with D, second letter L.'

'Blind. Why aren't you open?' She forwent any greeting, usual Peony style.

'Blind?' He typed.

'You're brilliant.'

'Why isn't the pub open for lunch?'

'What do you mean?' He stood up from his comfortable armchair and walked to the window and looked down on the street and saw Peony standing in the middle of the road, the phone up to her ear, looking up at him with a frown.

He sighed, 'I'm coming,' he said and he went down the stairs to where Peony was standing in the pub as Dora came out to the bar from the back room.

'Hello love,' said Dora to his daughter.

'Hi Dora,' Peony smiled at the woman who had been working at the pub since Rob's wife, and Peony's mother had died. 'You well?' She asked her.

'Fine thanks, how are you?' the woman asked Peony.

'You know, up and down,' said Peony vaguely as Rob stepped forward.

'Sweets,' he said and pulled her into a hug. 'Why are you here with no warning? You're like the wind that came through, did you see it on the news?'

Peony shook her head. 'What wind?'

He placed his hands on each of her shoulders and looked at her face. 'What's wrong?'

'Nothing.' She shook her head and he noticed Dora trying to avoid listening to them.

'Come up then,' he said and Peony followed him as they traipsed up the back stairs to her old home. Rob knew not to push Peony. She would unfurl when she was ready and not before.

Peony sank into one of the large sofas and a squeak came out from under her bottom. She pulled a dog toy out and threw it on the ground and from the other room came Baggins, the lurcher who looked at Peony with disdain.

Baggins was licking his lips with a hint of icing sugar on his nose.

'Baggins, you've eaten my iced bun.' Robert pointed at the dog bed and Baggins slunk to it, and curled up with his back to the room.

'You look well,' Rob said with a raised eyebrow to Peony.

'Lies,' Peony sniffed. 'I look like the wreck of the Hesperus.'

She brushed some imaginary something off her jeans and then crossed her legs and tried to smooth down her hair.

'Coffee?' he asked.

'No thanks. So, why aren't you open for lunch?' She looked at him, her arms crossed. 'Where's the chef?'

'Chef is an overreach,' scoffed Rob. 'Why do you think you look like the wreck of the Hesperus, as you so artfully put it?'

The father and daughter stared at each other, neither willing to give in.

'I'm going to stay for a bit,' she said.

'Where?' Rob asked.

She looked around. 'Here. Unless you don't want me to stay.'

'No that would be lovely.' Robert nodded and he meant it. He didn't get enough time with his only child.

There was silence.

And then Robert broke first. 'I don't have a chef at the moment. The last one was terrible but he left before I could fire him. Upped in the night and took my KitchenAid with him. I think he's on the run from something, most likely food critics. His mashed potato is so thick, I nearly used it to wallpaper the downstairs loo.'

Peony leaned forward, her arms around her knees. 'God, Dad, did you report him to the police?'

'And say a man stole my teal KitchenAid from a pub that no one comes to anymore?' He laughed, although it sounded too strained to be pithy.

'So, no Fergus gracing us with his bad moods and commentary on my whiskey collection this time?' He asked lightly. Baggins sidled up to him and leaned against his thigh, as though waiting for Peony to reveal the truth while asking for his owner's forgiveness.

Rob never bore a grudge but he did find Fergus wearing on his good humour and wasn't sorry Peony hadn't brought him with her.

Peony lifted her dirty hair and pulled it into a bun which promptly fell without anything to hold it up.

'Not this time,' she said, lifting her chin. 'Actually, not anytime,' she added.

As much as he was pleased Fergus wasn't there, he could see the dark circles under her eyes.

'Do you want to talk about it?' Robert asked.

'No, I know you don't like that sort of chat,' she said and they sat in more uncomfortable silence for a moment. 'What's done is done.'

'Righto, well, you stay here as long as you need, Sweets,' he said as he stood up and went to the door, taking Baggins's lead from the hook.

'I'm talking Baggins for a walk in the woods, so I'll let you get settled in.' He paused. 'And have a shower.'

Baggins, unsure why his owner wanted to leave but thrilled to know there was a second walk in a day, jumped in joy while Robert tried to put the lead on him.

Peony put a pillow over her head. 'Thanks Dad,' she said, her voice muffled. 'I'm sorry I smell.'

'Love stinks huh?'

'To high heaven,' she answered.

He thought about the things Christina, his wife and Peony's mother might have said, about how Peony was a catch and how Fergus was a dunce and that life wasn't always fair but to stay open to love and you would find the right person like she and Robert had. But he didn't. Instead, he thought, he would pick her up an iced bun on the way home from Mabel's, along with another one for himself since Baggins had helped himself. That would make things better.

Anthea

Anthea McGregor was born with a gift, though unlike some who were frightened of their own potential, she had embraced it and used it to make a fortune. No, it wasn't the ability to read minds or to dream of the lottery numbers for the next night. Anthea had the rare ability to see scents. Yes, it's a thing, look it up. This ability was called synaesthesia, and no matter what Anthea did, she couldn't hide from the skill she was gifted upon her birth. Some people can see colours when they hear a name or can taste something when they look at a colour but Anthea's gift was different in that she could see all the parts of a scent.

Like most gifts of this nature, it emerged when Anthea was a child. It was discovered when she smelled the bottle of Joy perfume that had been given to her mother for her fortieth birthday. Anthea could still remember the moment. She had been sitting at the dressing table, and her mother had shown her the perfume. She had opened it and held it under Anthea's nose and a rush of visions came to her. Roses that lined the path to her grandmother's front door, the white flower that climbed the fence of the lane that she passed on the way to school, and the wooden box her father had given her mother when he came back from India. Sandalwood, her father had said, which for a very long time, Anthea thought it was made from sandals and that sandals must grow on trees.

As she'd described the scent to her mother, she saw a frown and then something that looked like fear. No, not fear, that was too strong a word, unease. Anthea's mother seemed uneasy with her child being so easily able to describe the scent.

It was a moment when she knew she was different. We all think we are different and we are, but Anthea's gift was rare. While this sounds lovely in theory, the truth was awful smells, such as body odour, old rubbish and worse, upset her so much that she carried with her a small Victorian vinaigrette case in the shape of a heart that she wore on a velvet ribbon around her neck. In Victorian times these would be filled with perfume and vinegar-soaked sponge or ammonium carbonate and lavender, as Queen Victoria loved a bit of lavender and what Victoria loved the society women loved too.

But Anthea filled her heart with citrus oils, sometimes bergamot from Tuscany, sometimes the oil of oranges from Corsica or lemons from the Amalfi Coast. She was particular with the oils she used, because not every lemon was the right scent for her needs.

She had once read a book about a man who had an exceptional sense of smell who became a perfumier and then a murderer after trying to capture the scent of young virgin girls. The book annoyed Anthea, with the trope of the virgins smelling the best to men, when in fact there was no scent more tantalising than that of sex and lust and, above all, love.

And then the gift was gone. Anthea caught Covid and thought she was fine but then she woke up in hospital, there had been machines keeping her alive, her doctor told her, and it took a long time for her to recover, but eventually she rallied and when she came out of hospital, she found she could no longer smell anything nor was she the owner of her own namesake company.

John, had left her, taken most of her company and the money she had made and gone to Spain with a woman named Natalie.

Losing John and her company was terrible but losing her sense of smell was worse. And it wasn't just because she couldn't see the things that the scents evoked in her mind, she could smell nothing at all.

And there was nothing the doctors could do.

'It might come back of its own accord.'

'We have tested you and there isn't anything we can pinpoint. Anosmia can be from anything, but most likely it's an after-effect of the virus and we just have to wait and see.'

And so, she waited. She waited through the messy divorce, the huge payout to her ex-husband she had to make to use her own name and trademark, and through the photos in every trashy paper in the UK of him and his TV star second wife Natalie, host of a popular morning show, at their wedding at Villa Lampara en la colina in Spain.

Still there was nothing.

Thus, Anthea decided to hide in plain sight. She had a private estate agent look for a house that needed renovating but not too much work, she didn't fancy a *Grand Designs* scenario where three years later the renovator has gone stark raving mad and is living on tinned beans in a caravan while they wait for the building to be finished.

Something that would need a light touch and heavy decorating. It needed to be in a picturesque place but not so far from London that she would have to fly or go by train. And it needed to be private. No sticky nosed tourists or locals taking photos and selling them for a tenner to a trashy publication. She could read the potential headlines should this happen.

The Perfume Queen's new scent – Regret – with notes of bitterness and humiliation.

This was an absolute, she told the agent, and she wanted land around her.

When the agent showed her Spindle Hall, she could see the potential but its location was more important. Would she be left alone?

The drive to Honeystone had been a non-event. No one looked at her as she drove through the village. She had stopped at Mabel's Table and had been served by a lovely woman named Mala whose husband Ajay cooked scones the size of soufflés and had a delicious raspberry jam which Anthea had bought four jars of when she left.

They were pleasant and polite and didn't ask her anything other than what she wanted in her order and that suited Anthea just fine.

The pub seemed to be closed the day she stopped at Mabel's which also suited her, since she didn't want people eying her Mercedes and wondering why she was in the area.

But she had other reasons she wanted to live in the country. She needed to feel again. She wanted to breathe in the country air and smell the soil and the chestnuts and flowers in the summer. She just had to be patient.

But still nothing.

And now she had a huge house, just for her to rattle around alone while waiting for the garden to be made and to grow. It had seemed like a good idea before Christmas, now it felt like a folly. She felt like an English Marie Antoinette with her pretend rural retreat on the grounds of Versailles. Next thing you know she would have pastel-dyed sheep wandering the grounds and a billy goat named Robespierre.

Anthea pulled her coat from the hook by the kitchen door and looked at her phone on the bench. Who would call other than London friends asking her to come to a party or a dinner, neither of which she'd wanted to attend even when she did live in London.

'Leave the phone here,' she said aloud and with a whistle, her dogs were running beside her as she made her way to the woods, trying to shake the unsettled mood that accompanied her.

She walked towards the woods and as she entered them, she was glad for her coat, feeling the temperature drop several degrees. There were still a few fallen leaves on the floor of the woods but there were also fresh, green shoots poking their heads out to see the new day. Anthea stood for a moment and looked up at the trees. The new buds on the branches were so hopeful, she thought, wondering what the canopy would look like in a few weeks. The branches closer to the top of the forest already had young leaves open, forming a delicate, lacy mantilla above her, with sunlight filtering through.

It was so beautiful, she thought, and she was sure it would have a scent, and she wondered what the notes of the forest would be. Chestnut, sap, broken leaves, soil, moss, earthy notes. But she couldn't imagine it, even though she knew the right words.

Losing her sense of smell had destabilised her life. No more nostalgic scents, reminding her of good times, great meals, simple pleasures and at times, she wondered if she was losing her memories too, so many of them tied up with scents. Her whole life had been signposted with aromas, taking her from success to success and now, as she stood in the woods of Spindle Hall, she wondered if her nose had finally led her the wrong way.

Peony

Peony had spent her first week back in Honeystone sleeping, in between wandering about the pub and checking her phone. The days and nights were blurring into one, until she woke up one morning and said, 'Enough'. She was going to do something today, she told herself. She wasn't sure what it was but she had to do something or she would go mad.

At least she was showering now, she told herself as she dried her hair with a towel and stood in the living room, noticing that Baggins was out, which meant her dad would be out. Probably avoiding her, she thought. She certainly hadn't been much fun since she came back to Honeystone.

'Rob?'

Peony heard a female voice call for her father. She narrowed her eyes and went out and looked down the stairs and saw Izzy Hinch standing at the bottom of them, and Connor's daughter Clover next to her.

'Izzy, hi,' she said.

Peony went down the stairs, two at a time – old habits die hard when you're back in your childhood home – and stood in front of Izzy, who still looked like a teenager. She was very pretty in an unusual way with her short brown hair cut in a pixie style, wearing a striped T-shirt, overalls and work boots.

'Oh, hey Peony! God, it's been a while, hasn't it?' Izzy seemed as surprised as Peony was. Peony didn't come back to Honeystone often throughout the year, only for Christmas, unless she was at Fergus's parents'. When she was in Honeystone, she avoided seeing the Hinch family as much as possible, to the point she hadn't spoken to either Izzy or Connor in twelve years. It wasn't easy but Connor didn't come into the village if Peony was around and she and Izzy had managed to ignore each other successfully until now.

Peony nodded.

Izzy looked at Clover.

'I was thirteen when I last saw Peony,' she told her. 'I was living with your gran and gramps, but they're gone now,' she added.

Clover nodded. 'They're dead from a truck accident.'

Peony shook her head, feeling like a puppet in a show she didn't want to be a part of.

'I'm sure we've seen each other since then,' she said.

Izzy seemed to think. 'Yes, it was the night you broke up with Connor. I remember because that's the night he started playing Radiohead's "Kid A" album and didn't stop for a year.'

Peony sighed, 'Yes, I'm sorry about that. I was going to write you both a sympathy card.'

'For the Radiohead or my parents dying so close together?' Peony shivered at Izzy's tone. Izzy could ice anyone at twenty feet and at this distance, Peony could feel the chilblains forming on her conscience.

Izzy looked down at the child and back to Peony. 'Have you met Clover?' She looked at the child intently, as though she was trying to see her through Peony's eyes.

Dark straight hair cut in a bob, her thin pale face and wide brown eyes with a pair of apple green framed glasses on her nose. She was small and slight in stature, willowy, Izzy would have said, bending with the winds and storms that came her way in her short years on the earth. Yet Clover kept coming upright again and again, with a resilience that only came from being underestimated from the moment you were born.

Clover was looking at Peony with curiosity, more out of

having a new person in her presence than interest in Peony, Izzy noted and gave a little laugh.

'This is Peony, she used to be friends with your dad until he woke up one day and Peony had run away with the circus.'

Peony glared at Izzy. 'You always were annoying, good to see you're still maintaining your brand,' she said to Izzy.

'And good to see you still come in and out of the village as though you're paying a royal visit.'

'I'd like to be in the circus but I would look after the animals,' Clover said.

'They don't have animals in the circus anymore,' said Izzy, holding Peony's glare. 'It's cruel.'

'Maybe my mum went to the circus,' said Clover confidently. 'We should look.'

Peony and Izzy glanced at each other. Peony knew Mel had left the hospital and had told Connor she didn't want to be a parent of a disabled child, and like everyone else they had assumed she would come back to her daughter. But Mel had never come back for Clover or Connor. Something Peony couldn't really understand.

Izzy's face lost its anger and she bent down to Clover. 'Your mum definitely loves you, I promise. She probably got lost somewhere.'

Peony bent down to see Clover's face. 'Hello Clover, it's nice to meet you,' she said with a smile.

Clover looked at Peony, her eyes running over Peony's face as though memorising it or perhaps remembering it? One couldn't be sure with Clover.

'Do you want some more artichokes? Izzy grows them.'

Izzy lifted the basket in her hand. 'I gave some to your dad last week, he said the cook was going to use them.'

'The cook ran away,' said Peony. 'With a KitchenAid.'

'Hey diddle,' said Izzy with a snort. 'Did he also take a dish and spoon?'

'Probably,' Peony said looking around the kitchen, wondering what else had been pilfered. She walked to the bench and wiped invisible crumbs from the top.

'Dad buys veg from you? That's great,' Peony said, trying to muster some enthusiasm.

Izzy stared at Peony and memories of watching her and Connor as teenagers came flooding back. There was always something about Izzy that made Peony doubt herself.

'It's OK, I wouldn't say it's great, that's a reach.'

The women stared at each other for longer than necessary, unspoken opinions lay out between them.

'You don't come back here much,' Izzy said as she put the basket on the stainless steel kitchen bench next to where Peony stood.

'No, I have a busy job. It's hard to get away.' Peony said this firmly but the adults in the room knew this was a lie. But there wasn't enough connection between Izzy and Peony to talk about why Peony stayed away and why Izzy couldn't leave.

'Is Rob around?' asked Izzy.

'No, he's taken the dog to Spindle for a walk,' Peony said.

'I saw a truck there this morning,' said Izzy, her tone changing from defensive to almost conspiratorial, or even gossipy. Talking about the possibilities for Spindle Hall was the one thing all Honeystonians could debate for hours no matter their differences.

'A truck? What sort of a truck? Has it sold?' Peony asked.

'A construction truck of sorts, it looked like, but I can't tell the difference between a digger and an excavator so I'm no use. Couldn't Rob tell us? He's the mayor after all.'

Peony laughed. 'I don't think he has any access to records and real estate, nor any actual mayoral powers.'

'Other than pissing Barry Mundy off,' said Izzy and Peony couldn't help but giggle. Barry Mundy was a bane in everyone's life.

Izzy shook her head and walked further into the kitchen and took a knife from the drawer and started to peel the artichokes, removing the tough outer leaves. 'I'll just clean these up for the cook.'

'The cook ran away, remember.' Peony reminded Izzy.

Clover walked to her side, swaying a little, concentrating with each step.

'Did he go to the circus as well?'

Peony and Izzy shared a smile, not a complete reconciliation but a start.

'Perhaps. He will be able to make some lovely cakes with that stand mixer,' Peony said.

Izzy was working her way through the artichokes. 'But if it has sold, Barry Mundy's going to throw an absolute wobbly.'

Peony looked at Clover who seemed unfazed by the idea of Barry Mundy throwing a wobbly, instead watching Izzy peel the vegetables with deep interest.

The kitchen door opened and Baggins came bounding into the kitchen with Rob following behind.

'Well, Barry Mundy is going to lose his mind, Spindle Hall's been sold,' he said. 'Apparently, it's been done up inside and none of us had seen a thing this whole time. Like magic, it seems.'

'Izzy said Barry would flip about the house,' Clover informed Rob who laughed harder than Peony had heard in a long time, not that she spent enough time with her father to know if this was a common occurrence or not.

'So? Who bought it?' asked Peony.

'No idea but there are signs up and some new fencing is being put in and the signs aren't exactly welcoming.'

Rob took off his jacket and opened the back door to the garden where Baggins ran outside.

'More artichokes?' He gave a concerned look at the artichokes Izzy was peeling.

'Did your cook use them last time?' asked Izzy. 'Clover told you they would be good with pasta.'

'Artichoke pasta? Here?'

'Would be a good special for the next week or so,' said Izzy as she expertly wielded the knife in a way that was both impressive and intimidating to Peony.

'It would be but since the cook left us high and dry, I won't be serving any specials for a while, if at all.'

'Shame,' said Izzy not sounding sorry at all.

'I could cook,' Peony burst out of nowhere. She looked around. Had she actually just said that aloud?

'You?' Robert frowned. 'You're a social worker, not a cook. You have a job.'

Peony wished Izzy wasn't here but she seemed to be very involved in her artichokes, as though her life depended on ensuring no tough leaf was left uncut.

'I've actually resigned, Dad,' she admitted.

'Resigned? Why?'

'Because I need a break. I need to be here for a while.'

'You hate Honeystone,' Robert said.

'I do not,' she said, unsure if that was true or not. Time would tell, she told herself.

'But you never come home,' Rob said and he looked at Izzy for what Peony supposed was validation of his point but Izzy shook her head.

'Don't bring me into it.' she said. 'Not my circus, not my monkeys.'

'You don't have any monkeys. And why do you keep talking about the circus?' Clover said, looking somewhat hopeful that Izzy did in fact have some monkeys somewhere that she hadn't told her about.

'You're my monkey,' Izzy stuck her tongue out at her niece. 'And this whole thing feels like a circus.' She gestured around her to the little girl.

But Peony wasn't listening to Clover and Izzy.

'I don't mean not to come home,' said Peony. 'I was just busy in London.'

They were silent for a long moment.

'I mean, maybe I avoided it for a while, you know, it was hard to come back.'

Both Robert and Peony looked at Izzy who shook her head.

'Don't bring me into this, I am not responsible for my brother.'

Robert turned back to Peony. 'You aren't a commercial cook,' he said. 'It gets busy.'

'Not that busy,' said Izzy. 'You haven't been ordering even half of what you used to.'

'Not helping Izzy,' Robert said but Peony glanced gratefully at Izzy.

'I can cook, I mean I'm not a chef, but it's lunch and dinner, and it's a small pub, it can't be that hard.'

'Famous last words,' Robert grumbled but he wasn't as opposed as she thought he might have been.

'I'm sorry, Dad, I know I'm a rubbish daughter,' she said but she felt clearer than she had in the past week. 'But I want to be here, I need to be here. Just let me try. I need to have something to do, to focus on. I love cooking, you know this.'

And it was true. For the first time in ten years, Peony felt as though she wasn't lying to everyone and herself. It wasn't anything she had planned but it felt right.

'So, you're going to stay?' Izzy asked, putting the knife down.

Peony nodded, 'Yes, I am,' she said, more and more certain as she spoke.

Izzy shook her head and looked at Rob. 'Oh God, Peony is back. Connor's going to—' and before she could finish the sentence, Clover chimed in for her.

'Throw a wobbly.'

3

Connor

Connor was on top of the ladder, assessing the blossoms on the sweet Sheep's Nose apple trees when he saw Izzy's car leave the house. After the strong winds, he'd expected to see the ground covered in white blossoms but so far, there wasn't too much loss and the little fruits were forming, for which he was grateful. He couldn't afford to lose the apples when the new cidery in Cirencester had said they would buy everything and for a fantastic price. Cider was incredibly popular and they were going to use his apples for their premium blend cider, to be sold across the country.

Connor wasn't much of a drinker, and didn't love cider, so he would have to take their word for it, he told them, but the money would be helpful since Clover was about to start at a private school in a month, in time for summer term.

He wondered where Izzy was off to with his daughter but knew it wouldn't be further than the village. Izzy didn't like to stray too far from the farm. He wasn't sure how she would be when Clover started at Cracklewood School. In recent days, Clover had started to call it Cacklewood School for Witches, which Izzy thought was hilarious.

But the school was perfect for Clover. Small classes and with a specialist teacher for when she needed extra support. She had been in a school for children with special needs since she was four but intellectually she was fine and needed an everyday school to learn and play at.

It annoyed him when people told him that he was a saint for raising Clover alone but what choice did he have? Would a woman be called a saint if he had walked out instead? There was never a question that he would care for Clover. And when Mel had told him she was pregnant, he had been excited to have a baby, though he had thought it would be with someone else, not Mel. They weren't in love, and she and Izzy didn't get along very well. But Connor had offered Mel his home and they had pretended to each other that they could make it work until Clover's traumatic birth. Then Mel was gone, leaving a note on the back of the menu sheet at the hospital telling Connor she couldn't be a parent to a child with special needs and she was handing him full custody.

Now, Connor climbed down the ladder and stretched. His back ached and he was sure he was getting sunburnt from the April sunshine. Lunch was on the agenda, he thought and he looked at the old Omega watch his father had left him. The watch and the farm were his inheritance, and Izzy was left a small amount of cash which she had used to buy the car she still drove eight years later.

It wasn't a fair deal but his parents hadn't thought a truck would drive through their car so he gave Izzy everything he had and all she needed.

Losing both parents within weeks of the other was tragic and then having Clover a few years later and Mel walking out on them was brutal but he had made it through, because what choice had he had? Sometimes you just have to get on with it. You don't know why things happen or why people do what they do.

But it was Izzy who saved him and who became the anchor for him and Clover.

He never imagined his angry little waspish sister would have the maternal instinct she did but it made sense since Izzy could make anything grow, including a very premature baby with cerebral palsy.

Connor walked through the orchards and past the few cherry trees and the damson trees that his grandfather had planted years before. The raspberry canes were looking excellent this year, he noted, and he wondered if Rob Grayling would want the extra fruits for the pub. They were always a popular fruit, he thought to himself and for a moment, a long-forgotten memory of Peony's raspberry galette flashed before him. It was still the best he had ever eaten, served with her always perfect clotted cream. Why she hadn't pursued her talent for cooking he'd never understood, but then Peony had always confused him.

He tried not to think of her but even after all these years, it felt like Peony was in the next room, ready to storm in at any moment, waving a spoon, asking him to taste something and ruffling his hair and leaving a kiss on his lips, tasting of whatever it was she was making in his parents' kitchen. His parents had adored her, and Izzy had secretly liked her, he could tell, because she didn't go to her room as much as she usually did.

Peony had a way with Izzy, as though she treaded carefully but also respectfully. Even though Izzy was only fifteen at the time and filled with hormones and disdain she would often chat to Peony longer than she spoke to Connor and their parents.

And then Peony was gone, the scent and taste of her disappearing after that terrible day and even though she was still physically in Honeystone, her spirit had gone with

45

the news. And it was all his fault. If Connor could have one wish, it would be to change the way he spoke to her that day, and make sure his parents didn't die, which were all tied up together. But there wasn't a time machine and he couldn't change what he'd said or how he'd made her feel.

Even now, he shook his head, as though trying to shake Peony Grayling loose from his mind, but she was stuck, like a bloody emotional barnacle, he thought.

Focus on now, he reminded himself and his stomach rumbled with hunger, pulling him back into the present.

He ran his hand through his hair. He needed a haircut, but he really couldn't be bothered to drive into town and sit and wait at the barbers when he could be doing something in the garden. His dark hair was curly and often had remnants of apple blossom in it, unless he was wearing his dad's straw sunhat that had seen better days but felt like a hug when he put it on his head. Clover had inherited his dark hair but nothing else. He had blue eyes where she had Mel's brown eyes. He was tall and broad shouldered, with brown skin in the summer that stayed all the way through until winter. Not that he let the weather bother him. He just exchanged his straw hat for a woollen hat and kept on in his little life. Why should he get a haircut? It wasn't as though he needed to look presentable to anyone. Clover loved him no matter what and Izzy thought of his appearance less than her own.

Lunch consisted of large slices of fresh bread, which he cut poorly. He knew Izzy would tell him off later for not using the proper knife but he was impatient and the Double Gloucester cheese he had bought from the farm on the way to the village was calling his name.

He slapped on some butter and cut five slices of cheese. Four for the sandwich and one to satiate him while he made the sandwich.

Not bothering to cut it in half he walked into the living room and switched off the television then went into the kitchen and turned on the kettle.

Tea was next and then maybe a slice of cake. Clover and Izzy had been trying to perfect a sponge cake, the results of which were a little hit and miss but Connor wasn't fussy. He would eat anything if offered to him.

He stood by the back door looking out over Izzy's garden. It was perfect as always, he thought as he noted the well-spaced vegetables, planted with a mix of flowers, waiting to be heavily populated by bees and butterflies in summer.

Izzy had been doing a beekeeping course online and was planning to bring in hives next. Another thing for her to care for, perhaps something to fill in the days when Clover started school.

It was time for his daughter to spread her wings but he knew his and Izzy's days would be quieter without her around every moment.

He made his tea and took the cake from the refrigerator and cut himself a generous slice and then ran his finger along the knife to collect the cream and jam from the strawberry sponge. Lucky Izzy wasn't there to see him, she would have swatted him with a tea towel.

Sitting outside on the wooden bench he had made for his mother when he was a teenager, he watched a chiffchaff jump from branch to branch, as though urging the berries to hurry up so he too could have his lunch.

Connor sipped his tea and ate his cake, slowly, enjoying the peace and quiet, pondering what he would do this afternoon. He only had to check the irrigation for the apple trees and then he would knock off for the day.

Perhaps he and Izzy and Clover could head into The Hare and Thistle for dinner. He liked Rob Grayling and the pub was always sure to be avoided when Peony was home, which thankfully was rare nowadays. She had a fancy boyfriend, a Scot, who Rob didn't like but Rob didn't like anyone for Peony but Connor, and that ship had long sailed.

The sound of Izzy's car broke through his thoughts and she tooted her horn loudly as she pulled into the parking spot.

She opened the door.

'Guess who's back?' she called. Her face was red and laughing and she looked slightly maniacal.

'You're going to throw a wobbly,' said Clover, now standing beside her aunt.

'I'm going to what?' he asked. What was happening? This was almost like the windstorm had come back but was in the form of the two women in his life.

'Peony's back,' said Izzy.

'So?' he shrugged.

'She's staying,' Clover said.

'She's going to be the cook at the pub.' Izzy continued. 'She's moved home again. Broke up with the boyfriend.'

And then Connor felt like the wind had really returned again, and this time Peony Grayling had flown back in on it and had upended more than just the roof of the potting shed.

Robert

'Baggins, come here,' Robert bellowed as the dog chased two spaniels through the woods and into the clearing.

There was a truck with an earth mover on the back and smoke coming from Spindle Hall.

The fences were still up, but Robert knew a way through and thought he would have a quick walk with Baggins before he opened the pub but Baggins had found new friends and now Rob's covert walk had been uncovered.

'Taggie, Rupert,' a female voice called and Rob saw a woman coming from the house, dressed in black with a coat flying out behind her.

'Baggins,' he called after the lurcher who was charging after one of the spaniels while the other one chased him.

'Did you not see the fences?' The woman snapped at Robert. 'Did you read the signs?'

Robert glanced at her. She had dark hair with a stripe of white through it and a pale face and red lipstick. She seemed to be a little younger than him and smelled wonderful.

'I didn't see them,' Robert lied, avoiding her glance.

'And would you have adhered to the request if you had?' she asked.

'Probably not,' he said and turned to her to see a smile at the corner of her mouth.

'Those signs won't bode well for you though.' He whistled loudly to Baggins who stopped and was bowled over by a spaniel.

'I'm not really interested in the thoughts of the villagers,' the woman said. 'I prefer to be left alone.'

Robert paused and then laughed. 'Goodness, you have quite the community spirit, don't you?'

'I didn't buy a house here to be overrun by villagers,' she snapped.

Rob looked around at the woods. 'I understand this is your land but it's been used by the villagers for decades for walking, collecting mushrooms and chestnuts. We have always walked here and never upset the grounds. It does seem a little aggressive to suddenly push people out who have only ever cared for the land.'

The woman was quiet and Robert whistled again and

Baggins came over and sat at his feet. Robert clipped the lead to his collar.

'And you know what happens in *Macbeth* with the chestnuts, that's a warning if I ever heard one.' He laughed to himself and nodded to the woman.

'What do you mean?' she asked and pulled her coat close around her body.

Rob pulled Baggins in tight. 'In *Macbeth*, the witches demand the sailor's wife shares her chestnuts and she insults them and says no. So, the witches then summon up wind that takes the sailor out to sea and he won't sleep for eighty-one days, being blown about the sea until he dies of hunger and thirst.'

'You think I am going to be sent out to sea in a storm?' she scoffed.

Rob shook his head. 'No, but I think that the new owner of Spindle Hall should be mindful and not selfish and continue to share their woods and the chestnuts, just in case they ended up being blown some bad luck about for eighty-one days.'

She snorted. 'Thank you for the literature lesson.'

Robert looked around the land, the digger on the back of the truck, the equipment ready for use in the garden.

'The Renshaws, who owned the place before the Dows, they were lovely people, well the Renshaws were very feudal, according to Old Ed. They had fences and fought with everyone surrounding the boundaries. In the end they put up fences and nothing grew on the land for years. There was nothing wrong with the soil, nothing that they could see or find out, but in the end, they left because the land wouldn't give back to them when they gave nothing in return.'

He then patted the head of one of the spaniels and left

with Baggins to walk back the way he came, feeling her eyes on his back until he came to the road.

Robert walked along the main road that went past Honeystone and then through the streets to the village, still enamoured by Honeystone after a lifetime of living there. It was so quintessential of the English with the eponymous honey-coloured stone cottages, and the different window boxes and climbing plants ready to show their blooms for spring.

The pub faced the village square and if Honeystone was a more popular village it would have been bustling with locals and tourists, but Barry Mundy didn't want to promote Honeystone to the tourists. It was a shame, Rob thought as he passed Biddy's Bits and Bites, closed indefinitely since Biddy had left the village and hadn't returned since last summer. But Biddy had put up a *Back Soon* sign and hadn't been back since. He had no idea what had happened, except that Barry Mundy had been bad mouthing her more than usual when she left.

Rob had never found out what happened with Barry and Biddy but he didn't like to pry, that was between them.

The scent of freshly baked bread wafted from Mabel's, and Rob wondered if Peony would like a fresh scone. He had some nice apricot jam from Clary, Old Ed's wife, which would be lovely with some of Old Ed's butter.

Rob came to the door of Mabel's and put his head inside where he could see Ajay and his wife Mala setting up for the day in the tea rooms.

'Any chance of a scone or two? Peony's back,' he said to them.

Mala went to the kitchen and came back with a paper bag, 'Is she OK?' she asked.

'Broke up with the boyfriend, thinks she's going to be the

new cook at the pub. I think it's a panic decision, I'm not expecting her to stay,' he said.

He took his wallet out but Mala waved it away.

'Come over for dinner this week with her, I'd like to see her,' Mala said.

Ajay came to her side and he put his arm around his wife's shoulders. They had come to Honeystone a year ago, looking for a change of pace after Ajay had been a successful pastry chef in London. They bought Mabel's hoping to make a nice little life with a busy tea room business but the tourist traffic wasn't what they had hoped and they had made bread, sold milk and other small bits and pieces to the locals to make ends meet but Rob knew it was hard, not to mention some racist idiot who had written a letter to the council questioning the suitability of an Indian man making England's iconic scone.

Rob was sure it was Barry but couldn't prove it, instead he wrote in the Honeystone newsletter that Jenn Carruthers edited that scones originated from Scotland and that people who ordered tikka in Cirencester for lunch in Cirencester (Rob had seen him at Bombay Nights on Dollar Street once) and then complained about traditional English food shouldn't be.

Barry ignored Mabel's after that but Rob had noticed his wife Dora, often bought a finger bun from them when she was at the pub working, as though trying to show them that not all Mundys were xenophobes.

Rob took the scones and wandered up to the pub, standing outside, trying to see it through the lens of a tourist.

There were no flowers in the hanging basket, the frost killed the begonias which in hindsight were the wrong choice. Perhaps with Peony's return, for however long it was, he should do a few things to make the pub a little more enticing. He would ask Izzy to plant up the baskets with something welcoming, and maybe he would arrange his Toby jug collection on the mantle in the dining room instead of the shelves far above the bar where they were hard to see.

Yes, that would help, he decided and he went inside to give Peony her scones and tell her about his ideas for the pub.

Izzy

The next morning, when Clover was awake and watching *The Great British Bake Off*, safe and tucked up on the sofa with toast and chocolate milk, Izzy texted Connor that she was heading out and he said he would come back to the house for a while.

Izzy grabbed her basket and walked to the fence line by the side of the house and slipped under the wire.

A few more steps and she was among the chestnuts and the woods of Spindle Hall. She knew what she was looking for as she moved among the trees, looking at their bases.

One by one she found them, pulling them out and putting them into the basket.

'Morning,' she heard a voice and looked up to see a woman with two dogs bounding towards her.

'Hi,' said Izzy.

'What are you collecting?' asked the woman, trying to peer into the basket on the ground.

Izzy waved a fungus at her. 'Morel mushrooms, incredible in pasta.'

'Are you a cook?' asked the woman.

'Not likely, I'm terrible but my niece loves to cook, so I'm trying to learn.' She laughed and looked in the basket. 'No these are for Peony Grayling at the pub. She's opening the restaurant again and I thought these would be a nice gift.'

'You could sell them,' said the woman, her hands in her black anorak. She was very glamorous, even for a country walk. Her dark hair had multiple white streaks in it, and she had wide blue eyes and the sort of skin that looked like it loved the great indoors.

Izzy instinctively touched her cheek, wishing she had remembered to put on moisturiser that morning.

'No, I don't own this land, so I don't sell anything I don't own. This is Spindle Hall's land, I mean people collect the chestnuts and the mushrooms, those who know about them and there are rumours of truffles being found here but I haven't been that lucky.' She laughed. 'But no one sells anything from here. It's kind of not the right thing to do, you know?'

The woman nodded. 'I'm Anthea,' she said.

'Izzy,' she answered. 'I live at Raspberry Hill Farm down there, with the red roof.'

The woman peered at the house. 'You have the fruit orchard?'

'Well, my brother does all the work in that, there are apples with a few cherries and damsons in the mix. I have a vegetable and flower garden which keeps me in some money. He sells apples for cider. He has a really big brewery buying them all this year, which is exciting.'

'How fantastic,' said the woman. 'Very bucolic,' she smiled.

'Or alcoholic,' said Izzy. 'The Bucolic Alcoholic should be the name of the next pub,' she said as she moved to the next tree and placed more mushrooms in the basket.

The woman laughed. 'You're a gardener?' she asked, as the dogs ran around them occasionally barking at nothing.

It was cold in the shadows of the trees and Izzy wished she had worn a thicker jacket.

'I am, I mean I'm not formally trained but things seem to grow for me,' she laughed. 'So who am I to argue with them.'

'What about you? Do you garden?' asked Izzy.

'I'm starting a garden,' she said, in a vague way.

'Good luck with it,' said Izzy with a smile. 'Soil around here is tricky, depending on where you are.'

'How so?'

'There's peat, clay, limestone rock, Oxford Clay, so get your soil tested to make sure the right things grow for the soil you have.'

Anthea looked like she was about to say something when Izzy heard her name being called.

'Morning Izzy,' Jenn Carruthers was walking past them, holding purple hand weights, and doing arm curls as she walked. She was dressed in matching aqua and silver active-wear and had a woollen turban on her head. She looked like a very fit, exotic mermaid. Her fat Cavalier, Otto, wandered behind her, looking disappointed to have Jenn as his owner and not a slightly inactive spinster.

'Good to see the fences are down and those rude signs,' Jenn was shaking her head. 'Whoever the new owner is of Spindle Hall, they didn't make any friends doing that as their first move into the area.'

Izzy glanced at Anthea who didn't respond.

'I won't keep you and your friend though. I'm compelled to walk, I can't seem to stop,' said Jenn almost surprised at this revelation as she was always happier to stop and chat than she was to focus on her exercise routine.

She picked up the pace and went into the distance.

Otto stopped and looked at Izzy and Anthea and then gave a heavy sigh and went on his way after her.

'I would have introduced you but she can be a pain in the arse,' said Izzy to Anthea. 'I mean that in a loving, caring way but if you want something shared with Honeystone then tell Jenn Carruthers.'

Anthea smiled. 'That's OK, I guess I'll meet her eventually. I've just moved to the area.'

'Oh wow, whereabouts are you living?' Izzy picked a particularly good mushroom and placed it carefully inside the basket.

'Up at Spindle Hall,' said Anthea. 'I'm the person who put the rude signs and fences up. Until a man told me I would have cursed chestnuts and barren land if I didn't take them down.'

Izzy gasped and then laughed, 'Oh you're the new owner. Wow. Good for you but yes, that's a lot of pressure re the fences, but I am glad you gave in, because I do love these woods.'

'It was some man with a dog named Baggins who threatened me,' Anthea sniffed.

'That's Rob Grayling. He threatened you?' Izzy asked. 'I'm shocked, he's lovely. What did he say?'

'He said that he would send me out to sea and I wouldn't eat or drink for eighty days or something, some *Macbeth* curse. I'm not exactly sure but he did make me feel guilty enough to have the workmen take them down.'

Izzy laughed, 'That's Rob, he's the fairest man in the district, a saint really.'

She lifted up the basket of mushrooms. 'I was going to offer his daughter these as she's just taken over as cook at the pub, but they belong to you.' She held the basket out to Anthea. 'I'm sorry for taking them. They're also great in a risotto or so Clover my niece tells me.'

Anthea shook her head. 'My mushrooms, your mushrooms,'

she said. 'Besides, imagine if I stopped you taking them I'd probably get a curse from Jenn Carruthers and end up eating a toadstool or the like.'

'You know what they say about mushroom picking?' Izzy asked.

Anthea shook her head, 'No?'

'Always leave some for the coroner.'

Anthea burst out laughing. 'You? I like. Come up to the house later and I can show you my plans for Spindle Hall. I think you might be interested if you're a gardener.'

'Thank you, I would love that.'

Anthea led them out of the woods and they walked into the sunlight and down towards the house.

'And you said the man with the dog was Rob?' Anthea asked.

'Rob Grayling,' Izzy said. 'Everyone loves Rob.'

Anthea's nose turned up a little.

'Except you, it seems,' Izzy laughed.

'I just didn't appreciate being told that I would be cursed if I didn't take the fences and signs down.'

'You would only be cursed if you believed it though,' Izzy said as they walked.

A flock of birds flew over them and Izzy looked up, 'Flock of birds before my eyes, when will I have a nice surprise?'

'What's that rhyme?' Anthea asked.

Izzy shrugged, 'My grandmother used to say it, she learned it as a kid in South Africa I think. Clover, my niece, and I always say it when we see a flock.'

'And do you get a nice surprise?' Anthea smiled.

Izzy paused for a moment, 'Yes. I met you.' And then she waved and went walking back to Raspberry Hill Farm with her mushrooms and the news that would turn Barry Mundy's knickers into a twist.

4

Peony

The rabbits landed with a lump on the kitchen bench.

'Caught this morning, skinned and gutted and ready for you to turn them into a pie that would satisfy Mr McGregor himself,' Robert said proudly.

'Did you go rabbit catching?' Peony made a face at him and then looked warily at the rabbits.

'No, they're from Old Ed, he left them on the doorstep. I saw them when I came in from my walk. He left a note stating they're good in a pie.'

Peony sighed. She had planned a menu and rabbit did not feature on it but who was she to say no to fresh meat. A rabbit pie couldn't be that hard to make. She had made every other sort of pie in her life.

Robert opened the door to the garden and looked at the sky.

'The weather is improving, so hopefully we will get a few more tourists in.' He walked inside again, leaving the door open.

'I was thinking I might move the Toby jugs, make them more viewable to the drinkers. They're a good conversation starter.'

Peony frowned. 'Toby jugs are awful, I find the ones that look like old men terrifying.'

He seemed to ignore her comment. 'Did you know they're named after Sir Toby Belch from *Twelfth Night*?'

'Yes Dad, you like to tell me every time you mention them which is far too often for me and to be honest there are more important things we need to do to the pub to bring people in.'

'Dost thou think, because thou art virtuous, there shall be no more cakes and ale?' Rob muttered as he washed his hands at the sink.

'I was going to take Baggins up to Spindle but with the fences up, I'll have to find a new place to walk him,' he said to Peony.

'They're down now. Whatever you said to the new owner made her take them down.'

Peony and Robert turned to see Izzy standing in the doorway, with a basket in her hand.

'Morning Izz,' said Robert with a smile.

'Morning both,' said Izzy. She placed the basket on the bench. 'Some morel mushrooms as a welcome gift.'

'Oh gosh, these are lovely, thank you Izzy.' Peony pounced on the mushrooms and held one up and then took a deep inhale of its scent.

'When did you speak to the new owner, Dad?' she asked.

'Yesterday,' Robert said. 'I snuck through the back way and then Baggins chased her dogs and then we exchanged some words.'

'You argued with the new owner?' Peony shook her head at her father. 'That's not very welcoming.'

'No, I simply told her that she wouldn't be helping herself if she kept the woods away from the visitors.'

'You said she would be facing eighty days of pestilence or something,' Izzy corrected and looked at Peony. 'I met her when I was mushrooming.'

'I did no such thing,' Robert harrumphed. 'I simply mentioned *Macbeth* and the witch's punishment for not sharing the chestnuts.'

Izzy leaned against the bench. 'To be honest, I don't think she realised how much the woods were used by the locals. She was totally cool about it and with me pilfering her mushrooms.'

'Did you find out anything else about her?' Robert asked. 'Is there another half? Children?'

'You're being a nosy parker,' Peony said. 'Meddlesome villager, you'll be in cahoots with Jenn Carruthers next.'

'I am nosy,' Robert said with no chagrin and looked to Izzy for the answers. 'So?'

'Nothing telling but she said she is planning a garden and invited me to take a look.'

Peony's phone rang and she pulled it from the back pocket of her jeans and saw it was Fergus and put it back in her pocket.

'You will have to speak to him sometime,' Robert called out to her.

'Thank you Nosy Nellie, but you can stay out of my business. He just wants to know when I'm getting the rest of my things so he can get rid of the flat. I don't want anything left there, I have everything I need.'

'You don't want your furniture and the rest of your clothes?' Robert asked.

'No, I don't want my boring clothes I used to wear to the hospital or the Ikea furniture that can be picked up at any charity shop for five pounds. It's all just stuff and none of it matters.'

It was true she didn't want anything left in the flat. She had taken the most important things including her mother's jewellery, some art she liked, some kitchen items she loved

61

and the clothes that felt the most like her. Everything else was Fergus's. It was depressing how little she had of herself in the relationship. It was always about Fergus.

As she thought about the flat, she remembered when she first went to Anstruther to meet Fergus's family after they had started seeing each other. She had been hoping for a happy, joyful, Scottish weekend of family and laughter. Instead, Fergus was sullen and childish around his parents and his younger sisters. He'd turned every conversation into an argument and was rude to Peony in front of the family. His mother, Claire was clearly spiritual, with a farmer's almanac by the backdoor for best planting times for the garden by the phases of the moon, and candles and bunches of herbs in corners of windows. Peony had no opinion on it but Fergus hated it, throwing some sprigs of lavender under their pillows into the bin.

'Mum's witchy tat,' he snorted. 'She thinks she's some sort of Stevie Nicks white witch. I hate it.'

Peony had been silent, but later, when he wasn't in the room, she had fished the lavender from the bin and placed it back under her pillow, because she liked that Claire had thought to do it and she liked the scent.

She hadn't seen that side of Fergus before but thought that perhaps the regression was some childhood stuff he hadn't unpacked yet.

There was time, she told herself, that's what she was good at, working through those familial patterns to come out wiser and kinder.

But when she was packing to leave the disastrous weekend, Fergus's mother Claire had come into the bedroom and closed the door behind her. She came to Peony's side and whispered. 'Peony, you have such light inside you, you are a healer.'

Peony had nodded. 'Thank you, Claire, it's been lovely here.'

Claire had shook her head, 'No it's been terrible. Fergus is difficult, always has been and when I look at you, and I see your light and healing energy, I worry.'

She had paused and the words she said next had stayed with Peony.

'Fergus, he's never been able to share. If you stay with him, he will take everything good from you and there will be nothing left. You will be empty.'

At the time Peony had nodded, smiled and said thank you for the advice but she had never told Fergus, because she realised, now, as she looked at the mushrooms that Izzy had left for her, that Claire was right.

There was nothing left of Peony.

She looked up from where she had been staring un-seeing at the mushrooms and noticed Rob and Izzy chatting happily about something she wasn't familiar with and she smiled. Perhaps she would find herself again in Honeystone, one dish at a time.

She needed to cook. She needed to feed and nurture and she needed to do it now. All through her schooling life Peony had been told she had potential. But potential for what?

Murder? Betrayal? Creation? Destruction? She had wished they were more specific but now she remembered something her father used to say when she would ask him what the teachers meant. *It's not in the stars to hold our destiny but in ourselves,* he would say when she asked what the teachers meant by potential. But perhaps she had put too much faith in the world to show her what to do and instead she had to take her fate into her own hands, one decision at a time, one dish at a time.

'Right, get out of my kitchen you two busybodies, I have food to make and mouths to feed.'

She flapped a tea towel at them as they laughed and Izzy went on her way.

'Izzy, thank you for the mushrooms,' she called out as Izzy went to the door.

'You're welcome,' Izzy said with a smile and then she was gone and a sense of peace and forgiveness came across Peony. All that time she had avoided Izzy when in fact, she was fine. It was Peony who had created the drama. She wondered if perhaps there wouldn't be more of these home truths that came up now that she was home.

Dora

Dora woke before her husband Barry.

Her morning routine hadn't changed much in forty years.

She would do some washing, ironing, folding and any cleaning around the house.

Then she would wake Barry and make him breakfast. He was watching his weight, so he would have a slice of wholemeal toast spread with butter and Marmite accompanied by a cup of tea, while he flicked through the newspaper.

Dora would hover, waiting for any instructions or things she had to attend to before he then went and showered.

She never showered before him. He liked to have the hottest water, he told her, so she would have to shower after him, even though she had a job to go to and he didn't, and even though he often left her little to no hot water.

Only then could she leave the house and head to work.

Work was a relief to Dora and even though Rob Grayling

was a lovely boss and the pub was fine and the patrons all known to her, the work was hard on her sixty-year-old feet.

The drive from her house to Honeystone wasn't long but far enough away that Dora could feel her body untensing as she left the house behind.

She had taken a few pounds from Barry's coin jar, so she could buy herself a coffee and cinnamon scroll from Mabel's before work. What a lovely treat that would be, she thought.

Dora made her way into Honeystone and parked her car at the back of the pub and wandered around to Mabel's. As she pushed open the creaking wooden door, the sweet scent of freshly baked scones and brewed tea welcomed her, wrapping her up in a cosy embrace. Dora felt herself relax, as Mala came to serve her.

'Hello Dora, how are you?' Mala was so lovely, in fact, if Dora had a daughter she would have wanted her to be like Mala, who only ever seemed to say nice things about other people behind their back.

'Fine thanks Mala, how are you?' Dora smiled at the young woman.

'Wonderful, every day is a blessing,' said Mala, 'Now, a scone? Cinnamon scroll? Fruit toast?'

'Scroll and a coffee thank you,' said Dora and she handed over the exact money. 'To take away thank you.'

The tea room's interior was a quaint and delightful tableau of country-style simplicity that Mala and Ajay had tweaked when they took over the business. The well-worn wooden floorboards, scuffed and faded by countless footsteps, added to the rustic ambiance. Soft, earthy tones painted the walls, adorned with floral wallpaper that seemed to have been plucked from a vintage cottage.

Antique wooden tables, each with its own distinctive character, were dressed in white tablecloths, surrounded by comfortable, cushioned chairs that invited guests to linger, and wooden benches along the wall near the door that provided extra seating for those who were waiting for a table or for a take away treat. On each table, Mala had replaced the stern white crockery with pretty, mismatched teacups and saucers, each telling a story of its own.

The soft hum of friendly conversation which filled the air, occasionally punctuated by the gentle laughter of customers was soothing to Dora. She loved hearing and seeing people living happy lives.

Opening for breakfast had been a brilliant idea, she thought, as she looked around at the tables.

There were some new faces and some old ones, and she saw Jenn Carruthers waving at her.

'Dora, come and sit, the pub doesn't open for another half an hour,' Jenn called.

Dora looked around nervously. She had lied to Barry about the opening hours so she could leave earlier, and now Jenn was singing it from the rafters.

Dora gave Mala her order and went and sat opposite Jenn, who was in a pink shiny tracksuit top with a thick aqua zip that pulled the top up under Jenn's chin.

She looked like she was encased in a pink sausage skin and for some reason, this gave Dora the giggles.

'You seem happy,' said Jenn.

Dora raised her eyebrows, 'Do I?'

Jenn smiled at her. 'Now I was thinking Dora, why don't we get you to do the Spring at Honeystone flyers. Maybe you can draw something? I love your drawings of the village, you could do one in colour with all the flowers around?'

Dora shook her head. 'I don't have time to draw much at the moment,' she said, which was partly true.

'We could pay you one hundred pounds.'

Dora paused. One hundred pounds would help her a lot. It would certainly move her towards her goal, but if Barry knew.

She looked at Jenn. 'I'm sorry, I can't,' she said, trying to keep the sadness from her voice.

Jenn frowned, 'But you're so talented Dora, you really should be drawing, not working in a pub.'

Dora was silent. *I should be doing a lot of things*, she thought but she wouldn't say as much to Jenn Carruthers because she was a gossip and, God knows, Dora didn't need to have more to worry about.

Mala brought over her coffee and cinnamon scroll.

'You said take away?' Mala asked Dora who nodded.

'Yes, thanks so much.' Dora said and she gave Mala the right money and stood up.

'Thanks for asking,' said Dora to Jenn. 'I do wish I had more time.'

Jenn nodded and then looked into Dora's eyes in a way that unnerved her.

'You know you can always ask me for anything Dora, or tell me anything,' she said. 'I have been through a lot you know. People might think my life is all beer and skittles but there was a time, in my first marriage, yes, I was married before, that I wondered if I would ever survive.'

Dora was silent. How much did Jenn know? God knows Dora tried to keep her marriage private but people didn't like Barry and she was sure they couldn't understand why she was married to him, so she kept to herself.

For a moment, Dora thought about sitting down with Jenn and telling her everything. Maybe Jenn could help? They weren't friends but there was something in Jenn's face that made her think twice about leaving.

The sound of a text on her phone rang out and she put

down the coffee and took her phone from her bag and read the message.

I know you took money from my jar. I count it every day. There should be a good reason for you to take it and not tell me. I look forward to your explanation.

Dora felt her stomach drop and she blinked a few times, as though trying to focus on the screen and then she slipped her phone away.

'Another time perhaps,' she said to Jenn and she took the scroll for which she didn't have an appetite for anymore and went to the pub.

Rob would be more than happy with it, she thought and she wondered what she was going to tell Barry about the missing money.

Robert

Robert set up for the lunchtime session, still thinking about the cinnamon scroll that Dora had bought for him.

She wasn't always so friendly or giving, so he wondered how she was. Dora Mundy was an odd bod, as his Mum used to say. But he was happy she wanted to work at the pub, and the locals liked her enough.

As he adjusted the cutlery on the table, he tried not to worry about how Peony was travelling in the kitchen but aware he would probably be a hindrance more than a help.

Christina had always told him to get up and would flap tea towels at him when she was alive, and Robert was secretly happy with this instruction as he wasn't comfortable with kitchens. Bars were much more his comfortable place.

He had written the lunchtime specials on the board and put it outside on the street but wasn't sure that anyone would care or come, even though Dora Mundy had spread the news about Peony joining as the new chef by telling Jenn Carruthers who popped in to tell her the signs at Spindle Hall were down.

The dining room was set up for lunch. Calling it a dining room was a stretch as it was really a smaller room in the little pub, that had a fireplace and a mantle and his collection of Toby jugs that had been collected and given to him and his family over the years.

If Robert was honest with Peony he would have admitted he hated the jugs and their ugly, smug faces, but he just smiled and accepted them when a new one came into the collection. His great-great-grandfather had started the collection and he felt he was betraying his ancestry by getting rid of them, but the ugly faces in the tricorn hats and ruddy cheeks really were an eyesore.

The pub door opened and there stood Old Ed and his wife, Clary.

'You're in early Ed,' said Robert starting to pour Old Ed's pint. 'And nice to see you Clary.' He nodded to Old Ed's rarely seen wife.

'We're here for Peony's rabbit pie,' Old Ed said.

Clary was dressed in a teal raincoat and see-through bonnet tied under her chin, but there wasn't a drop of rain on them.

'Prepared for rain, are we?' asked Robert as he placed the pint on the counter. 'I didn't see anything on the forecast.'

'The swallows were flying low this morning,' was all Clary said as she undid her raincoat and bonnet and carefully folded them into small squares and placed them into little matching plastic envelopes.

'I love those little superstitions,' said Robert. 'Can I get you a drink, Clary?'

Clary frowned at him as she smoothed down her short grey hair.

'It's not a superstition. It's when the birds fly lower to look for food because of the thermal pressure in the air the insects and bugs seek protection in the grasses and trees.'

Robert was taken aback at her comment. 'Is that so? I never knew.'

'Well, now you do,' said Clary. 'I'll have a lemonade please.'

In all the years of Rob working and living in the pub, Old Ed and Clary had never come for a meal. She had come for a lemonade when Christina had died, always nodded at him in the street and had given Peony a little handmade rag doll when she was a child which Peony had loved to death. But mostly Clary kept to herself. Some children once called her a witch when she passed them on the street to which Clary stopped and told them it was a compliment and if she was a witch, she would have boiled them all up for tea. The children avoided her after that.

'Lunch for two it is,' said Robert.

He gestured to the little dining nook. 'Take your pick of the tables,' he offered. 'Your rabbits will make a wonderful pie.'

'Not my rabbits, God's own,' Old Ed stated as he groaned, lowering himself into a wooden dining chair.

Robert went to the bar where he told Dora the order.

He then carried the drinks to the table and put them down.

'Pie for both of you?' he asked.

'Just me,' stated Old Ed.

'Roast chicken for me,' Clary ordered.

'What's for afters?' asked Old Ed. 'I do like a bit of sweet after dinner.'

Rob panicked. 'Hang on, I'll check,' he said.

He hadn't thought about dessert and he wondered if Peony had.

Robert went to the kitchen and opened the door.

'Old Ed and Clary are in,' he said as he watched Peony baste chickens in the oven.

'For lunch?' she asked.

'Yes, and they're very standoffish, I feel like the reviewers from the *Telegraph* are here.'

Peony grimaced. 'What do they want? Two rabbit pies?'

Robert shook his head. 'One pie, one roast chicken. Also, they want to know if there is dessert?'

Peony nodded, 'Apple pie with ice cream or lemon tart with Chantilly cream.'

'When did you whip those up?' he asked, surprised.

'I didn't, they were in the freezer. They're not homemade but they'll do for today,' she said.

'Well done, Sweets,' Robert said. He heard the bell on the pub door announce a new arrival and went to the bar.

'Hello Barry,' he said. 'Lunch? Would you like Dora to join you?'

Barry was wearing his 'Keep Honeystone Clean' fleece jacket that he had tried to say was about litter but most people understood the hidden meaning.

'Yes please,' said Barry, his arms crossed, as though he was ready for a confrontation.

Robert looked at Dora who was behind the bar, her face tight and strained.

'Do you want to join Barry?' asked Rob but Dora shook her head.

'I have to help Peony serve.'

'You're going to make me eat alone?' Barry hissed and Dora took off her apron and went and sat down.

By the look on Dora's face, Rob wished he hadn't said anything.

He had always known Barry was hard work and that Dora bore the burden but Dora had seemed down more often at work, and then there was the issue with the wine, which he would have to talk to her about when he had got to the bottom of the missing bottles.

Robert gestured to the room. 'Take your pick,' he said and Barry and Dora sat at the little table next to one side of the fireplace. 'Drink?'

Soon Dora and Barry had ordered two roast chickens and a glass of white wine and a pint for Barry.

Robert was back from the kitchen, as two Americans had come into the bar and ordered a pint each.

'Alright Dad?' asked Peony, poking her head through the doorway from the kitchen.

'Busier than usual but it's good.' He beamed at Peony.

'Old Ed and Clary's meals are ready.'

He came into the kitchen and she handed him a white cloth.

'The plates are hot,' she said. 'Make sure you warn them.'

Robert did as he was told and carried the plates out to the older couple. The pie looked delicious and the chicken was perfectly juicy and smelled amazing.

It was much better than anything that had been served at The Hare and Thistle in years, maybe ever, he thought and pride rippled through him as he carefully placed the meals in front of Old Ed and Clary.

They leaned over and sniffed the food and then Old Ed tucked his napkin into the top of his knitted jumper and proceeded to start on the dish.

'We have apple pie and lemon tart for afters,' he said to them both.

'Apple pie please,' said Clary and Old Ed nodded his approval.

'Same thanks, Rob.'

'Table for one please,' Robert heard and turned and stopped in surprise.

It was the woman from Spindle Hall.

'Hello,' he said with a smile, hoping she might meet him halfway. 'I'm Robert Grayling, welcome to The Hare and Thistle.'

'Robert,' she smiled at him in a cool classy way. 'Anthea McGregor.'

'Here for lunch?' he asked.

'Yes, I was told there would be rabbit pie, which were caught on the grounds of Spindle Hall. Isn't that right, Ed?'

Ed nodded, wiping his mouth on his napkin, leaving a smear of gravy across the white linen.

'Mrs McGregor is right, I caught those rabbits at Spindle. I offered them to her but she said she was fine, so then I told her they would be on the menu today at The Hare and Thistle, so here we are.'

Anthea McGregor. Why did that name seem so familiar, he wondered. Peony would know, he thought, tucking the name away in his mental to-be-sorted box for later.

'One rabbit pie it is,' said Robert and he rushed into the kitchen to tell Peony that the rabbits had actually come from Mrs McGregor's garden.

Joe

'Dr Fisher?' Joe heard his name and turned around and saw a man coming towards him from the pub.

'Barry Mundy,' said the man, putting out his hand for Joe to shake. 'Deputy Mayor of Honeystone. My wife, Dora is the medical secretary, she was told from the council she would be needed back as we had a new doctor. Great news for everyone.'

'Joe, please,' he said shaking the man's hand. Barry Mundy was a non-descript sort of a person, in a plain blue shirt and V-necked jumper and blue trousers with black lace up shoes. He might have been coming from work, where perhaps he had a desk job, with a fake plant by his computer.

His sandy hair was brushed to one side, and he wore transition lens glasses that seemed to be stuck in-between changing, giving his eyes a slightly eerie look.

'I'm so pleased you have decided to become our new village doctor,' gushed Barry. 'I don't usually like new people to come into the area, they're usually just weekenders, not volunteering for anything, not sending their children to the local schools, just bringing in their fancy food from London. We need people to stay, not treat the place like a holiday village.'

'I'm only here until the permanent replacement can start,' Joe reminded Barry.

'Once you come to Honeystone, you won't want to leave,' said Barry and Joe tried not to feel alarmed. It sounded slightly ominous, like the lyrics from 'Hotel California', a song Joe had always turned off when he heard it. Why wouldn't you want to leave somewhere? Having being stuck in Australia finishing his medical degree the moment he could head to England and work he did. And in-between assignments he travelled to Croatia, Switzerland, Germany and Italy. But he was running out of money, so needed to stop somewhere for a while until he could save up again.

'You're from Queensland then?' asked Barry as he pulled out the keys and opened the door to the surgery. 'Very hot there, right near the Barrier Reef,' Barry stated knowingly.

Joe nodded. He couldn't be bothered explaining to people that Brisbane was not exactly on the doorstep of the Great Barrier Reef. It only went in one ear and out the other.

The surgery, as it was, was a small stone building with empty window boxes and a red front door.

The inside waiting room was fine, albeit sterile but that was a good thing for a doctor's surgery, he thought, as he passed the reception desk and office area.

'I've arranged for my wife Dora to come and help you the three days you're here,' said Barry. 'She was the receptionist when the last doc was here for a while, then she left and went to the pub, which is a step down in my opinion but she tells me she can do both again.'

Joe listened to the man waffle on and followed him into the surgery, noting all the necessary equipment and the clean environment.

'It's great,' he said, meaning it. Because Joe only ever said what he meant. Sometimes this got him into trouble but mostly it made him a fine doctor and liked by patients.

Barry showed him through the rest of the downstairs and then took out another key and opened the door that had a sign on it reading, **PRIVATE QUARTERS**.

Barry gestured for Joe to go first up the narrow staircase.

Joe climbed the stairs and walked into a perfectly service-able sitting room that looked slightly like someone who decorated motels for a living had had a stab at this interior.

Plain sofas with stiff-looking pillows on them, and a plain wood coffee table. A small galley kitchen was to the side, with everything he would need, he thought as he noticed the coffee cups hanging on a metal stand. It reminded him of a country motel, he thought, thinking of the many he had stayed at driving between Sydney and Brisbane.

The bedroom was as expected, with a dull bed cover and what looked to be a painting of Honeystone over the bed in case he forgot where he was.

'Does this suit you?' Barry asked.

'Absolutely, it's all I'll need,' said Joe.

Barry clapped his hands in glee. 'So Honeystone has a quack once again, good news. I'll be sure to tell Jenn Carruthers who is the editor of the *Honeystone Herald*. It's online but she does print a few copies and leaves them at the pub across the road. It's not a great paper, I would do more with it if I had time but Jenn does her best.'

Joe nodded as he and Barry walked downstairs again. He had no idea what this man was going on about but presumed it best that he stayed on the good side of him.

'And it comes with a little runabout. Just a little Astra but it runs well.' Barry handed Joe a bundle of keys in a plastic sandwich bag. 'That's parked around the back.'

They stood awkwardly in the reception area for a moment.

'Well, I should get my things from the rental car,' said Joe. 'If you could perhaps drive the Astra into town tomorrow so I can return the rental and you could drive me back, I'd be so grateful?'

Barry looked like he had been asked to put bamboo stakes under his fingernails.

'I will see what I can do but I have a very busy schedule. I have a tennis party tomorrow.'

Joe nodded. 'Of course, no worries if you can't.'

Barry moved to the door. 'Probably not, but I'll let you get settled, perhaps head over to the pub tonight and I'll introduce you to a few people.'

'I might take a rain check on that,' said Joe. 'Get settled and so on and don't want to drink and have the village think I'm a drunken Aussie.'

He was about to laugh but he saw Barry nodding in agreement.

'Good idea,' he said and he whispered as though people were listening.

'It's not a great pub anyway, I had lunch there and the chicken was dry.'

Joe was disappointed to hear this, since he loved a good pub feed, but he could always drive into the next villages, in the actual Cotswolds.

They walked to the door and Barry shook Joe's hand again and went down the street, a spring in his step.

Joe went to the rental car and opened the boot and pulled out his bags and doctor's kit and then walked to the front door.

'Hello, are you the new doctor?' he heard and he turned around to see a very pretty young woman, a small child with a splint on her legs standing next to her.

'I am, I'm Joe. Joe Fisher,' he said.

'I saw you talking to Barry, I assume he was your welcome party,' she said.

'I guess he was.' Joe smiled. 'Is he a friend of yours?'

The woman made a face, 'No, not at all.'

He laughed. 'Good to know then.'

'I'm Izzy Hinch and this is Clover Hinch,' she said with a smile.

Clover looked at him suspiciously. 'Barry said Izzy couldn't park in the special spot even though I sometimes have a wheelchair.'

Joe was taken aback. 'Did he? That's not very fair.'

'That's Barry Mundy for you,' said Izzy.

'Did you need me to write you a letter for a permit?'

'We have a permit,' said Izzy with a look that spoke volumes about her opinion of Barry Mundy.

'Izzy said that Barry is a pain in her arse,' Clover stated.

Joe burst out laughing as Izzy looked around nervously. 'Shhh, he might hear you.'

'You're Australian,' Izzy said and he nodded.

'Guilty as charged. An escaped convict.'

'I thought we sent you there to stay, not to come back,' she teased.

'I couldn't help myself,' he said. 'I just love the weather here.'

Izzy laughed. 'Well I hope we never see you again unless it's socially,' she said.

'Do you like cake?' asked Clover suddenly.

'I do,' he said and smiled at the little girl.

Izzy pulled the girl to her side in a hug and looked at Joe. 'Clover likes to bake.'

'Oh fantastic, I love lemon drizzle cake, just in case you're planning on making one,' he joked. 'Do you have them here in England?'

'Yes, we do,' said the small voice.

'Of course, you do,' said Joe. 'I should have known.'

He smiled at Izzy and then back to Clover. 'You don't have to make one, I was teasing.'

'No trust me, it would be doing her a favour, she loves a reason to bake.' She leaned down and kissed the child's head.

'I can't bake or cook, I need to teach myself,' he said. 'Or I will be starving while I'm here.'

'You can eat at the pub,' Izzy said as she looked over at the pub across the road from the surgery. 'They have a new cook, she's just started today. She's going to be great, I can feel it, can't you Clo?'

Clover stepped out, 'I recommended an artichoke pasta.'

Joe tried not to laugh, 'Wow, that sounds fancy.'

'Clover knows a thing or two about food,' said Izzy. 'Which you wouldn't know judging by the size of her.'

'You must have hollow legs,' he said to Clover.

'I don't, my legs have veins and bones in them and blood,' Clover said with authority.

'I know, it's a saying my aunt used to state about me.' He smiled.

'See? Aunts know things,' Izzy said to Clover. 'I'm always telling her this but she just rolls her eyes at me.'

'You're her aunt then? I was wondering why she called you Izzy, thought it was modern parenting and all that,' Joe asked.

'And a very proud one at that,' Izzy said with a smile.

Dammit, she was gorgeous. That cute short hair and the striped T-shirt and overalls, she was like an earthy Audrey Hepburn.

No, he reminded himself. No lovers in Honeystone. He couldn't take the risk of having his heart broken. It would ruin all the carefree bachelor plans he had for the year ahead.

But as much as Joe hated to admit it, he was a one girl guy and one-night-stands always left him feeling a little depressed afterwards, because sex was sex but sex with love was something else.

He smiled back at her and then lifted the bag in his hand like a shield between them.

'I should get these inside,' he said.

'We won't keep you, we were just passing and wanted to

79

say hello and welcome to Honeystone,' Izzy said with that dazzling smile again. Double damn.

'Nice to meet you both,' he said and he watched them for a little while as they walked away, chattering happily like a pair of canaries, hoping like hell neither of them would want medical care while he was in Honeystone.

5

Izzy

Izzy had never been in love. Mostly because the boys she grew up with in Honeystone and the surrounding areas didn't like that she could run faster than them, could jump higher, and could hit a cricket ball for six as easily as buttering toast.

Naturally the boys then teased her about everything from her sexuality and the way she wore her hair short. She could have explained to them that she kept her hair short because she hated the feeling of it on her neck and she was also madly in love with Leo DiCaprio and Tobey Maguire when she was at school but they wouldn't have listened. People decided what they wanted about people and it was a rare person who could have their mind changed.

Instead, she'd ignored boys at secondary school because she didn't have a mum to ask about boy things, and she would never ask Connor, and then she went to university at Swindon to study science. She partied a lot on weekends and lost her virginity with her eyes closed in a single bed in a university dorm room.

It was all very unfulfilling and Izzy didn't have the patience for it and despite the cajoling from her friends from school, she stayed in Honeystone.

She had tried sex, she didn't like it the first, second or

third time, and a few more times after that. In the end, she felt it wasn't worth the effort to just lie there and pretend it was special and fun. It was perfunctory and without any purpose other than making a mess and then trying to find an excuse to leave straight afterwards.

After leaving the doctor's surgery, Izzy didn't have any opinion on the new doctor. She didn't look at him with any lens on except would he be kind to Clover, because she knew, despite their joking, that he would be seeing Clover again.

She was often sick, no matter what Izzy did to try and build up her immune system or how much she protected her at home. It was only going to become worse once Clover started at school with all those extra germs.

Clover, however, had viewed Joe with rose-coloured glasses. 'He's smart,' she said.

'Is he?' Izzy asked. 'How do you know?'

'I just know,' said Clover decisively. 'And I am going to make him a cake.'

'That's nice,' said Izzy as she drove home.

'And then I'm going to write him a letter,' said Clover. 'And do a drawing for him.'

Izzy looked at her niece in the rear-view mirror and smiled.

'What will you write to him about?' asked Izzy.

'It's private,' said Clover and she crossed her arms to seal her decision.

Izzy laughed as they drove. 'Well, I won't ask about the drawing then.'

Izzy saw Connor walking past with a ladder as they pulled into the driveway and she lowered her car window.

'There's a new doctor in town,' she said to him.

Connor nodded. 'That's good,' he said in his usual taciturn way and he kept walking.

Izzy was about to say more but she realised Connor was in a mood.

She wanted to yell that it was good because she was the one who had to take Clover further out of Honeystone to find a doctor and having one in the village meant she could keep Clover's care in one place. One card, one record, one doctor.

But Connor didn't want to hear any of that.

She helped Clover out of her seat and they walked inside the house.

'I'm going to do the drawing now,' Clover said and she went to her room.

Izzy watched her go and then sighed.

There was a list of things she had to do but she didn't want to do any of them.

The restlessness had become worse lately.

The need to do something new, see something different, talk to someone else other than Clover and Connor.

Izzy looked out of the window and saw Connor was putting his things away and soon he would be coming inside to do the accounts probably.

The need to walk was powerful and Izzy went back through the front door and walked around the house and up the embankment and towards the fence and without a look back, she slipped under the fence and made her way into the woods of Spindle Hall.

Anthea

Anthea lay her napkin down on the table after she had eaten her lunch at The Hare and Thistle.

She was thankful for not having lost her sense of taste as well as her sense of smell because the pie she had just eaten was perfection.

A rich buttery pastry on the top and bottom made it a true pie, as far as Anthea was concerned. It had to have a pastry bottom to be a pie, she had always thought but the meat filling was where the pie took her to a new level.

She waved at Robert who was behind the bar. 'Can I speak to the chef?' she asked. 'It's your daughter, isn't it?'

Robert looked around. 'Is there a problem?'

'Not at all. I simply wanted to ask her about the pie.' Anthea looked him in the eye and raised one of her eyebrows.

Robert frowned. 'She's busy so why don't you come to the kitchen?'

Anthea nodded and stood up and followed him to the kitchen.

'Sweet, this is Anthea who has moved into Spindle Hall, she wants to talk to you about your pie.'

Anthea saw the back of a woman – thin, tall, hunched shoulders – before she turned to face her.

'Was everything all right?' the woman asked.

'It was amazing,' said Anthea, taking in the woman's heat-flushed cheeks and hair pulled into a scraggly bun. She was mid-thirties and had a worried air about her.

'Oh wonderful.' The relief was palpable on the woman's face.

'This is Peony, my daughter,' said Robert, somewhat proudly. 'This is her first lunch service.'

'Well done, you,' Anthea said, glancing around the kitchen.

Everything seemed in top condition: clean, organised and efficient.

'I must ask, what was the slightly fruity taste in the meat? It was delicious.'

Peony wiped her hand on the towel hanging from her apron and smiled.

'Cider,' she said. 'I make the gravy with apple cider, it pulls the flavour of the rabbit out more than anything else I've found.'

Anthea nodded slowly. 'Cider, of course.'

If her sense of smell was working, she would have been able to pull apart the scents from the dish and would have picked up the apple but she had to rely on her taste buds now and they were not even close to her sense of smell when it worked.

'I used the cider from the Raspberry Hill Farm orchard. Connor, I think you met his sister Izzy from there, he made a small batch and Dad gave me some. Izzy also gave me the mushrooms from your woods.'

A wave of something like recognition but more similar to when you finally understand the solution to a problem, washed over Anthea. It felt like everything was clear but she hadn't known it was foggy until now.

'Yes, I met her, she's lovely.'

She saw Peony glance at Robert who made a face.

'What?' asked Anthea.

'Izzy is many things but I wouldn't say she's lovely.' Robert laughed. 'She can be very direct and perhaps rude, you must have got her on a good day. But if you win her heart, she'd do anything for you.'

Peony giggled. 'Izzy is the truthteller of the village, so if you want to know how things are or where you stand, Izzy will tell you.'

Anthea smiled at them both. 'So, what does that make you two then? In the archetypes of Honeystone village?'

It was a reasonable question, and one Robert looked like he might have answered if he had more time and a glass of something in hand. But Peony seemed lost.

'I don't know, I mean I've been away for a long time,' said Peony. 'I've just had a change of direction. I lived in London for ten years or so.'

Anthea nodded, 'Me too, except for thirty years. This is where my change of direction led me.'

Peony nodded, 'Welcome,' she said.

'We should have a drink sometime and share London stories,' Anthea said, surprising herself.

'Oh yes please, I have no friends here, so that would be amazing.' Peony laughed.

'Wonderful, give me your number and I will text you,' Anthea said, taking her phone from her bag.

With Peony's number in her phone and hers in Peony's, she said her goodbyes and went to her car.

There was a man with a beard outside the doctor's surgery taking down the sign. He gave her a wave as she opened her car door.

She gave a small wave back as she got into the car and drove towards home. A wave of anger at herself came over her for suggesting a drink to Peony. She had said to herself no friends in the country. The plan had been that she would see a chosen few who wanted to come from London but mostly she wanted to lose herself in her work. One rabbit pie and suddenly she was Miss Congeniality.

No friends, she told herself as she drove up through the large gates and through the woods and to the clearing outside the house where she saw someone sitting on the front steps.

She peered at them as she slowed the car and then smiled as the person waved at her.

She stopped the car and opened the door.

'Izzy,' she said. 'This is a surprise.'

God, was she a friendship charmer? Why were all these women popping out of the woods?

Izzy shuffled her feet in the gravel looking like a teenager.

'You mentioned the garden plans? I thought I might be able to give you some more knowledge about the soil, and what grows in what if you like, you probably have people to do that but still...' Izzy's voice trailed away.

'I don't, I mean I do but not with the personal knowledge of you,' Anthea said. 'As a local.'

She held up a container of lemon tart. Perhaps she should just give into the moment and the connection.

'Peony gave me this. Feel like sharing it? We can have some tea.'

Izzy nodded. 'I would love that,' she said.

'Come on then, let's go.'

Anthea walked around to the side of the house and through the door once meant for the staff, of which she had none. She had had a housekeeper in London but she went after she had found out she was giving John information about Anthea's whereabouts after they split up. Not that Anthea was doing anything untoward, but which friends she was seeing and where she was going was none of John's business.

The kitchen was warm and inviting and she gestured to Izzy to sit down at the kitchen table.

'This is such a beautiful kitchen,' Izzy said. 'I bet Peony would die to have this.'

Anthea looked around at the green cupboards with brass

handles and marble benches. It was her perfect kitchen except she hadn't cooked anything in it since moving in, existing instead on a diet of things that needed heating up.

'It is, but it feels like a waste, I don't really cook for myself,' Anthea said as she filled up the kettle and put it on the hob. 'I always thought I would have a family, loads of children and loads of animals and so on but it never happened for me.'

Izzy shrugged, 'Kids and animals are overrated.'

'Do you have either?' Anthea smiled at the young woman.

'I have a cat, who is a total shit and has been missing since the winds. No, don't worry, he's not in trouble, he will be off under the house somewhere, playing survival games until I get worried enough and he'll return like the prodigal feline and we will all make a fuss of him.'

'What's his name?'

'Cat.'

'Yes, the cat,' Anthea said.

'His name is Cat.'

'That's inspired.' She laughed.

'I got him when I was fourteen and I was trying to be edgy, and that's what Holly Golightly called her cat in *Breakfast at Tiffany's*. I also think that because my parents had died the year before, I didn't really have any creativity in me to name him more than Cat.'

Anthea reached out and touched Izzy's arm. 'I'm sorry to hear that.'

'That's OK, we all have sad stories.' Izzy smiled at Anthea and she saw she bore no malice.

'Who is the "we" you mentioned?' asked Anthea warming her favourite teapot.

'My niece, Clover and my brother Connor, he's a single dad so I help with Clover, she has cerebral palsy,' Izzy said. 'Born prem and had some struggles.'

'Where is mum?' asked Anthea.

'God knows. Left Clover at the hospital, and a note to Connor saying she didn't want to be a parent to a child with disabilities.'

'Ouch,' said Anthea sitting at the kitchen table.

'Yes, it was pretty awful. Clover doesn't ask about her, well not much but Connor and I know it's coming and it will be hard for her.'

'Have you ever tried to find the mother?'

Izzy shook her head. 'I haven't, I know Connor had tried her family, but nothing. We haven't moved, she knows where we are. Clover is seven and brilliant and deserves everything and more in life but if your mum doesn't want you, what does that say to your little soul?'

Anthea sighed. 'I can only imagine.'

The kettle started to sing and Anthea went and filled the teapot.

'What do you do Izzy, besides collect mushrooms? You mention you have a garden at your house?'

'I do, a small vegetable plot but it yields more than enough for us and some extra for the pub that Rob Grayling buys.'

Anthea nodded. 'Did you study horticulture?'

Izzy snorted. 'No, I just have a way with gardens. I read a lot and watch videos but mostly I just get the feel of it, you know?'

Anthea nodded, she did know, or she had known.

'Now, tell me about your garden,' Izzy asked as Anthea plated up the lemon tart. 'I want to know your grand plans and dreams.'

Anthea took a moment to think and then she gathered her thoughts.

'So, what I was thinking was ...'

Peony

'Is this yours?' Rob walked into the kitchen holding a black shawl.

Peony glanced at it and shook her head. 'Nope, not mine.'

Rob looked at the label. 'Johnstons of Elgin,' he read. 'We don't have any Johnstons around here? From Elgin, I'm not familiar with it?'

Peony laughed, 'It's a label, Dad, not a name tag and it's probably cashmere.'

Rob turned the label over. 'It is,' he said. 'I wonder who left it.'

Peony wiped her hands dry on a clean tea towel, wet from the last of the cleaning up in the kitchen.

'I know who this belongs to,' she said taking it from her father. 'Anthea McGregor.'

Rob shrugged. 'I'll let her know that it's here when she calls and asks. If it's expensive then she will want it back.

Peony held the shawl to her face and inhaled the scent, part lemon, part jasmine, maybe some roses.

'It's OK, I will take it back to her, I want to have a peek at Spindle Hall.'

'Now who's a nosy parker? You'll be putting Jenn Carruthers out of a job soon. She's our gossip barometer.' Rob laughed.

'Not gossiping, just seeing,' said Peony, putting the shawl on the bench. 'You all right here?' she asked her father.

'Right as rain,' said Rob. 'Dora's coming for a shift in the bar this evening and I'll be closing at nine.'

'I'll be home before then,' laughed Peony.

The road to Spindle Hall wasn't long but it brought her

past Raspberry Hill Farm and she could see Connor standing at the gate at the top of his driveway.

'Please don't see me,' she said aloud as she drove past the house and towards Spindle Hall's driveway.

She kept her eyes straight ahead as she passed the house but she knew Connor had seen her, she could feel it, she had always felt seen by him and never more so than now.

She turned off at Spindle Hall driveway and drove up to the house, where a Range Rover was parked.

Peony parked next to it and got out of the car, the shawl in hand.

There was no answer at the front door when she rang the bell, so she walked around the house, pleased to see it looking less forlorn than it had in the past.

Peony had always hoped someone would care for Spindle Hall again and the fact it was a successful woman made her feel powerful just by being on the property.

Peony knew who Anthea was, most women who love perfumes and skincare did, not that Peony owned any of Anthea's products. She'd had a candle once that someone gave her for her thirtieth birthday. Fig and Amber were the scent and Peony had loved it so much she refused to burn it for years. When she finally did, the scent had faded to nothing almost and Peony had wondered why she left things so late until they were ruined. It seemed to be the theme of her life.

She walked around the side of the house and saw the kitchen door was open. There were two mugs on the kitchen table and a teapot with the empty container that had held the lemon tart. Peony looked around the kitchen quickly and felt her heart skip a beat for such a homely yet elegant space. It was exactly the sort of kitchen she would have had if she owned a house like Spindle Hall.

Peony carefully folded the shawl and left it on the table and walked out and looked down over the view.

There were two figures waving at her in the distance and she covered her eyes with her hand to see them.

Anthea and Izzy were walking towards her.

She put her hands in her pockets and waited, feeling nervous in case Anthea did think she was a Jenn Carruthers type.

'Hello,' called Anthea.

'Hi,' Peony called back. 'You left your shawl at the pub, I was returning it. I popped it on the kitchen table.'

Izzy waved at her with a shy smile.

'I'm giving Izzy a tour of the garden and my plans, want to join in?' Anthea asked as she came closer.

Peony thought for a moment. All that was waiting for her back at the pub was her dad and Baggins, neither of who were begging for her company.

'I'd love to,' said Peony and the three of them traipsed across the lawn towards a walled garden.

Anthea looked to be in her element as she walked and talked about her plans for Spindle Hall.

'The whole place will be filled with all the flowers and herbs and trees I need to start my new business.'

'Your new business?' asked Peony as they walked around the overgrown garden.

'My ex-husband managed to take half of everything and my name,' said Anthea pulling at a rose hip and dropping it on the ground.

'Your name? How can that be right?' asked Izzy.

Anthea gave a sharp little laugh that didn't sound like anything was funny about the situation.

'He owns my name and my brand. It's not right but he did it,' said Anthea 'And I was ill and unable to fight the way

I would have if I wasn't on life support. I had Covid and it was touch and go for a while.'

Peony looked at Izzy whose face was mutinous.

'What a bastard,' Izzy muttered.

'It's OK,' Anthea said, 'I can't fight it anymore and I don't care, he will probably sell it off to some huge parent company and become even richer from my name.'

Anthea turned around in a circle, slowly, her arms out-stretched. 'But this, this is mine,' she cried.

Her voice echoed in the walled garden and she beamed at Peony and Izzy.

'Your ex-husband is a bastard,' Izzy called and the phrase came back to them several times over.

'My ex-husband is a bastard, and a prick,' Anthea called and laughed as the sound bounced around them like a pinball. 'And he was rubbish in bed,' she screamed laughing as it echoed back.

'I hate Honeystone,' yelled Izzy and then laughed as it shot back at her.

'You have to yell it,' instructed Izzy to Peony. 'But it needs to be something you haven't said to anyone else.'

'For the first time in my life, I have no idea what I'm doing,' yelled Anthea.

'I've never known what I'm doing,' Izzy yelled, laughing uproariously.

'I plan exotic and unusual ways to kill my ex-husband when I'm going to sleep, I find it soothes me.'

Izzy was bent over laughing as Anthea yelled out her secret.

'I think someone put a spell on me and I'm stuck in Honeystone forever and sometimes I think about running away in the night but don't because it would break Clover and Connor's hearts.'

Anthea made a face at Izzy.

'I know, that was a bit heavy, sorry,' Izzy said and she turned to Peony, 'Go on, your turn.'

Peony looked at Anthea and Izzy laughing and felt her eyes fill with tears so she closed them and called out into the air.

'I'm pregnant.'

6

Anthea

Anthea led the way to Spindle Hall with a sobbing Peony and a silent Izzy.

'A cup of tea, and a chat will help,' Anthea said as they came to the kitchen door, opening it as Izzy and Peony stepped inside.

Anthea closed the door and saw a rainbow in the distance near the village.

'There's a rainbow, that's a good sign I think,' she said and she refilled the kettle and brought a box of tissues to the table and sat down opposite Peony.

'How far along are you?'

Peony shook her head. 'I don't know, maybe eight weeks.'

'Do you want to keep it?' Izzy asked, ever the pragmatist.

'I don't know that either. I always thought I would have children but I would be married, the father would be a good person, not a cheating shit of a partner like Fergus.'

'Did he cheat?' Izzy asked.

'I think so, with a woman from his football club.'

Izzy rolled her eyes.

Peony took a tissue and blew her nose loudly.

'And I have nothing, I mean, nothing to show for my relationship with me. I left my job, I left my flat, all I have is the pub which is Dad's anyway and this.' She put her hand on her stomach.

Anthea leaned back in her chair. 'I can't tell you what to do, but I will say, if you want children, then there is no right time to have them. How old are you?'

'Thirty-four, turning thirty-five in September.'

'That's getting old,' said Izzy. 'You don't want to wait too much longer.'

Peony glared at Izzy and turned her nose up at her. 'Thanks for that reminder.'

'If you did have the baby, your dad would help you, wouldn't he?' Anthea asked.

Peony nodded. 'He would, yes.'

'He's the nicest man in the world, so of course he would help, and he would love being a grandfather. He's so good with Clover, makes her feel very important when she comes with me to the pub,' Izzy told Anthea.

Peony was silent. 'I just wonder if he would be disappointed in me, because I would be a single parent.'

'He's a single parent,' said Izzy with a snort.

'My mum died, not really the same,' Peony snapped.

'And Clover's mum up and left her at the hospital because she didn't want a child with a disability, that doesn't make Connor a disappointment,' Izzy snapped back.

Anthea got up and made the tea and searched the cupboard and found a packet of gingerbread biscuits that were a gift in a hamper from when she had moved in.

'No one is disappointing anyone,' Anthea said firmly. 'It sounds like you're judging yourself, Peony.'

She brought the mugs and biscuits to the table.

'You will need to see a doctor to confirm the dates and discuss your options with them.'

'You can see the new Australian doctor in the village,'

said Izzy eagerly, wiggling her eyebrows at Peony. 'Tell him I said hi.'

'God you're just as annoying now as you were at thirteen,' said Peony.

'I hope I am,' said Izzy, 'I really try to stay true to myself.' Anthea laughed at Izzy.

'And you can't tell Connor,' said Peony to Izzy. 'This isn't gossip, OK?'

'I won't,' said Izzy, and Anthea believed her. Izzy was exactly what she said she was and did what she said she would. There was an honesty about her that was both charming and disarming to Anthea. Women like Izzy were rarely understood, particularly by men, because they refused to play the games men expected them to play to survive.

'Didn't you want children?' Izzy asked Anthea.

'I did but my husband didn't and by the time I turned forty, I had left my run a bit late. I tried fertility treatments but it was interfering with work and in the end I thought it best if I treated my business as a child, which ended up backfiring on me.'

'Why?' Izzy asked.

'Because my stupid ex took my baby. I am left with some hope to start again but you know, it's a lot,' Anthea admitted as she looked around the kitchen. 'And I'm no spring chicken.'

'You're not a wizened old lady, either,' Peony said. 'Look at JLo, she's fifty and thriving.'

'Can I not look at JLo please?' Anthea said. 'She's not really anything I aspire to be, far too much exercise, but each to their own.'

'I think she looks amazing,' said Izzy. 'But I agree, there's a lot of work in that body. Just get in the garden and everyone would be toned up and fit in no time.'

Anthea sighed. 'I wasn't actually planning to do the work myself, I'm just responsible for the vision. But enough about me. Let's talk about you, Peony.'

Peony closed her eyes. 'I'd rather talk about JLo if we could.'

'Have you told your ex?'

Peony shook her head.

'Are you going to tell your ex?' Izzy asked.

'I will but he won't want it, I already know that and then it will be a whole thing about money and so on.'

It was true it would become about money. In Anthea's experience, everything with men became about money.

'If you want to have the baby then you can do it alone, lots of people do without half of the support you have here,' Anthea said.

Peony looked at her. 'Do you think so?'

'Of course. I have all the faith in the world in you. And you have Izzy and me, doesn't she, Izzy?'

Izzy looked at Peony and then to Anthea. 'I guess, I mean it's not like Peony and I are friends though. Just because we lived here together doesn't make us besties.'

'No, please be more honest,' groaned Peony.

'What?' Izzy said. 'I'm just saying it as it is. You left my brother when my parents died and he was broken and you said he was too sad. And then he ended up with Mel and she turned out to be a nightmare and the only thing he was left with was Clover, who, by the way, I do the majority of caring for.'

Anthea watched Peony's face spin through a series of emotions but she wasn't quite sure which one the arrow landed on.

'Are you fucking serious? Is that what he told you?'

Anger, it seemed, was where the spinner landed.

Peony was leaning towards Izzy, over the kitchen table, as though she was about to leap at her. Izzy, to her credit didn't flinch.

'Yes, that's what he implied.'

Peony stood up, the kitchen chair making a scraping sound on the floor.

'Where are you going?' Anthea asked.

'To see Connor.' And then Peony was gone.

Izzy looked at Anthea. 'Well, that got her moving, didn't it?'

'What do you mean?' asked Anthea.

Izzy laughed, 'He didn't say that in so many words but I think they need to see each other and Peony in full flight is always the best mode for her to see Connor.'

'So, he never said that to you? About her leaving after he broke down?' Anthea was confused.

Izzy took a biscuit and dunked it in her tea. 'Nope, I knew he broke up with her but I also know he's regretted it every day since. Peony and Connor are meant to be together, they just can't see it yet. Why else would her relationship with her idiot ex have gone to the dogs?'

Anthea shook her head, 'Izzy, you shouldn't meddle in their affairs.'

But Izzy laughed. 'Why not? If they aren't going to do it then who will? Sometimes people just need a push in the right direction.'

'You're a little witch,' said Anthea with a smile. She had the feeling that Izzy would need her own push eventually but where to was up to Izzy to find out.

Peony

'Excuse me,' Peony called out to Connor, who was walking up the driveway.

'Hello Peony,' Connor said, as though he had been expecting her. He lifted his red cap off his head and ran his hand through his dark hair. It was a small gesture but it was enough to make Peony's blood boil.

She had forgotten about his self-assured nature, as though nothing would ever trouble him, even in the worst of times. His lack of vulnerability was one of the things that made her furious when they went out as teenagers, and it was clearly something he was still carrying around like a prize.

'Nice to see you, I hear you're back for a while,' he said in that casual way that was both simultaneously dismissive and attractive.

'You need a haircut,' she shot at him. 'And why did you tell Izzy I broke up with you after your parents died?'

Connor grimaced. 'Nice to see you too, thanks for noticing my hair and I have no idea what you're talking about,' he said. 'And it was ten years ago, why do you care?'

'Because if you've told people in the village, that I dumped you days after your parents died then I look like an awful person, don't I?'

'You've always said you never cared about what people in the village think of you, it seems that isn't true?' Connor scoffed at her in a way that brought everything back to her like a bucket of cold water being thrown in her face.

'I care if people think that I've been a bad person all these years.' She could hear her voice rise but couldn't stop the pitch it was heading toward.

'Do you honestly think that everyone has been sitting

around all these years saying that you're a bad person? That no one else has had anything happen in their life but you? As though the entire village has been paused for your return?'

He shook his head at her and started to walk away then turned for a moment.

'That's the difference between you and me, I know I'm not a bad person so it doesn't matter what people think of me. It's what I think about myself.'

He started to walk towards the orchard and Peony ran several steps to keep up as she kept talking.

'There are many ways we are different Connor but that is the least interesting one in the list,' she snapped.

'In what other ways are we different?' he asked as he walked at a steady stride, in a way that was like a challenge to Peony's ears.

'You always said you would leave here and yet you're still here,' she said. 'But I went away. I managed to leave after all your carrying on that you were too good for Honeystone and its backward ways. How different we are.'

He stared at her for a moment longer than was comfortable. 'Are we? You're back now, aren't you?'

His reasoning angered her. 'God you're an arrogant prick,' she said.

He nodded. 'If you think so.' He shrugged and put his cap back on. 'Is that all? I don't know why you're here, Peony. I never think about you, and I am sure you never think about me. This all seems a bit pointless.'

'You never think about us? What happened?' she asked.

'We were teenagers, things happen,' he said.

'You were twenty-four,' she said. 'Not really a teenager.'

'Boys take longer to mature,' he said and she rolled her eyes.

Peony was about to continue when she saw Clover

walking carefully towards them, her face a picture of concentration as she took each step.

'You're the lady who took the artichokes,' Clover said.

Peony plastered a smile onto her face, 'I am,' she said.

'Remember Izzy said Dad would throw a wobbly when he found out you were coming back to stay,' Clover said and Peony watched Connor shoot his daughter a look of pain.

'That's not true,' he said. 'I haven't, I didn't. Not in the least wobbly.'

Peony looked at Clover. 'Did he?'

Clover held onto her father's leg. 'He's been pretty grumpy since then but he's always a bit grumpy.'

Peony laughed. 'Good to see some things haven't changed.'

Clover looked up at Peony. 'I want to make a cake for the new doctor, can you help me?'

Connor shook his head, 'I can help you, Clo. You don't need to ask Peony, she's busy.'

'You can't cook and Izzy can't bake,' Clover replied. 'And I can't get around the kitchen fast enough.'

Connor was silent and he looked at Peony. 'You don't have to,' he started to say but Peony had crouched down to be at Clover's height.

'I would love to make a cake for the doctor for you. A lemon drizzle cake, you say? With extra lemon?'

Clover nodded and Peony's eyes ran over the little girl's face. She had brown eyes like her father and had inherited his long dark lashes. Is this what their child would have looked like if she had stayed with Connor?

'What about you get Izzy to come to the pub next week and we can make it in the kitchen there? You can be a professional chef for the day.'

Clover grabbed Connor's leg to steady herself as she did a little wiggle with excitement.

'Can I come tomorrow?' she asked, eyes wide.

Peony looked at Connor. 'How about you come on Monday? We aren't open for lunch then.'

Connor took a long breath in through his nose, and then nodded. 'Fine.' He leaned down and picked Clover up as though she weighed less than a silk scarf.

'Nice to see you again, Peony.' He turned and walked down towards the house.

'Daddy,' Peony heard Clover's voice carry on the breeze.

'What is a wobbly and why did Izzy say you would throw one when you saw Peony? I didn't see you wobble at all. I'm the one who wobbles sometimes when my legs are tired.'

'Sweetie, it's a saying when some people get upset about something, like having a tantrum.'

'Oh OK,' Clover said. 'Like when Izzy yells about you using the last teabag?'

'Yes, exactly like Izzy, she's an extreme wobbly thrower. The Queen of Wobbly throwing.'

And Peony couldn't help but giggle as she got into the car and drove back to the village.

Izzy

Something had changed since Peony was back and Anthea was in Spindle Hall.

Izzy woke each day with the sense that something exciting was coming and she realised she hadn't been excited by anything since she was a small child, probably Clover's age or less.

Clover, however, was easily excited and since Peony's visit to the farm, that was all she had talked about.

'Peony is pretty.'

'What does a Peony mean?'

'Why don't we grow peonies?'

'Did you and Peony go to school together?'

'Were you friends?'

'Why was she angry when she was talking to you in the driveway?'

'She was angry because she had her hands on her hips.'

'Why do you want me to stop talking about her, Daddy?'

Izzy had enjoyed watching Connor squirm under Clover's questions and comments. There was no more distracting her from her need for knowledge about everything and everyone. It was funny to see Connor try to circumvent the line of questioning and Clover bring it back on course, like a little barrister at the kitchen table. Intellectually Clover was more than ready for a mainstream school Izzy knew that, but it was still hard to think that this little girl would be physically able to keep up with the other children.

Connor however was furious with Izzy for saying to Peony what she had said and since the Friday, he had been courteous and polite to her but nothing more.

Now it was Monday, the day of the cake making, and Izzy watched Connor fill his Thermos with tea.

'You have to take Clover to the pub.'

He looked up from his task. 'Can't you?'

'No, I have an appointment,' she said. 'I can pick her up later but I can't take her.'

Connor was about to say something and then he closed his mouth.

'What time is she expecting you?' he asked Clover.

'Ten,' Izzy answered on behalf of Clover who hadn't seen the texts between Izzy and Peony.

Anthea had taken their phone numbers and had started

a group text, which was fun and funny and something Izzy was enjoying more than she thought she might.

'Fine,' said Connor. 'Who is your appointment with?'

'None of your business.' Izzy smiled sweetly at him. She leaned down and kissed Clover's head. 'I'll be back to see you later and we can take the cake to the doctor.'

'What doctor?' Connor asked.

'The doctor in the village that Clover's been talking about all weekend, when she wasn't interrogating you about Peony.' Izzy shook her head at Clover. 'He doesn't listen, does he? We should ask the doctor to see if Daddy has potatoes in his ears.'

Clover grabbed her ears. 'Ewww.'

Izzy turned and left the house, happy to be in her warm coat despite the spring sunshine that was weaker than a cheap teabag.

After Peony had left her and Anthea at the house on Friday, she had talked to Anthea about Clover, and Anthea being the smartest woman Izzy currently knew, asked why Izzy was playing mother to Clover.

Izzy hadn't stopped thinking about the question all weekend and she knew that she had to step back somehow and Connor needed to step forward.

It wasn't going to be easy and the first step was today when she had asked Connor to take Clover to the pub.

Izzy turned her car at the end of the driveway, knowing Connor was watching from the window. He was so nosy. She laughed and drove the long way around and soon was travelling up the driveway to Anthea's house where a flurry of workmen were moving about, and a digger on the back of a truck was being backed onto the grass.

'Morning,' called Anthea from the back door, a mug in hand.

'Gosh it's all go, isn't it?' Izzy said, looking around and stepping over a pile of fence posts that were not there on Friday.

'Yes, it's all go, but in a good way.' Anthea said. 'Tea?'

'No thanks,' said Izzy, hands in the pocket of her coat.

'Then let's get started.' Anthea said, taking her coat from the hook, putting her mug down on the counter and whistling. The dogs came running from another room and went bounding ahead of them.

The pair walked into the garden and down towards the barn. The ground was wet beneath their feet and Izzy looked at Anthea's fancy boots.

'You need some wellies,' Izzy said.

'I know, I do, I have been meaning to buy some online,' Anthea said.

'What size are you?'

'Eight.' Anthea said.

'I have a spare pair, I'll bring them over,' Izzy said.

'You don't have to do that,' Anthea said.

'Remember, I don't do anything I don't want to do,' Izzy said cheerily. 'So it's no trouble.'

They stopped at the barn, while the dogs ran around but not too far away.

'This is it,' said Anthea and she pushed open the door and Izzy looked up at the roof, which was a little like a colander, but the eaves were beautiful and the wood in good condition.

'This is where I think I will press the botanicals,' Anthea said, looking up at the roof.

'It's a great spot,' Izzy said, looking around. 'You could do a whole thing, like a pressing area and have people come and make their own scents and perfumes from the flowers and botanicals they pick from the garden. Little baskets at the end of each garden area,' she said with a smile.

'Go on,' said Anthea.

Izzy shrugged. 'I mean I'm not a business person like you, I'm just thinking about what I would have liked as a kid or what Clover would like. There's something about being a child and pulverising leaves and berries and pretending you're a witch or a mad scientist and taking jam jars from the kitchen and making potions. God how I loved to do that when I was little.'

'I loved it too,' said Anthea. 'So much that I made a career out of it but I never thought about other people coming to do it here.'

Izzy walked to the barn door and looked out to the nearby stables.

'You could have a café in there and a shop where everyone could buy your things. It could be lovely and it would be great for Honeystone to have some more traffic, we seem to get passed over by the tourists.'

Anthea came and stood next to her, looking out at the stables.

'I wasn't really thinking about making it a tourist thing, I was looking for a quieter existence here.'

'Nothing wrong with that either,' said Izzy. 'Don't listen to my ideas, I'm just thinking aloud and honestly I don't know what I'm talking about most of the time.' She gave a little laugh and Anthea elbowed her gently.

'Don't say that about yourself, OK?'

Izzy turned to look at the older woman. 'What?'

'Don't be mean to yourself, it's not good for you. You have to say something nice about yourself now.'

'What?'

'Say something nice about yourself.'

Izzy started to laugh. 'I don't know what to say.'

'What do you like about yourself?' Anthea asked.

She paused, thinking, 'I like that I know when it's time to plant seeds and when to harvest carrots.'

Anthea burst out laughing. 'Well that's great, I would have no idea but carrots have excellent antioxidant properties for the skin, so I will be planting those. I will have to get you to tell me when to harvest them.'

Izzy smiled. 'I can do that.'

'Let's go to the stables,' said Anthea and they walked the short distance to the beautiful stone building.

'Have you always gardened?' asked Anthea.

'No, not until Clover came home from hospital and I wanted to give her the best vegetables possible when she could eat solid food. I found out I was good at growing things and feeding Clover the best quality food I could kind of became an obsession.'

'A worthy endeavour,' said Anthea. 'Did it help her?'

'I think so, I mean the cleaner the food the better. Right?' Izzy said.

'You can tell by the way the soil smells if it's going to be good quality vegetables,' Izzy said and she walked to an area that had been dug up and crouched down. She moved some grass aside, took a handful of earth and held it to her nose and inhaled.

'Everything will grow here, smell that.' She held it to Anthea's nose.

Anthea shook her head. 'I can't.'

'Can't what?' asked Izzy.

'Smell it.' Anthea gave a large sigh.

'Why not?' Izzy threw the dirt onto the ground.

'I was sick, very sick and I lost my sense of smell,' Anthea said. 'It's been two years and it hasn't come back.'

'Can you taste things?' Izzy asked.

'Yes but it's dulled, not like it used to be.' Anthea turned and looked out over the fields.

'My sense of smell, that's what my gift is and that's how I made my name, and now I don't have it. It's part of how my ex-husband managed to push me out of my own business. By saying I wasn't of any benefit now even though it was my ideas, marketing, style, design, everything that made the Anthea McGregor brand what it is.'

'Do you think it will come back?' asked Izzy.

She couldn't imagine not being able to smell, it would feel like the world was somehow turned down.

'I don't know, I have seen specialists, tried sprays, steroids, had my nose cleaned out in surgery, it is just refusing to return. It's probably too late now.'

'There's a new doctor in the village, maybe he can help?'

Izzy laughed to herself just a little.

'You just want to go and see him again,' Anthea said.

'I'm going to see him again, after being here. Clover is at the pub making a cake with Peony and then we will take it to him and say hello. See if he still thinks I'm pretty. It's been a long time since anyone looked at me the way he did.'

Anthea sighed. 'I can't remember when a man last looked at me like that. But that's nice of Peony to make the cake and very welcoming of you too.'

'I am nothing but welcome incarnate,' said Izzy with a bow.

'Now, let's look at these plans again, I have a feeling your roses might be facing the wrong way.'

'Nothing worse,' exclaimed Anthea and the woman walked back to Spindle Hall, the dogs following and the garden a hive of activity.

7

Connor

There are some people who cling to others in the worst times of their lives. They want company to keep the ghosts at bay, want food and cups of tea made for them, someone to sit with, someone to answer the phone and collect the flowers and organise the small details that seem like a rude interruption to the process of grief.

And then there are people like Connor. When his parents died within weeks of each other, he had taken care of all the small details, and caring for Izzy. It didn't matter that Peony tried to help, or that Robert had tried to assist, explaining that he understood death from when his wife, Christina, had died, leaving Peony bereft at the age of twelve, but Connor hadn't needed his advice or assistance.

Instead, he organised the funeral for his father, like his father had organised for his wife a few weeks before and got on with it.

Peony tried to help, he remembered that but he pushed her away. He needed to be there for Izzy. He didn't have time for teenage romance, he'd told Peony, whose look of pain still haunted him when he lay in bed and wondered how he could have got it so wrong.

'Do you think Peony will let me put the cake in the

oven?' Clover asked as they drove towards the pub. 'Izzy never lets me,' she said with a heavy sigh.

'I don't know,' he said.

'Izzy said I would fall into the oven, like the children in Hansel and Gretel and I would be turned into a stew by the witch.'

Connor shook his head. Izzy could be so macabre at times it was unsettling.

The street was quiet when he parked the car and he went around to the back seat and helped Clover out and held her hand as they walked to the kitchen entrance of the pub.

As he walked towards the open door, he could hear someone retching and he paused.

'Peony?' He called and he heard a tap turn on and then Peony appeared in the doorway wiping her hands on a tea towel.

'Are you OK?' he asked, scanning her pale face and tired eyes.

'Yes, fine,' she said, barely looking at Connor before she crouched down to Clover.

'Are you ready to bake?' she asked and Clover nodded.

'I have my own apron,' she said to Peony and she touched her bag that Connor was holding.

'That's smart. I have three types of cake tins for you to choose from, a heart, a circle and a square.'

Clover gasped, 'I have to choose the heart, don't I, Daddy?'

Connor smiled at his daughter. 'Whatever you think the new doctor would like will be right.'

He looked at Peony again. 'This is very kind of you,' he said, aware of the stilted tone of his voice.

'No, it's fine, I like to bake and I'd like to get to know Clover.' She turned and gestured for Clover to come into the kitchen as Connor held the bag out for Peony to take.

'Izzy is picking her up, just text her when you're ready. She's out somewhere, no idea where,' he said.

Peony nodded. 'Will do.'

He paused and then took a chance.

'Ginger helps,' he said.

'Helps what?' Peony looked at him.

'With the nausea.'

Peony seemed to freeze and he saw the muscle in her jaw twitch. Gosh she was thin, he thought, too thin.

'Thank you,' she said and then she closed the door in his face.

Connor stood for a moment and then went back to his car.

He shouldn't have said anything, he told himself, the last thing Peony would want is him interfering in her life and making comments on her health.

But gosh she looked unwell, and he wondered if Robert had seen it in his daughter.

None of your business, he told himself silently as he drove back to the farm.

He couldn't give Peony any of his energy, he thought, he had spent enough time obsessing over her since she had left Honeystone and so much had happened since then.

As he came back to the farm, he could feel his phone ringing in his pocket and he took it out and saw it was the cidery calling.

'Connor Hinch,' he said as he opened the door to the house.

'Connor, hi, it's Pete from Cotswold Cidery.'

'Ringing to check on the apples? They're going marvellously,' he said. 'You will have a bumper load in the autumn.'

There was a pause and with it, Connor felt his stomach drop.

'The thing is, Connor, we aren't going to need the apples now,' Pete said.

'What do you mean?' He sat down on the lounge chair.

'We have been struggling for a while, and unfortunately, we are going into administration.'

Connor slumped back into the lounge chair, his head felt like it was fizzing and he couldn't speak but he could also hear the pain in Pete's voice.

'But I'm sending Clover to a new school,' he said. 'I was paying the fees with the money from the apples.'

'Who's Clover?' asked Pete and Connor realised Pete didn't know Clover from grass and he closed his eyes.

'Doesn't matter,' he said. 'I'm sorry to hear about the cidery, I wish I could do something to help us both.'

'I'm sorry,' Pete said and Connor was sure he could hear his voice breaking.

'It's OK, things happen.' Connor said. 'You take care of yourself and remember, it's just a hiccup, don't lose your mind over money.'

He put his phone away in his pocket and sat in thought. It might be only money but he had to pay for Clover's school, a whole year of fees and all her uniform costs and more.

And he wondered if the school would take a few tons of Sheep's Nose apples as payment.

Izzy

'Hello?' Izzy called as she opened the kitchen door of the pub.

Clover was sitting at the bench on a stool with a perfect heart-shaped cake next to her and Peony was taking photos on her phone of the cake, the child, and the cake and the child. There was a lot of posing and Izzy laughed at them both.

'Look how wonderful she is and this cake would win a prize,' gushed Peony, and Izzy laughed.

'Wow, look at you both, and look at that cake.'

Clover beamed at Izzy. 'It was so much fun and Peony let me put the cake into the oven, which you don't do.' Her tone was accusatory and Izzy pretended to flick her ear.

'Quiet, small one,' she said. 'All fine?' she asked Peony.

'She's terrific, we had a blast,' said Peony.

'Peony was sick,' Clover said. 'She needs to see the doctor.'

'Sick?' Izzy frowned at Peony.

'Just a bit of nausea, nothing to worry about.' Peony looked at Izzy and shook her head and nodded towards Clover.

'Peony probably ate too many apples, and felt sick, like you did that time.' Izzy explained to Clover but then looked at Peony.

'You should probably go to the doctor's at some point to make sure it's just the apples.'

'I will,' she answered unconvincingly.

'So, are we taking this cake to the doc or what?' Izzy asked Clover, who started to carefully climb down from the stool.

Izzy reached out to help but Clover slapped her hand away. 'I'll do it,' she said firmly.

'Yes, chef,' she said and looked at Peony who was laughing.

'OK, well are you going to come and say hello to the doctor?' asked Izzy to Peony.

But Peony shook her head, 'No I might have a nap, I'm tired.'

'I'll text you,' said Izzy.

Izzy carried the cake outside with Clover following and they waited at the side of the road.

'Look to the left, look to the right, look left again.' Following Izzy's instructions, they crossed and walked to the surgery. Izzy opened the door and ushered Clover into the waiting area, helping Clover hold the cake.

'Hi, we're not actually seeing patients yet,' Izzy heard Joe say as his head popped around the doorway of the surgery.

'Good, as we're not ill,' said Izzy. 'We come bearing cake.'

Clover held out the cake and Joe stepped forward. 'You made this?' he asked and she nodded. 'With Peony at the pub.'

'Peony at the pub, that's lovely alliteration and this cake looks even better.'

Joe bent down and looked Clover in the eye, 'You have the gift of baking and now you must come and eat it with me. Let me put the kettle on.'

Clover looked up at Izzy and beamed. 'Can we stay?' she asked.

Izzy smiled, 'Yes, we can stay for a bit as long as we're not in your way.'

'Not even the slightest,' he said as he led the way up the stairs carrying the cake, while Izzy carried Clover.

They entered his living area and Izzy looked around at the plain, soulless interior.

'This is very,' Izzy paused to find a word, 'Functional.'

Joe laughed and put down the cake. 'Yes, it's basic but it's all I need, I'm just a fill-in for a while, I'm travelling and working.'

He turned on the kettle and opened a few cupboards, taking out mugs and plates.

'How long have you been a doctor for?' she asked.

'I'm thirty-four now, so a while.'

Izzy calculated the age difference. He was Connor's age.

Nine years seems like a lot but then again, she felt closer to forty than she did to thirty.

Clover sat on the sofa, looking around the room. 'This doesn't look like my house,' she said. 'We have cushions on the sofa, and pictures in frames. They're mostly of me but some of Izzy and my dad.'

Joe smiled. 'No, I don't have any photos yet but maybe I will. I keep the good memories in my head.' He tapped the side of his skull. 'So, I can see them whenever I want.'

Clover thought for a moment, 'I have photos in there too,' she said, as though surprised by the revelation.

'That's great, we all have them,' Joe replied, pouring tea into two mugs.

'Would you like some milk or water?' he asked Clover.

'Tea is fine, one sugar,' she said to him and Joe smiled at Izzy.

'A young tea drinker,' he said.

'You know how in France they give young children a thimble full of wine at the dinner table? We do that here but with tea and it's usually a mug,' she laughed.

'Ah yes, we do that with beer in Australia,' he joked, bringing the tea to the coffee table and then the cake and plates.

'Did you want to cut the cake, Clover?' he asked but she shook her head.

'You can,' she said.

Joe served the cake and handed the Hinch women a plate each.

'Have you always lived here?' he asked Clover which Izzy appreciated.

Clover nodded. 'I have since I was six months old,' she said.

'And where did you live before that?' asked Joe.

'At the hospital,' she said. 'I was born too early.'

Joe nodded. 'Well, that can happen.'

Clover chewed her cake and shrugged. 'Life happens,' she said and Joe burst out laughing.

'That's very Buddhist of you,' he said.

'What's that?' she asked Izzy.

'It's a religion,' Izzy answered.

Clover accepted this answer and kept eating.

'And have you always lived in Honeystone?' he asked Izzy, and she felt herself redden under his gaze. It was a simple question but he asked it as though he wanted to know. Izzy was so used to people asking about Clover or talking to Clover she forgot she was also someone who people might want to get to know.

She cleared her throat. 'Yes, I mean I went to university for a while but my parents and grandparents and those before them have always lived here.'

'Honeystone blood,' he said with a smile.

'I suppose, but it gets a bit thick at times, doesn't course through your veins the way it should, can make you lazy.' She half joked.

'So you don't like living here?' he asked and she noticed the way he sat back on the chair and crossed his long legs.

Izzy glanced at Clover who was concentrating on her cake.

'I'm here, aren't I?' Izzy tried to keep the edge out of her tone.

She could feel Joe's eyes on her but she kept her eyes on her niece.

'I've helped with Clover since she was born. We're like two peas in a pod now, aren't we?' Clover was picking up crumbs of her cake with her finger and then sucking them.

'I'm going to big school soon, so I will have new friends,' she said and Izzy looked at Joe and made a face.

'Looks like I'll be yesterday's news soon enough.'

Joe laughed. 'The young people are as fickle as a pickle nowadays.'

'Fickle as a pickle, I like that,' Izzy said.

'Whereabouts in Australia are you from?' she asked.

'Brisbane, Queensland.'

'Nice and warm,' Izzy said. 'I'd love to go to Australia.'

This was true, Izzy wanted to see the world but only if she could take Clover. Who else would make sure the child had everything she needed? But the idea that she would take Clover further than London was out of the question and when all was said and done, Izzy was only her aunt.

'You should come, it's beautiful and there's lots of work. You could get a visa and travel, like I'm doing,' Joe encouraged.

'Do you have family?' she asked.

'Yes, two parents still alive and kicking, and a sister who is a lawyer.'

'A doctor and a lawyer, your parents must be pleased with their investment in you both,' Izzy said.

'They're happy we're happy,' Joe answered.

'Where to after Honeystone?' she asked.

'Canada, I think,' he smiled.

'It's colder there than here,' said Izzy.

'Indeed, it is but I want to see the world.'

'Don't you miss the weather in Queensland?'

'Not really but ask me in winter. I haven't been here for winter yet.'

'Do you have a girlfriend back in Australia?'

He shook his head, 'I feel like I'm being interviewed.' He smiled.

'You are,' said Izzy. 'Because if we are to be friends, you and I and Clover, we must know all.'

Joe sighed. 'No girlfriend in Australia, or here either.'

Izzy looked at Clover, 'Any questions for the doctor?'

Clover thought for a minute. 'What's your favourite flower?'

'Oh good one,' she said to her niece. 'The answers are always very telling.'

'Daisies,' he said and Izzy looked at Clover who nodded.

'Unusual answer, why is that?'

'Is it unusual?' Joe sat back and crossed his legs.

Izzy nodded, 'Very. Men usually say roses because that's all they know. Why daisies?'

'They remind me of my granny's house, She had a big bush of them by the front gate and I used to pick the petals off to see if Shelly Ashby loved me or loved me not in grade five.'

Izzy laughed, 'That's a nice memory.'

Joe gasped, 'But it isn't because she never did love me, she loved me not.'

Izzy sipped her tea. 'When are you starting to see patients?'

'Not so fast, I have questions for you both, if this is to be friendship based on equal knowledge of the others.'

Izzy made a face, 'You want to ask us questions?'

He nodded and turned his attention to Clover.

'Pasta or rice based dish?'

'Pasta.'

'Your choice of sauce on the pasta is?'

'Pesto made from Izzy's basil.'

Izzy couldn't help but preen a little. The basil she grew was always flavourful and lasted all summer.

'Taylor Swift or Billie Eilish?'

'Abba,' said Clover. '*Mamma Mia!* Is my favourite film.'

Joe laughed, 'Nice answer. Didn't see that coming.'

Izzy made an apologetic face. 'I'm not sure she gets the complete storyline but we love the songs don't we?'

Joe turned to Izzy. 'Do you have a boy or girlfriend?'

She shook her head, 'Nope, neither.'

'Siblings besides your brother?'

'None and my parents are dead,' she shrugged. 'I'm incredibly boring.'

'I don't think that makes you boring, there's probably quite a complex story in there about you but since we have just met, I won't pry.'

She laughed, 'Thank you.'

'Ever think about travelling?' he asked.

'Never,' she lied.

'You said you wanted to see Australia.' He reminded her.

'Oh yes,' she said, 'I mean yes to Australia, not sure about the rest of the world.' She was aware Clover was listening intently.

'And did you go to university?'

'Tried it, wasn't for me,' she said, leaving out the fact she came home for Clover.

'Where would you like to be in five years?' he asked.

Izzy paused. She never thought about life further than the day ahead, it helped her to not think beyond dinner because then she didn't get that odd feeling of her heart falling through her feet and then just emptiness inside her.

'Right here,' she lied. 'Hanging out with Clover and in my garden. Nowhere else I would rather be. I love Honeystone, it's home.' She smiled brightly at him but there was a look of something on his face she couldn't place. Bemusement? Disbelief? Humouring her?

He cleared his throat.

'So, I'm starting work on Wednesday, Dora, Barry Mundy's

121

wife is coming over tomorrow to go through everything with me. She will be the receptionist.'

'Doesn't she work at the pub?' Izzy asked.

'Yes, she will keep doing a few evening shifts and working here,' he said. 'She said she likes to keep busy.'

'Don't blame her, I'd work every day to not be with Barry,' said Izzy.

'Oh, he seems all right,' said Joe but Izzy snorted.

'You wait, he's a control freak and the moment you step out of the lane he has you in, you're done for. I planted the hanging baskets for the pub. I put in red geraniums, very bright, as Rob wanted something fun, and Barry wrote a letter to the pub stating the geraniums were too Italian-looking and instead he wanted to see white primulas. Rob ignored him and then the following week all the geraniums were pulled out and thrown into the gutter.'

Joe's mouth dropped. 'Was it Barry?'

'He said no, but it was Barry, it had to be.'

'So, what happened then?' Joe leaned forward.

'Rob installed a camera and told everyone he would be watching 24/7 and I replanted the geraniums and they have stayed.'

'And Barry, or whoever, never came back? Did they show on the camera?' Joe seemed very invested.

'You know, and this is just between you and me, but the camera is just a play one from the pound shop. It's sort of tacked to the wall, my brother Connor did it but no one else knows it doesn't actually work. Rob can't afford that sort of technology but the hanging baskets have been left alone since.'

Joe leaned back. 'Intrigue at Honeystone, who knew?'

Izzy snorted. 'It's just small village drama, nothing major

ever happens here. Every day is very much the same. You'll be bored soon enough.'

Joe furrowed his brow. 'Are you bored?'

Izzy looked at Clover and back to Joe. 'Never. Boredom is for people who lack vision.'

'I like that, I'm going to steal it,' he said.

'I took your pickle comment so we're even.' She smiled at him and he smiled back in a way that made his eyes crinkle, a real genuine smile, that gave her butterflies, then she felt her eyes sting with tears.

How long had it been since she had been smiled at like that by a man? She wasn't even sure she had ever been so entirely smitten as she was in that moment.

True to Izzy's contrary nature, she stood up and took Clover's plate from her.

'I want some more of the cake,' complained Clover but Izzy had already put the plates in the sink.

'We shouldn't take up your time,' she said to Joe.

'Actually, I have a favour to ask,' he said.

'OK?' Izzy put her hands in the pockets of her jacket.

'I have to take my rental car back and I need someone to follow me there and drive me home. It's not so far but the buses are slightly unpredictable here.'

Izzy laughed. 'You can say that again.'

'I did ask Barry but he wasn't so keen on helping me. He said he's the deputy mayor, so I assume he's very busy.'

Izzy laughed, 'Deputy Mayor? God, the nerve on that man, he's made himself Deputy Mayor, there isn't even a real Mayor, I mean it's Rob from the pub but he only did it so Barry wouldn't get the Mayorship. He would be even more unbearable with more power.' She laughed to herself as she imagined Barry in ermine robes and carrying an orb around the village.

'You could ask Jenn Carruthers, but she is a huge gossip and by the time you return back here you will know all the village secrets.'

'Oh yes, I will definitely ask her then. Can I have her number?' he asked.

She couldn't tell if he was joking or not.

'I'm joking.' He laughed. 'I'm not interested in anyone's secrets unless it's medical related.'

Izzy thought for a moment and dug her phone from her bag and checked the time.

'You know what? Go and get in your car, and we will follow you now. We love a drive, don't we Clo? A chance to sing more Abba.'

'Really?' he asked.

She waved him towards the cake.

'Cover the cake and get your keys then we can head off,' said Izzy and she carried Clover down the stairs.

'When I go to school, I will have to do the stairs by myself,' said Clover, her hand on the back of Izzy's neck, playing with her hair.

The thought of it made Izzy's heart sink but she smiled brightly.

'You will and you can,' she said. 'We're just in a hurry now as we have to get Joe's car returned.'

'I like him, he's so nice,' Clover announced as Izzy buckled her into her seat.

'He is, very nice.' Izzy said and she went to the driver's seat and sat in it, as Joe pulled out in his rental car and waved and tooted his horn at her to follow him.

'Daisies,' she muttered as she got into the driver's seat. Who on earth would have thought?

Anthea

The idea that Anthea could have recreated her perfume brand again at fifty-five was ambitious but her decision to buy Spindle Hall and grow her own flowers and botanicals to provide the ingredients felt enormous.

After Izzy had left to pick up Clover, she looked around the garden with the equipment and people walking in bright orange safety vests and wondered if she shouldn't just throw the towel in and take her money and move to Lake Como and host parties and become friends with Amal Clooney.

Was she trying to recreate her brand to upset her ex-husband? Or was she truly trying to start something new and wonderful?

There was already an Anthea McGregor brand, they didn't need another one.

The questions rattled around in her head all afternoon until she couldn't bear them anymore. She needed company and after she'd fed the dogs, she drove into the village for a drink at the pub.

The pub seemed dark when she arrived and she went to the front door and peered inside. Closed. *Damn*, she thought.

Walking back to her car, she saw Peony look out of the window and she waved up to her.

Peony smiled and put her hand out as though to tell Anthea to stay where she was.

Soon enough she came downstairs.

'We're not open on a Monday,' Peony said apologetically.

'I realise that now,' Anthea said with a smile.

'Come up and have some dinner with me and Dad,' Peony said. 'We'd love the company, otherwise I have to listen to him give me the etymology of the names of the food we're eating.'

'I can't intrude,' Anthea said but Peony shook her head.

'You're not intruding, you're being invited and I have a lovely chicken pie and salad and Dad makes a great G&T, as you know.'

Anthea sighed, she didn't have anywhere else to be and it did sound rather pleasant.

'OK, arm twisted,' she said and she followed Peony into the pub and up the stairs to a surprisingly cosy and lovely upstairs area.

'Anthea, you remember my father, Rob?' Peony said as she wandered through and gestured to Anthea to take a seat on one of the soft sofas.

She smiled at Rob, who had stood up at her arrival. 'Of course, how are you?'

'Fine thank you,' she smiled at him. He had a lovely warm sort of an energy, like a well-knitted sweater. 'G&T?' he asked.

'Yes please.'

Rob set about making them a drink. 'One for you, Sweets?' he asked Peony.

'Just the tonic, thanks Dad, not feeling like the gin part tonight,' Peony said and Anthea watched her body language. She hadn't told her father yet, she realised. Perhaps she wouldn't be keeping it. No judgement from Anthea – women had to do what was right for them.

Rob seemed unsurprised by Peony's request for only tonic water. He served them all drinks and sat down again, moving the crossword from *The Times* that he had been doing.

'How are things at Spindle Hall?' he asked.

Anthea thought about saying the right things that people

wanted to hear and then thought about what she was really feeling.

'Terrible. I have no idea why I am doing what I'm doing,' she admitted and immediately felt relief at saying the words aloud.

'Do any of us have any idea what we are doing?' Rob laughed. 'But do you feel you have bitten off more than you can chew?'

She thought for a moment. 'I think I have gone in with the wrong intention,' she said.

Peony came over with her drink and listened intently.

'How so?' Rob crossed his legs, like she imagined a therapist would.

If she could have a gin and tonic in a therapy session then she would have gone in a heartbeat, but she wasn't usually the sort of person who liked to talk about her problems. Now, however, as she sat with Rob and Peony, she realised that perhaps it wasn't healthy to not speak about what troubled her.

John always said that therapists were head shrinkers, and her mother had avoided speaking about emotions till the day she died.

She looked at Rob, his handsome worn face, his lovely daughter standing behind him and wondered why she hadn't married someone like him instead of John.

'I think I'm doing it to prove a point to my ex-husband. That I can do it again, and he is nothing without my ideas and creativity and smarts.'

Rob nodded. 'And is he watching?' he asked.

'What do you mean?'

'I mean you're doing this with Spindle Hall to show him something and I'm wondering if he's aware. Is he checking in? Coming to see the progress?'

Anthea swallowed some of her drink and then laughed and coughed.

'I don't think he is,' she said. And then she started to laugh, really laugh. She put her drink down on the table and laughed from the belly until Peony and Rob joined in.

'What is so funny?' Peony asked.

'Is he watching?' Anthea screamed, laughing again. 'Imagine doing all of this trying to prove a point to someone and they aren't even watching.'

She shook her head and wiped her eyes. 'Honestly Rob, that is the most brilliant question I have ever encountered. It's so simple and perfect and yet shows me how blind I have been. I've being doing this with the wrong intention all along.'

Rob laughed as Peony giggled and went back to making a salad.

'So, if you could do the house just for you, what would you do? What would you make of it?'

Anthea sat back and thought for a moment. 'I don't know to be honest.'

Peony bought over some plates and cutlery.

'You know I've been thinking a lot about what I wanted to be as a child, because I think we know what we are supposed to be as children and somehow we lose sight of it from teachers telling us what we are bad or good at or parents pushing their dreams onto us.' She put her hand on Rob's shoulder. 'Don't worry, Dad, you never did that.'

Anthea listened. 'So, what did you want to be when you were a child?'

'I wanted to own a café or a restaurant and now, only through circumstance and heartbreak, am I doing what I wanted. I mean it's early days but I love it and I know it will be successful.'

Rob looked up at his daughter and smiled. 'I have no doubt, love.'

'What did you want to be when you were a child?' she asked Anthea.

Anthea picked up her drink, took a sip and closed her eyes for a moment.

'I wanted to be a witch,' she said and she laughed. 'Which I kind of have done with my potions and lotions but I suppose I wanted to right wrongs, make people happy, change loves, more Glinda the Good Witch than the Wicked Witch of the West.'

Peony smiled. 'I can see you have those qualities, healing people. I did it for years as a social worker. It can be reward- ing but also really hard.'

'I don't think I want to go and do that as much as I want to make life better for others, make it lovely and beautiful and easier.'

Baggins the dog wandered over to Rob and laid his head on his lap and Rob patted it softly.

'You can still do that though,' Rob said. 'At Spindle Hall.'

She frowned. 'How?'

'Make it a place for everyone, like the woods are. If you're going to plant a garden let people come and see it, pick the flowers, I don't know, make their own perfumes and lotions and potions. That's healing, isn't it? You could have a whole intuitive garden, I read about those, where you take what resonates with you. Spindle Hall was once the lifeblood of Honeystone, bringing with it all sorts of visitors and the gardens were visit-worthy, and so much of the land was farmed with produce that kept the village and neighbouring farms alive during World War Two.'

Anthea sat up straight. 'Oh my God, you're right. Izzy said we should have a café but it's bigger than that.'

She thought for a moment. 'Imagine you come to the gardens at Spindle Hall and you walk around with a basket and you can pick what you like, and you can have the flowers turned into something in a lotion or a perfume but you can also take home a bunch. Or you can pick the raspberries and strawberries for pudding that night, or the vegetables for your soup that will feed your poorly grandmother. I mean, that's the dream, isn't it? A beautiful healing garden.'

Peony beamed at her and Anthea felt her eyes prick with tears.

'You are brilliant,' she pointed at Rob and then Peony. 'Utterly brilliant. I could kiss you both.'

Rob blushed and laughed. 'Sometimes we just need to be led in the right direction to find the path we are meant to take, just some simple questions and here you are.'

Anthea raised her glass to them both. 'To Spindle Hall, may she finally have her purpose in Honeystone again.'

Dora

Dora had once read that if you put a frog into a saucepan of cold water and slowly raised the temperature, it would only realise it was in danger of being boiled alive when it was too late and it would not be able to get out of the saucepan.

She knew the water was at a rapid boil now. Barry had organised the tennis party and she had made little pinwheel sandwiches that she thought looked elegant with cream cheese and smoked salmon, and egg and cress and ham and cheese. There was a lovely roast chicken from the pub that Peony had given her, telling her it would only go to waste, and a green salad, and Dora had made a cheese board and Eton Mess for dessert.

Everything was set up next to the tennis court, on a white linen tablecloth and little napkins with navy tennis racquets embroidered on them that Dora had made years ago when she cared about such things. There were bottles of Pimm's and wine and elderflower cordial in ice buckets and lovely coloured glasses that Dora had bought from a charity shop but told Barry they were from John Lewis.

It looked perfect, as things usually did in their life, except none of the guests had arrived. The invitation said 1 p.m. and it was now nearly two and there wasn't a single person waiting for a drink, chatting about the weather or commenting on how nice the table looked.

At quarter past two, Barry went inside the house and Dora sat by the table, wishing she could have a glass of wine, and waving flies and dragonflies away from the food.

At two thirty, Barry walked calmly out of the house, and Dora felt her stomach drop. The calmness was a red flag, something was coming, and as Barry came closer, she shrunk back in her chair. Barry came to the end of the table and, without even looking at Dora, lifted the entire thing on its end, tipping the lot onto the edge of the tennis court.

Dora watched as the carefully prepared food slid onto the grass. The sandwiches rolled across to centre court and the salad lay in a sad mess on the doubles alley.

She felt her mouth drop open but no words came out.

'No one is coming, because no one has any manners nowadays.' He looked at Dora with a venom that made her bones shake.

'You told me they RSVP'd yes.'

She shook her head. 'I didn't. I didn't know anything, you just told me what to make and I did it.'

'You're accusing me of not following up? Of lying to you?' he asked. He had asked her to press his white shorts with a crease down the front, and she had but realised now, they were uneven. She hoped he hadn't noticed.

'No Barry, I am just saying I wasn't even sure who you invited this year.'

'Well since everyone is my friend but you're so socially awkward and don't have any friends, I didn't bother to tell you who was coming. I assumed you would have received some phone calls from them stating if they were attending or not.'

'We haven't had any calls from people cancelling,' she said.

'You're an idiot, you're probably why no one came today,' he spat at her, coming closer. She tried to shrink herself down.

'But I can't leave you, can I, because you're a drunk and have no money and no skills and can't contribute, so you suck the life out of me and my dreams.'

Dora had heard it before but it still hurt and she felt a tear fall. She clasped her hands together, then dug her fingernail into the pad of her thumb, trying not to sob.

'Clean this up, you pig,' he said and as a last gesture, he attempted to kick a leg of chicken and nearly slipped in the salad.

Mumbling he walked back inside the house and Dora sat staring at the mess.

At what point had she allowed her life to become this? She wondered. And what would it take for it to change?

8

Peony

The waiting room was quiet. Peony sat on one of the few chairs, alone, as Dora walked into the surgery.

'Peony, how are you?' she said and then she shook her head. 'Well, you're at the doctor's, so I guess you can't be 100 per cent.' She sighed. 'Sorry, I'm rambling.'

She went to the computer and started to log in.

Peony looked at Dora, noticing her face was pale and drawn. Rob had mentioned that he thought Dora was taking wine from the bar. Peony wasn't sure this was Dora's style but she certainly didn't look well this morning.

'Fine, thanks Dora. You're working here and the pub? You're busy!' she said to the woman.

'Needs must, since Barry isn't working,' she said.

'Any luck for him on the job front?' Peony asked.

'Not yet, but he is applying,' said Dora, not looking at Peony.

The doctor came into the waiting room. 'Dora, you're here, wonderful. And you must be Peony Grayling? I'm Joe Fisher, the new doctor, come through.'

Peony followed Joe into his rooms and sat on the chair as he closed the door.

'How can I help you?' he said.

She paused. 'I'm pregnant, or I think I am … the twelve tests say I am.'

He nodded. 'OK, well twelve seems fairly certain but do a lucky thirteen to be sure.' He smiled and he went to the cupboard and took out a plastic jar and handed it to her and gestured to the door.

'Bathroom's in there, give me a sample and I will do another test.'

Peony was out again in a moment with her sample and he took it from her and put it on the bench next to the basin. He took out a test, dipped it in the urine and laid it on a piece of paper towel.

She sat still, looking ahead at the wall, wishing there was a painting of some sort she could focus on.

'Well, yes, this test also confirms it – you're definitely pregnant.' Joe came back to his desk.

She blew the air out of her cheeks and slumped in the chair.

'Not good news?' he asked. 'How far along do you think you are? When did you have your last period?'

She had calculated this one thousand times in her head before today.

'February the first was the last time. I think,' she said. 'Pretty sure.'

He typed on the computer and then turned the screen to show her. 'You're about eight weeks and your due date would be the eighth of November or thereabouts …' His voice trailed off.

Peony looked up at him. 'I'm keeping it,' she said.

'Is the father aware or involved?' he asked.

'No, he's not aware but I will tell him. We broke up not long ago,' she said.

Joe nodded and typed. 'You need to have an ultrasound

to check exact dates and you need some prenatal vitamins.'
He looked at her. 'I will need to do some blood tests as well,
check iron and so on.'

She nodded.

'Any sickness?'

'Yes, every morning till lunchtime.'

'Standard but if it gets worse, let me know. We don't want
you getting dehydrated. There are some home remedies that
seem to work. Ginger tea or ginger biscuits help, I've heard.'

Peony thought about Connor's comment to her when he'd
heard her retching. Did he realise? God, how embarrassing.

The doctor was handing her pamphlets and she took them
mindlessly and put them into her bag.

'Are you working?' he asked.

'I'm a cook, at the pub,' she said.

'That's a lot of hours on your feet,' he said. 'You will want
to ensure you're getting enough rest.'

She nodded. 'We only do a few sittings, it's not like
Honeystone is the tourist village of the year.'

'I must come for dinner,' Joe said with a smile and she
noticed his very good teeth and handsome face. It was no
wonder Izzy thought he was cute.

'Please do, we're open tonight. I'm making artichoke pasta
if you like that sort of thing.'

Joe laughed, 'I was recommended that by a young lady,
Clover Hinch.'

Peony smiled. 'How was your cake?'

'So good, I have had it for dinner for the last three nights
as I haven't been shopping yet.'

Peony gasped. 'That sounds like you need some of your
own vitamins.'

'Yes, not great, a bit of a bachelor's diet at the moment

but I have transport now and I can get some things to make actual food.' He laughed.

'Come to the pub tonight and I'll make you something nourishing,' she said.

'Deal,' he said and handed her some paperwork. 'You can book the ultrasound through this group in Cheltenham, get the bloods done and then make another appointment with me. I can help look after you during the pregnancy.'

Peony nodded. 'So I'm about eight weeks along?'

'Give or take,' he said.

'OK,' she said and she stood up and went to the door.

'Before I go, I just wanted to mention that the last doctor who was here, he wasn't great and he seemed to share information about villagers with certain people.'

Joe gasped. 'He didn't?!'

'He did, and I know that Dora is lovely and I think she's trustworthy but just watch her husband.'

Joe frowned, 'Gosh that's terrible, I would never and I will make sure Dora doesn't either.'

Peony nodded. 'Thank you, I'll see you soon.'

Outside the surgery, Peony looked at the pub. She thought about what she imagined her little restaurant would look like when she was a child. She used to line her toys up in little groups, with pillows and pretty napkins, and she would even draw little vases of flowers for the tables.

The Hare and Thistle interiors weren't exactly the bastion of country chic. There was a lot of wood and a lot of leather, like an old-fashioned men's club. But Peony knew what it needed. She went to the pub and pushed open the door and walked into the dining area as her father came out from behind the bar.

'You OK love?' he asked. 'I saw you coming out of the doctor's. What's he like? Any good? God knows the last one wasn't, he told me I had cancer of the eye when it was a stye and then Barry asked me if I had my affairs in order. Terrible man.'

Peony wasn't sure if he meant Barry or the doctor and then decided on both. She looked around the pub.

'I need to make some changes to this place if we want to make it more comfortable, so I'll need some money,' she said.

Robert laughed, 'You think I can just spin money like a latter-day Rumpelstiltskin?'

'I know you have money, Dad, at least a bit. It won't be more than window dressing but these chairs, they're awful.' She touched the restuarant chair, high-backed and hard to sit on.

'And we need more cushions, more colour, fewer Toby jugs.' She made a face at them.

'Don't you take my Toby jugs away from me!'

'You can put them whenever you want, Dad, just not in here.' She smiled.

'You're really staying then?' he asked, leaning on the bar.

'Yes, I'm staying,' she snapped at him. 'Did you think this was just a phase?'

'I don't know what it is Peony, you hardly ever come home and now you're here and wanting to turn the world upside down.'

'Putting new cushions on the chairs is hardly turning the world upside down,' she said.

'I know but it seems very quick, sudden, and you're not really a quick and sudden sort of a decision maker.'

Peony sat down on one of the uncomfortable chairs. 'I know and that's probably why I stayed away for so long. I was so afraid of making the wrong decision I didn't make any decision.'

This truth felt like a glass of cool water on a hot summer's day and she smiled at her father.

'I should have come back sooner, but I stayed away because I wanted to make it work with Fergus, because I was avoiding Connor and his little girl, and because I didn't want to be stuck in Honeystone. But now I see I wouldn't be stuck, I would be doing what I wanted to do, with you, because I love you, Dad. You're so great and I haven't appreciated you enough. You're a wonderful father, really.'

Robert smiled at his only child. 'Parenting you has been my privilege, Sweet pea, so yes, you can have your cushions and while you're sticking around, I might as well pop your name on the title of the pub.'

'Really?'

'Why not? If it's going to stay in the family, who knows, you might even want to pass it on to your children one day if you decide to have any,' he said cheerfully.

Peony put a leg out in front of her and arched her foot and then looked up at her father.

'Actually, about that.'

Izzy

Connor was even more taciturn than usual, short with her, vague with Clover and spending more time indoors than out in the orchard, which was driving Izzy insane.

She had things she wanted to do and Connor's energy in the house was making her tired and on edge until she had enough.

'What's wrong?' she asked for the eighth time in four days.

He had just come back from taking Clover to her physiotherapy appointment, something he always made a special time for Clover. They would go to physiotherapy and then head to a new café to try a cake and have a coffee for Connor and juice for Clover and Clover would come back and review the cake and café to Izzy. It was their little ritual and there was always a new café to try and a new cake. But today he had come inside and set Clover at the living room coffee table with her drawing things and now he was pacing the kitchen floor.

'Nothing,' said Connor, refolding a tea towel and laying it down on the kitchen bench and then picking it up and folding it once again.

'There is something, and unless you tell me I am going to follow you around the house, the orchard and the garden.'

'It's fine, I'll work it out,' he said.

'Work what out?'

She waited for him to reveal the burden she could see hanging over his head.

'It's fine, you can't help anyway.'

'Try me,' she said, her hands on her hips. She was wearing her overalls and a T-shirt and was planning to go and plant up the garden at the doctor's surgery because it was ugly and because she might see Joe again. The fact that she would be wearing an unflattering and worn T-shirt when she saw the person she might have an interest in, didn't occur to Izzy. What she wore had nothing to do with her feelings. She didn't look at what people wore and decide things about them, so why would she worry about what she wore?

'Talk to me, for God's sake,' she demanded, her voice louder than she intended.

'Shhh,' he said and then he went to the back door and opened it and gestured for her to follow him outside.

'What's with all the secrecy?' she asked, wishing she had brought a coat as she rubbed her bare arms.

'The cidery called, they're going under,' he said, his hands in his pockets. 'I can't send Clover to school, I can't pay the fees.'

The wind was knocked out of Izzy. 'What do you mean? They said they wanted them.'

'I have all these apples growing and nowhere to sell them at the price they're worth.' He looked down at the orchard. 'It's such a waste. You know when I was a kid, I thought I would take over this place one day and make my own cider and things, maybe even plant a few vines, I don't know, do something for myself and here I am stuck, growing fruit for other people's dreams.'

Izzy understood more than he knew about how he felt.

'Now I have to tell Clover I can't send her to the school, she will have to go to the local one where I know she won't get the sort of support she needs. They're understaffed anyway, those poor teachers can't help her the way she needs until she gets stronger and more confident.'

She nodded. 'Don't take her out yet, don't tell her. We have to find a way to do something, find the money, you know?'

'I can't draw on the mortgage, not without the contract to sell the fruit.'

Izzy scratched her head, thinking. 'Something will work out, I promise, it always does. You just go look after that blossom and get the best apples you can.'

Connor sighed. 'Thanks Izzy, sorry I'm such a miserable bastard, you're right, we have to stay focused on the positives. Thank you.' He pulled his sister into a big hug.

'And thank you for everything you do with Clover. We would both be lost without you.'

Connor wasn't a sentimental man, and this was the most

vulnerable he had been since Clover was born. Izzy hugged him in return.

'Go on, I'll take Clover with me for the rest of the day, you go get out into the orchard, the apples miss you.'

Connor laughed. 'Let me get my tea and I'll get out of your hair.'

A few moments later, after he had his Thermos of tea in hand and had kissed Clover goodbye, Izzy watched him head to the orchard.

The loss of the sale of the apples was huge, and she wondered how on earth they could manage without that money. She could get a job but then who would look after Clover all the time?

She needed to get her hands in the dirt and think, it was where she did her best ruminating and she could think about what to plant in the garden at the front of the surgery.

'Clo, I'm going to be in the garden,' she said to her niece, who was drawing in her sketchbook.

'OK, I'm drawing a wedding cake,' said Clover.

'Ooh, who is getting married?' she asked as she peered over the top of her to look at the drawing of the three-tiered cake with many iced roses.

'I don't know yet but when they do, they can have this cake, I'll make it for them with Peony.'

Izzy kissed her on the top of the head and went outside.

At first the idea of Clover leaving her to go to school was awful but now that Connor said she might not be able to go, it made her realise that Clover needed the experience. Izzy couldn't keep her wrapped up at home forever. Sure, she was physically weaker than some children but she was also more resilient in other ways.

Izzy walked around the beds of the garden and started to do a mental inventory of what she could plant in the garden at the surgery. The soil wasn't great and she could bring some in but money was tight now and she wasn't about to ask Joe to pay for it when it was supposed to be a gift.

She had a small cutting of a buddleia from last year that was forming well, and some nice lavenders and sedums that would work nicely. A few foxgloves for summer and the garden would come up well, she thought.

As she dug the plants out and re-potted and put everything into boxes to take to the surgery, she pondered over the apples and Connor saying he he wished he could make his own product. There was no reason why he couldn't, in theory, except for the large amount of money it would take to turn the dream into a reality. Plus it could take years for them to turn a profit enough to send Clover to school.

Izzy wiped her hands on her overalls and looked down to the orchard where she could see Connor, probably running over the same questions and worries as her.

He had only ever wanted the best for Clover, even if her mother didn't and he was a wonderful father, better than his own. Patient, kind, and playful when he wasn't being a grump.

The time he put into Clover's physical recovery as a baby was unparalleled, with him doing all the exercises the physiotherapist asked and taking her to the hydrotherapy pool when she was old enough. The way he told Clover she was helping him so he could be strong when he became old, so she wouldn't feel different or a burden. The way he spent every spare moment away from Clover working, giving up his life and dreams for his child. It brought Izzy to tears thinking about it.

Izzy went inside the house. 'I'm going to Joe's to drop some plants off. Do you want to come or go and hang out with your dad in the orchard?'

Clover looked up from her wedding cake drawing. 'Can we call in and see Peony?'

Izzy shrugged. 'I guess but she's working so we can't bother her too much.'

Clover got up from the sofa.

'Leg braces,' Izzy reminded her, picking them up off the floor.

'I don't want to wear them,' said Clover impatiently.

'I know but you need them, just for a while longer,' Izzy coaxed and Clover sat down in a huff.

'I know, it's annoying but better for your balance when you walk,' Izzy said as she slipped her little legs into the braces.

Soon they were on their way to the village and parked at the front of the pub.

The door was open and there was the sound of talking coming from inside and the smell of something heavenly.

'What's for lunch, I wonder.'

Clover sniffed. 'Fish,' she said.

'Can you really tell it's fish?' asked Izzy.

'Yep,' said Clover. 'Can we go and see Peony?'

'Quickly,' Izzy said and she ushered Clover across the street and around the back of the pub to the kitchen door. Peony was standing at the bench, plating up some dishes.

'Thank goodness you're here, Clover, wash your hands and you can help me chop the dill.'

Clover gave a little squeal. 'Can I help please?' She looked at Izzy with pleading eyes.

'Only if you're helping and not getting in the way.' Izzy said.

Peony looked up. 'Clover knows her way around a kitchen, she won't be a hindrance.'

'What's a hindrance?' the child asked.

'Something that gets in the way,' Izzy said and she helped Clover to the sink to wash her hands.

'I'm doing some gardening at the surgery, won't be too long but if she's too much pop her in the cool room.'

Clover gasped and then laughed when Izzy winked at her.

'At the surgery, hey?' Peony wiggled her eyebrows at Izzy who ignored her.

'I'm doing my municipal duty, that garden bed outside his place is awful.'

'Sure, sure,' said Peony. 'Now Clover, what I was thinking with the dill was...'

Izzy left them to it and went back across the road and opened up her car boot and unloaded everything onto the ground.

'Hello Izzy,' she heard and looked up to see Dora walking up the path.

'Hi,' she said. 'I'm doing the garden for Dr Fisher.'

'That's nice of you,' said Dora, stopping for a moment.

Izzy shaded her eyes with her hand and smiled at the woman.

'You're back with the doctor again. You are always so busy Dora, it's impressive. You must be making heaps of money.'

Izzy wondered how much being a receptionist at a doctor's surgery would pay, maybe she could do it to help with Clover's school fees.

Dora looked like she was about to say something but instead she just gave Izzy a weird smile and then scuttled inside the surgery.

Poor Dora, Izzy thought, as she grabbed her fork and started clearing the flower bed.

'Morning,' she heard and looked up to see Joe standing by the flower bed.

'Hello,' she said.

'Is this part of the deal for having a new doctor in the village?' he asked. 'A garden makeover? Can you do the living room upstairs also? Could do with a bit of art.'

Izzy smiled at him. 'Sadly, I don't do interiors but I can promise some flowers for a vase mid-summer.'

'That sounds lovely,' he said as he watched her dig. 'I don't know much about gardening.'

'And I don't know much about doctoring,' she laughed. 'We can't know everything, stick to what you love.'

Joe laughed.

'Do you love being a doctor?' she asked.

He shrugged, 'I don't know, sometimes I do, sometimes I don't but that's having a job, isn't it? Not every day is going to be amazing.'

Izzy turned the soil over. 'You're right, I mean I love being in the garden but it's not really a job for me, it's like a hobby that I make some money from.'

'Do you? That's pretty cool,' Joe said and she looked up at him.

'Is it? I don't know, it's hard to find work around here when I have Clover to care for.'

Joe nodded as Old Ed's wife Clary came walking past Izzy's plants and she quickly moved a lavender that could have been a tripping hazard.

'I better go, my first patient is here,' he said. 'Want to meet at the pub for a drink later?'

Izzy wasn't prepared for him to ask her anywhere, let alone for a drink.

'Sure, but I have to put Clover to bed first,' she said. 'Seven thirty?'

'Perfect. There's lunch on today at the pub, not dinner, so I will eat upstairs first,' he said. 'See you then.' He went to the front door and opened it as Clary came walking up the path.

'Good morning, Mrs Maynard, I'm Dr Joe Fisher. Come inside and let's have a chat.'

A drink with the new doctor, Izzy smiled to herself as she threw some fertiliser onto the soil. Yes, things were definitely more interesting in Honeystone than they had ever been.

Connor

Izzy was stirring the pot in every sense of the word, Connor thought when he came into the kitchen after his shower.

'You're not going to school, we're putting you to work in the kitchen at the pub,' she teased Clover as she heated up Bolognese sauce. Clover snorted at her.

'Good, better than going to Miss Cacklewood's school for naughty children.'

'And Peony will make you peel a barrel of potatoes every day.'

'Good, I like peeling potatoes.' Clover leaned on her elbows at the kitchen table.

'And then Peony will make you put the skins back on, like a weird vegetable jigsaw puzzle.'

'I'm good at puzzles,' Clover sniffed.

'You, small pixie child, have an answer for everything,' Izzy said as the doorbell rang.

Connor looked at Izzy, 'You expecting anyone?'

'Nope,' she said as Clover stood up, ready to move to the door.

'No, I'll go,' said Connor firmly to his daughter.

He went to the door and turned on the light and opened it and there was Peony. She was wearing lipstick and a pink shirt and was holding a container and a bottle of wine.

'Hello,' he said.

'Hi,' she smiled at him. 'This is weird but thank you for inviting me.'

Connor frowned, and then nodded. 'OK, I didn't but Izzy must have. Come in.'

Izzy came out of the kitchen and walked up behind him. 'Peony, what a nice surprise,' she said and Peony gasped.

'Oh God, Clover didn't tell you?'

'Tell us what?'

Peony seemed to twist to look around Connor and he turned to see his daughter looking sheepish by the kitchen door frame.

'I invited Peony for dinner,' she said.

'Oh, OK,' said Connor, looking at Izzy who was biting her lip.

'I'll go, it's fine, I should have checked,' Peony said quickly and she turned and walked away towards her car.

'No, wait,' Connor called and he followed her. 'What's in the container?' he asked.

'Raspberry galette,' she said as she opened her car door.

'You can't go then, because that's my favourite dessert you've ever made. Is there clothed cream?'

Peony turned to him. 'It's weird, I'm sorry. Clover did a very convincing job of telling me how much you wanted me to come. I should have known, but I took her at her word. I'm not used to the trickeries of small children.'

He noticed her hand went to her belly for a moment.

'Come on, it's just spaghetti Bolognese but it's comfort food and you're here now and Clover does seem to adore you. You're all she talks about.'

Peony seemed to soften and she handed him the container. 'OK, well I won't stay long.'

They walked back into the house where Izzy was now

cooking pasta and Clover was sitting at the table, drawing as though butter wouldn't melt in her mouth.

'It seems Peony was invited to dinner with no word given to the staff,' he said and he leaned down and whispered in Clover's ear. 'I know what you're up to.'

Clover seemed to have a quick case of hearing loss and instead she patted the seat next to her.

'Come and sit with me, I'm drawing wedding cakes.'

Peony sat down and looked at the drawing. 'Oh, don't ask me to make one of those, my piping skills are terrible.'

'We can learn, that's what my dad says, that we can always learn how to do things.'

Peony looked up at Connor who was leaning against the wall, feeling awkward.

'That's very true,' she said and she smiled at him and there it was, all the old feelings of being eighteen and deeply in love. Had he ever stopped loving her?

He knew the answer to that, and as Clover sat chatting like a magpie to Peony, who listened intently and answered appropriately, he felt every inch of her presence though her attention wasn't on him.

Izzy drained the pasta and turned to him. 'Right, you can be dad. I'm going to get ready, I'm off for a drink at the pub. You lot are on your own.'

Connor looked at his sister. 'You can't,' he said.

'Can so.' Izzy wiped her hands on the tea towel and then laid it over his shoulder.

'You made dinner,' he said, his eyes imploring her to stay.

'I did and I have already eaten, and now I'm going to shower and put on something nice and you can eat, clean up and put your daughter to bed.'

She turned to Peony. 'Nice to see you and I apologise in advance for my average Bolognese sauce. Please don't judge me, however I did grow the onions, garlic, and tomatoes in the sauce, so that counts for something.'

Connor could have strangled her as she swanned past him and gave him a wink.

Connor picked up the wine from the table. 'Can I get you a glass?'

Peony shook her head. 'Not for me, thanks, I'm working tomorrow.'

'I might save it then,' he said. 'I don't really drink much.'

Peony nodded, 'You never were much of a drinker I remember.'

'Still aren't,' Connor said. 'I don't like waking up with a woolly head. Righto, who wants some spaghetti?' he asked and started to serve the dinner up.

Izzy had made a salad for them and there was a fresh baguette with butter on the table. All in all, it wasn't a terrible dinner, probably not what Peony would have served, he was sure, but it was more than fine.

Clover couldn't have been more pleased with the outcome, he thought, as he put her bowl of pasta in front of her.

Soon enough they were eating and Clover dominated the conversation with Peony and he tried not to let himself think about what could have been.

Mel was never forever, even he could see that, but he did think that a child was forever.

He pushed the thoughts from his mind and focused on the moment.

'I hope dinner is OK,' he said to Peony who was mopping up some sauce with some bread.

'More than OK, it's terrific,' Peony said. 'I don't know why Izzy was concerned, it's delicious.'

He watched her eat with gusto and smiled.

'Can we play Uno after dinner, Dad?' Clover asked.

She had a pasta sauce mouth and a smile bigger than he had seen in a long time.

'I'm very good at Uno,' said Clover to Peony.

'Are you? I'm also very good, so we might need to see who is best,' Peony challenged and Clover clapped her hands.

'We will go to the living room and wait for you, Daddy,' Clover said.

Peony stood up. 'Let's help clean up first,' she said. 'A good chef always leaves a clean kitchen.'

Clover sighed, 'I don't like that part of cooking,' she admitted.

'No one does but it's nice to come into a clean and organised kitchen, trust me.'

Connor had a little laugh. 'Clover isn't convinced by your argument but it's a valid one.'

After the dishes were packed into the dishwasher and the galette had been warmed and put onto sweet pink plates by Clover – who told Peony they were the birthday cake plates – along with a generous scoop of clotted cream, Clover was ready to claim Peony all to herself.

'Come and play,' demanded Clover and Connor watched her take Peony's hand and walk carefully to the living room as he turned the kettle on for tea.

Clover came back within moments to the kitchen and pulled at Connor's jumper.

'She's my best friend now, so don't say anything mean to her and don't be a grump.'

Connor felt his mouth drop open. 'I wasn't planning on doing either,' he said.

'Good,' she hissed and made her way back to the living area.

'Uno time,' she squealed as he came into the living room.

Peony was sitting on the floor, just like he remembered she liked to do as a teenager.

And in that moment, he realised he had wasted all those years. Pushing her away, wanting her to stay away from Honeystone was useless. Peony was always going to find her way back to him, like an estuary finds the source.

9

Anthea

If Anthea was honest with herself, and she often wasn't due to an overbearing mother and an even more controlling husband, she would have said she hadn't been happy in the business or the marriage for years. But McGregor women didn't give up, according to her mother.

This included when Anthea told her mother she wanted to leave John, about ten years into their marriage.

'You don't leave, darling, you stick it out,' she had told Anthea firmly. 'Look at your father and me, we stuck it out.'

Anthea would have liked to have mentioned the screaming rows, her mother throwing things, her father's affairs, her mother drinking and the endless crying and apologies until it would stop for a while and start up again.

In the end it was John who left, after Anthea had resigned herself to a loveless, empty marriage where the only connection they had was in the boardroom of the head office.

Peony's question about what she wanted to be as a child had stuck with her for the last few days. So had Robert Grayling. He was the calmest man she had ever met, and he was smart, no, he was more than smart, he was wise. There was a sort of softness to him, as though he had been overlooked for much of his life and didn't care.

The dinner had been perfectly lovely and afterwards,

Peony had begged off to shower and go to bed, saying she thought she was coming down with something. Rob had offered to change the sheets on her bed so she would have fresh ones to hop into after the shower.

Peony had declined but Anthea wondered if John had ever thought to do anything for anyone that way, he certainly hadn't for her when they were married.

Why had she expected so little for so long? It wasn't until she came out of hospital that she started to really think about leaving John and selling the business. And it was only after he left that she saw how deeply unhappy she had been.

But she was fifty-five now. She didn't need to remain in the past, so she told herself every morning when she woke up, but still things she would have played out differently kept running through her mind.

On this morning, Anthea woke, aware the sun was coming up earlier than it had for the past week. She pulled on her clothes, washed her face, cleaned her teeth and went downstairs to let the dogs out. As she opened the door, Baggins was sitting patiently and next to him was a black and white cat.

'Hello, where are you two from?' The cat looked her up and down and then walked inside. Anthea tried to shoo it out but the cat took a swipe at her and then took off and ran into the hall of the house and upstairs.

'Seriously?' She called after the cat and as she turned around Baggins was there behind her.

'What am I? Dr Dolittle?' she muttered as she dragged Baggins by the collar outside, where Taggie and Rupert were running towards them.

'Rob?' she called but there was no answer and she saw Baggins run with Taggie and Rupert on the grass and through the mud. She walked around the house looking for

Rob but he wasn't anywhere to be seen and she went inside and texted Peony that her father's dog and a cat was at her house and did Rob know.

Anthea watched as the dogs played and chased each other when a text came back telling her that Rob was on his way but they didn't own a cat.

Anthea ran upstairs and looked for the cat, but couldn't find it anywhere, so she put on a slick of lipstick and a spritz of perfume that she knew smelled like jasmine even if she could barely remember what that smelled like. She went downstairs and made two mugs of tea and waited with the kitchen door open.

Her stomach was nervous and she tried to tell herself that this was nothing, and Rob wasn't at all interested in her and that they didn't know anything about the other besides surface information.

His wife had died of a cancer the doctor caught too late. Rob hated the doctor who stayed in the village for another ten years and proceeded to remind Rob every day that he was there that he was an incompetent fool.

Rob knew Anthea had an idiot ex-husband and not much else. She didn't share much about herself, not because she was as private as people thought she was but because she didn't think she was very interesting. Until Rob.

He asked her questions, about what she read, the music she liked, the wine she drank, the places she had travelled to.

The sound of a car coming up the driveway made her look out of the kitchen door and she saw Rob in his little runabout.

'I'm so sorry,' he said, shaking his head as he got out of the car. 'I was planning on taking him for a walk in the woods, and then I got distracted and I left the bloody door open and he's made his own way here. I'm very sorry and I hope he hasn't caused any trouble.' Anthea laughed. 'He's fine, he seems to be very friendly with my two, so they're playing, it's all fine. I'm glad he wasn't hit by a car or anything.'

'He knows not to go on the roads, he would have made his way through the back woods,' Rob said, whistling to Baggins who looked at him, and then kept chasing Rupert the dog.

Anthea asked, 'Also, a cat has come into my house and is now hiding upstairs. He's not a stray, he has a collar on, a black and white thing.'

Rob shook his head. 'I don't know whose cat it is. Have you asked Izzy?'

'Oh it could be hers, she did say her cat had been missing. I'll text her. Tea?'

'Why not?' Rob smiled and she gestured for him to come into the kitchen.

'This is lovely,' he said, looking around.

'Would you like the tour?' she asked him. 'We can also look for the cat so you don't seem nosy if you're worried.' She laughed.

'I would love it but yes, I don't want to seem too nosy.'

'Come on, be nosy, Spindle Hall is an icon, you must have explored it when you were a child?'

'You know, it was always very well-cared for, despite being empty, no vagrants or break-ins. I think the Honeystonians have always made sure she was safe.'

'Honeystonians, I like that. I wonder when I will be considered a Honeystonian,' she asked as she led him into the hall of the home.

'Probably by the fourth generation, maybe fifth,' he said and she laughed.

'Like that, is it?'

He shook his head and smiled. 'Not for me but for some

people like those in the Historical, or Hysterical Society, as we call it, so keen to keep a keen eye on interlopers and those who haven't earned the right to call themselves a local. Barry and Jenn Carruthers are at loggerheads over this very issue, as Jenn came here when she married Bill Carruthers, and she thinks ancestral claims are rubbish, and she is correct but Barry loathes her. He calls her a foreigner but she's only from Leeds.'

'I will make a note to let him know I'm from Dorset originally, that will throw the cat amongst the pigeons,' she laughed.

Anthea showed him the house, aware as she did how little she lived in the other rooms. She was either in the kitchen, the little TV snug or her bedroom. There was a lot being wasted, she thought but it was only her to fill up all the rooms which would be impossible.

After Rob had looked at every room, including looking on top of cupboards and under beds for the cat, and Rob had commented on all that he loved, which was everything, they sat down at the kitchen table and she handed him his tea and opened a tin of delicious looking biscuits.

'Still hot,' she said, taking a sip.

'Peony's pregnant,' he said.

'I know,' Anthea took a custard cream from the tin.

'Thought you might,' he said shaking his head. 'She's keeping it.'

'OK. Good for her.'

'She also wants to do up the dining room.'

'Fair enough.'

'She wants to get rid of my Toby jugs.'

'Good for her.'

'It's all giving me indigestion,' he said and frowned and rubbed his grey hair.

Anthea smiled. 'The pregnancy, the dining room spruce up or the Toby jogs needing a new home?'

'All of it actually.' He paused. 'Nothing has happened for ten years and now suddenly everything is changing, it's a lot for a bumpkin like me.'

'For a bumpkin, you're very well read and have lovely manners and an excellent reputation from people I've spoken to,' she said.

'Thank you.' He let out a big sigh.

'Which change worries you the most?' she asked him.

'Honestly?' He looked her in the eyes.

'Yes, which one?'

He took a deep breath in and then let it out through his nose.

'The Toby jugs, I've been collecting them for years and I don't actually like them very much but people seem to think of me when they see them which is slightly insulting since the men portrayed on them are always very ugly.'

Anthea burst out laughing. 'Get rid of them then.'

'But my grandfather collected them and his before that, I would be throwing away my collected heritage.'

'Did you ever think that perhaps they may not have liked them either and felt compelled because one Grayling male started the collection and no one has the courage to stop the Toby jug madness?'

Rob laughed. 'Maybe the Toby jugs are the curse I need to break.'

'Or maybe just break the Toby jugs. I'm with Peony on this one, they're ugly.'

Rob made a sad face, 'Do you think the ghost of Horatio Grayling, coachman of Honeystone will come and haunt me if I do?'

'No, I don't and I don't believe in ghosts being able to hurt people. If they could, there would be no one left because everyone holds a grudge, even if they can't admit it. I still haven't forgiven Simone Tophill for cheating on the spelling test in Year Six when I was at Miss Hilda's Girls' School and winning the top prize for English, when I knew she had written the words on her thighs, because she kept hiking her dress up during the test.'

'That's appalling, I will seek her out and Anthea McGregor will have justice and the prize. What was the prize?'

'A five-pound voucher for Boots.'

'Oh yes, I can definitely sort that for you.' He laughed.

Anthea looked at him.

'Honestly, if the Toby jugs are your biggest worry then I think everything will work out just fine.' Anthea leaned back in her chair. 'And I think Peony will be a beautiful parent.'

'She will,' said Rob. 'I'll help her as much as I can but she has to tell her idiot ex though.'

'Yes, she does.' Anthea agreed.

'And the pub does need a spruce up,' he said. 'And Peony can cook, really cook, and when she can't, I'll hire someone and she can oversee it.'

'Everything is OK then,' Anthea said.

'I suppose it is, I just needed to say what was happening out loud to make it real.' He laughed.

'Should we walk these dogs?' she asked as she noticed her dog Taggie running past.

'Why not?' he said and they left the house and walked towards the woods, the dogs running behind them.

The woods lay ahead, the new leaves on the trees creating a natural tapestry of colours, like a cloak unfurling as the sun became warmer, the limbs of the branches stretching after being asleep for so long.

Even as Anthea and Rob walked, she felt their steps fall into a slower, more relaxed rhythm. There was no hurry, nowhere to be, nothing to do but be here now, she thought.

This gentle pace wasn't something Anthea had expected since moving to Honeystone but she was starting to enjoy the new wisdom that came with slowing down. It felt at times she could finally hear her own thoughts without all the brown noise that came from the city.

'I've been thinking about your idea, about making Spindle Hall a place for everyone,' she said as they walked.

'Have you? And any conclusions from your ruminations?' he asked, turning his head to her.

'Maybe. I think it's the right idea, but I also think I want to do something different than flowers and perfumes. I've done that and I did it well but it would mean the brand would always be second to myself. There is already an Anthea McGregor brand out there, they don't need another one.'

Rob was silent as they walked, his hands in his pockets of his jacket.

'Look, bluebells,' Anthea said as they came into the woods. 'That's so exciting, I didn't know they were here. They weren't here when I came a few days ago.'

'Can't you smell them?' asked Rob. 'They're just so beautiful.'

Anthea said nothing but stood in the quiet, the sound of the breeze in the trees, the rustle of the dogs in the undergrowth, a blackbird singing.

'It's so lovely here,' she said, looking up at the canopy overhead. 'If I listen closely, it's as though the woods are trying to tell me something.'

Rob stood and listened with her.

'I'm a bit deaf in this ear,' he whispered to her and she burst out laughing.

'I was having a moment,' she said to him.

'Sorry, as you were,' he said and they stood in silence.

'Nope, it's gone, I could only hear them say one piece of advice.' She nodded slowly, processing what she had heard.

'What?' Rob seemed intrigued.

Anthea closed her eyes and put her fingers to her temples and then looked him in the eye.

'Send the Toby jugs to the charity shop. Nobody wants a mug of a man's face, nobody, I promise you.'

'But my dad said I was never to let them go,' he admitted.

'And my mother wanted me to stay in a terrible marriage. It doesn't mean we have to continue what our parents wanted for us, even in our fifties.'

And without thinking a moment longer, Anthea leaned up and kissed him softly on the mouth.

'Sometimes we just have to grow up,' she said, before she kissed him again and felt his arms envelope her close.

'I'm feeling very grown-up right now,' he said and they kissed again.

Anthea pulled away, 'I'm sorry, I shouldn't have done that. I'm not usually so forward.' She hadn't kissed anyone since John and God knows it had been a long time since they had shared any passion.

Rob laughed, 'OK Jane Austen, I think we're past that now?' and he pulled her into him again. 'I think you should have, and please don't stop because you think I don't want this. I have wanted to kiss you since you tried to tell me why those silly signs were up.'

'I was trying to create boundaries,' she laughed.

'Oh, we don't do boundaries very well in Honeystone,' he smiled.

'I can tell,' she said and then Rob kissed her again and Anthea wondered if she was actually Sleeping Beauty and she had just woken up for the first time in her fifty-five years of life.

Dora

Dora stood behind the bar serving as the dinner crowd came into the pub. It was busier than ever and Peony had organised Izzy to help serve and work in the kitchen to help plate up the meals.

She could hear them laughing and talking and wished she had the sort of friendship they were creating but all her friends had left since she married Barry. He wasn't a fan of any of her friends, said they were a bit low brow for the friends he had in mind for them when they married.

But since then, only Barry had friends and Dora knew their wives, all of whom seemed to dislike Barry.

She used to stand up for him once. Telling people he was a lovely husband and just a bit abrupt. That he didn't like to get close to people. That he was tired.

She had a litany of excuses until she ran out of them and people had stopped listening anyway. People said Barry was a bore which was a shame because his wife was lovely and very creative, have you seen the drawings she does? Barry likes to show them off to people, he even sold some, not that Dora saw any of the money.

At sixty years old, she was without a rudder and Barry was becoming more erratic at home.

He needed a job yet Dora had more work than ever now Dr Joe was in the village and Barry was furious.

As though she had just conjured him up, Barry walked

into the pub and looked around. He saw Dora behind the bar and came towards her.

'Hiya,' she said brightly.

'Don't say hiya, makes you sound cheap.'

Dora thought about reminding him she was a barmaid but knew to say nothing.

'Can I get you something?' she asked him. 'A pint?'

'I can't find the bread,' he said.

Dora looked at him and felt her stomach turn. 'I haven't been to the shop yet,' she said, trying to keep her voice steady.

'You've left me with beans and no toast for dinner,' he said as Izzy passed with a delicious-looking and smelling burger and chips.

'I haven't been to the shops, sorry love, I came here from the surgery. I'm sure I can rustle up some bread for you from here, let me go and look.'

'I won't take charity from here,' snapped Barry and then he looked at her and turned and left the pub.

Dora's heart was pumping so fast, she leaned against the fridge to steady herself.

'Is he not capable of buying his own bread then?' Dora heard and saw Anthea McGregor sitting by the bar. She hadn't seen her come in or sit down and jumped at her voice.

'He's not good at housekeeping,' said Dora loyally.

'What is he good at then?' asked Anthea.

Dora paused. 'What do you mean?'

'If he's not good at buying his own bread, then what can he do?'

Anthea's stare went through Dora like a hot knife through butter and she blinked a few times.

'Nothing,' she said.

'Does he work?'

'No, he was fired but tells everyone he was made redundant.'

Anthea nodded. 'Male ego at its finest. And you're working?'

'Here and at the doctor's surgery,' Dora said.

'Gin and tonic thanks,' Anthea said as someone came to the bar and grabbed some napkins. 'So, he doesn't work and wants you to take care of the food as well?' Anthea's eyes seemed to bore into her brain.

She nodded.

'That doesn't seem very fair, does it?'

Dora swallowed. 'It's fine, I will get some bread tomorrow.'

She made Anthea's drink and put it down on the bar and then cleared the glasses around the pub.

Why did Anthea make her feel like she could see something more than the story Dora showed the world? No one ever asked her any questions, she was just reliable Dora Mundy who could draw a bit and was always there to help out.

When Dora came back to the bar, Anthea was sipping on her drink.

'You're the illustrator, aren't you?' Anthea dug into her handbag and pulled out the 'Guide to Honeystone' with drawings in it that she had picked up when she first came to the area.

'This is your work.' She didn't pose it as a question but as a statement.

Dora looked at the guidebook. 'Oh yes, that's very old now,' she said. 'I'm not really an illustrator as in the job, just a bit of drawing here and there.'

'You're an illustrator,' Anthea said.

Dora shrugged; she had no idea who she was anymore.

Robert came downstairs and said hello to her and to Anthea, and she noticed a little smile between them. And she knew that Barry would love to know that tidbit. In the past Dora had told him things about other people she had heard because gossip was currency to people like Barry and the more focused he was on other people the less he was on her.

But she stopped that long ago when she realised nothing, she told him would keep him from finding faults with her.

There was a large part of Dora that felt guilty for the times she had betrayed people's confidences and told Barry and perhaps she deserved what she had now with her marriage and work. She would never live the way she wanted, because she was bad at life. Bad decision making, bad choice in husbands, bad at being a friend.

The night went on and after the dinners were served and the kitchen cleaned up, Anthea and Izzy and Peony and Robert were sitting around a table, all drinking wine except Peony.

'Come and have a drink, Dora,' called Robert from the table. She could see his foot and Anthea's foot were intertwined under the table and it made her happy to see. Robert was a lovely man who deserved so much happiness.

'I can't, I have to get home to Barry,' said Dora, pulling on her coat, thinking about the two bottles of wine from the cellar she had in her bag. She went to her bag and took them out. She shouldn't steal from Robert. He had been so good to her.

She went down to the cellar and put the wine back and then went out the back door and to her car.

That was the only thing left of her freedom. Barry didn't mind her driving because he didn't want to have to drive her from place to place but he controlled the petrol, the maintenance and insisted she clean it weekly even though she never ate or drank when inside.

Dora started the car and drove out of the car park and towards home, wondering what sort of mood Barry would be in, probably a bad one or he would be in bed and he would ignore her for the next week, making fun of her whenever she spoke.

He liked to pretend she was a chicken or a turkey or even a pig, making animal noises at her.

The lights were on when she drove into the driveway and she could see the television light flickering as she went to the door and pulled out her keys.

Her house key was missing. How odd, she thought, maybe it had fallen off?

She dug through her handbag and felt at the bottom of the bag. There was nothing there, so she knocked on the door.

'Barry love, my key seems to have fallen off,' she said.

There was no response. She knocked again.

Nothing.

Dora walked around to the front door and rang the door-bell but Barry didn't come. Bile rose in her throat and she felt the faint feeling of nerves coming up.

'Barry, love?' She went to the flower bed and knocked on the window. She could see Barry in his armchair, watching *Inspector Morse*, and he was eating what appeared to be a take away curry.

He never let them have take away … where had he gotten curry from? Had he driven into Cirencester and got a curry?

She knocked on the window, loudly and she saw his head turn for a moment and then back to the television.

'Barry,' she yelled, and he stood up. Maybe the television was too loud, and he hadn't heard her?

But then Barry stood up, walked to the window and, looking her in the eye through the glass, drew the curtains closed.

Dora went back to her car and sat inside it, her stomach churning. Where would she go? She didn't have any money, not enough for a motel nearby, and Barry didn't allow her to have more than fifty pounds on the debit card as he said he didn't trust her with any more than that.

She could drive back to the pub and sleep in the car park in her car but there was every chance Rob or Peony would see her.

There was the little spot near the church hall but it was a little way out of the village but Barry had said he saw some youths there a while ago, smoking and drawing on the fences with spray cans.

There was the car park at the back of Mabel's, built with hope that it would be a busy tea spot but so far that hadn't happened. And Dora knew that Ajay and Mala didn't use it, as they parked around the side near the private door. It was hidden, quiet and she was sure no one would see her, she thought as she drove back to Honeystone.

Dora could see lights on in the pub and wondered if it was still the women and Rob chatting. She would have liked so much to have been included but Barry would never have it.

She drove carefully into the back of Mabel's and parked, turning her lights off and locking the car doors.

This was her home for the night until Barry calmed down, but he hadn't done this before. He had threatened to kick her out but now he had done it. What would she do if it was forever? How would she start again?

Dora did up her coat and rubbed her arms. It was already cool and the temperature would get down lower in the night. She wouldn't freeze but it would be uncomfortable and then she needed a wee.

She couldn't get out and do it on the side of the car park, imagine if someone saw her? She was a sixty-year-old woman without a pot to piss in, as the saying goes, and she started to cry.

Sobs came from her body as she felt snot and tears mix together but she closed her eyes and let them come, the windows steaming up and her heart aching. How could she have let her life come to this?

She would have to drive to a fast food place in Cirencester and use the loo there and then come back, she thought and she searched in her bag for a tissue when she heard a knock at the window and a torch shone at her.

Was it Barry? Was he coming to apologise and tell her to come home? It was all a mistake and wasn't he silly and mad?

She wound down the window and there was Ajay with a torch.

'Dora, why are you here? Are you OK?' Ajay asked and Dora's heart sank.

'Oh yes,' she said. 'Just going home.'

Ajay peered closely at her. He was wearing a dressing gown and a concerned expression.

'Dora, come inside, I will get Mala to make some tea and we can talk.'

His kindness was an arrow to her soul and she started to cry again.

'I can't intrude,' she said. 'I'll go to the pub. It's OK.'

She wound up the window and opened the door and stepped out into the cool night air.

'He locked me out,' she cried, 'He won't let me back inside because I forgot to buy the bread.'

Ajay put her arms through his. 'It's OK now Dora. You're safe, I promise. Let me take you to the pub.'

He walked with her to the pub and went to the door and tapped on it and looked through the window while Dora stood feeling shame in every part of her body.

Rob opened the door. 'Ajay. What's wrong? You all right? Mala OK?' Rob sounded concerned but Ajay stepped to the side and pulled Dora gently to him to show her to Rob.

'Hello Rob, I am fine and so is Mala, but I think it is Dora who needs our help tonight.'

Izzy

Clary was sitting at the bar with Old Ed, when Izzy came into the pub and was making herself comfortable at the bar with them when Anthea came in not far behind her to wait for Rob to close up the pub.

'Hello all,' Anthea said to them as Peony came out of the kitchen and waved at her.

'You going to get married then?' asked Old Ed to Peony as she untied her apron.

Peony laughed as she poured Anthea a gin and tonic and Izzy a white wine.

'No Ed, why, what have you heard?'

Ed shrugged, as he sipped his pint, 'Nothing, but at least if you're here you can cook for us and not for your husband. That steak and kidney pie was better than Clary's.'

'I'm sorry Clary, that's not nice to say,' Peony admonished but Clary laughed, 'No, he's right, it's better than mine and mine is very good.'

'Well, you have a very patient wife Ed, and no I'm not getting married, I have no potential husband in mind either.'

Clary nodded, 'If you want to dream of your future husband, you have to fast on St Agnes Eve and get into bed backwards.'

Izzy laughed. 'Really?'

'Indeed,' said Clary, sipping on her shandy.

'You also told me that if Clover ever got whooping cough to pass her under the belly of a donkey.'

Anthea and Peony laughed but not unkindly as Clary and Old Ed finished their drinks and said their goodbyes while Rob closed up.

The women moved to a table and sat down, Peony bringing some crisps from behind the bar with her.

'How is Joe?' asked Anthea to Izzy who laughed.

'We had a drink and a bit of banter, that's all. Nothing else. I mean I tried to flirt but it's not a natural state for me, I prefer to snarl at people,' Izzy said to Peony and Anthea.

'Is he nice?' asked Anthea.

'He's lovely,' said Peony, 'Well he was to me when I went and saw him about this.' She pointed at her belly.

'Have you told Fergus yet?' asked Izzy, eating a crisp from the torn open packet on the table.

'Nope, because I am a coward and scared shitless,' said Peony.

'At least you're honest,' said Izzy. 'Speaking of which, how was my grumpy brother at dinner the other night?'

'It was great,' Peony said. 'Clover is a riot. Seeing her in her own environment was great.'

'A riot is a perfect name for her.' Izzy laughed.

'She's very excited about going to school,' said Peony eating a crisp.

Izzy sighed. 'Yeah, well we will see about that.'

'Why? What's wrong?' Anthea asked as she poured Izzy more wine.

'Don't, I have to drive,' said Izzy, putting her hand over the glass.

'You can stay here,' said Peony and Izzy moved her hand away without further encouragement.

'OK, and only because I am slightly tipsy, I will tell you both, but you can't mention it to Connor.'

Anthea and Peony leaned forward.

'They didn't buy the apples,' she said and shook her head sadly.

Peony and Anthea looked at each other.

'A sip from the cup of context might help us here,' said Anthea.

Izzy laughed wryly and then told them the disappointing news about the drama with the apples.

Peony gasped.

'Oh no, that's terrible, he didn't say a thing about it the other night.'

'Because Clover doesn't know,' Izzy said. 'I am going to try and get some more work to help out but it's hard because Clover needs someone with her. She can't be in the orchard all day.'

'Cider?' Anthea asked. 'How hard is it to make his own cider?'

'Hard,' replied Izzy. 'He would need to find somewhere to make it, a cidery or a brewery with the right equipment, plus it's expensive and he would need to sell it. It's not easy.'

Anthea nodded. 'You're right.'

Robert turned off the lights outside and came to sit down, bringing more wine.

'This is a lovely bottle,' he said to Anthea, 'It's a local winery and they do small batches of sparkling, just lovely with a light meal.'

'A local winery? I didn't know there were wineries around here,' she said, looking at the label on the bottle.

'Yes, some lovely little places, we can go on a day trip if you like, visit a few cellar doors.'

Izzy watched the way Anthea looked at Rob and kicked Peony under the table but she wasn't listening.

'Also Izzy, I think your cat is at my house.'

'Oh?' Izzy rolled her eyes.

'Yes, he ran inside when Baggins came for a playdate and I haven't seen him since but I've left food out and it's been eaten. I have no idea where he's relieving himself or where he's sleeping.'

'He probably realises he's onto a better thing at Spindle Hall and not at our place, he always did have tickets on himself. I can come and look for him tomorrow if you want but he will probably just come back again. He needs to come home on his own accord.'

Anthea shrugged. 'It's fine. He must be going outside, I've been leaving the kitchen door open, so I suppose he's using my garden as his litterbox.'

'If you have a warm spot in the house, near the pipes or the airing cupboard, I'd check there,' Izzy said.

A knocking at the pub door startled them. 'Who would that be?' Asked Peony standing up.

'It's all right, I'll go,' said Rob and as he stood, Izzy could see Ajay's face in the window.

'It's Ajay,' she said to Peony and Anthea.

The women watched as Rob opened the door and they could hear talking and then Ajay, wearing a dressing gown and slippers, walked in with Dora who looked worn out, her face red and splotchy.

'What's happened?' Robert asked but Izzy stepped forward and pulled Dora into a hug.

172

'It's OK, you're safe.' She looked at Peony and Anthea shaking her head and mouthing the word Barry at them. Ajay and Rob spoke quietly on the side and then Ajay came to Izzy and Dora's side.

'Dora, you have friends here, with me and Mala and this lovely group of people. You can come and stay with us if you wish, and we will look after you, OK?'

Dora nodded.

'You never sleep in your car again, we will always have a bed for you.'

Izzy looked at Peony and Anthea whose faces registered the shock Izzy was feeling. Sleeping in her car? What had Barry done?

Dora sobbed for a long time while Izzy held her, knowing not to let go until Dora did, because she was sure the hug felt like a lifeline to her in this moment.

When Dora finally let go of Izzy, Peony had made tea and Izzy led her to the bar and they sat her in the armchair by the dying fire.

Rob stoked it up again and put a log on it and they sat around Dora, waiting for her to speak but Dora stared into the fire.

'What did he do, Dora?' Peony asked in a quiet, calm voice.

Dora shook her head. 'I don't think he meant to, he's just very upset at the moment. He hasn't had work for a long time, and I'm tired. I forgot the bread, you know?' Dora looked up at Peony who nodded. 'I know,' was all she said in reply.

Izzy was confused but knew this wasn't the moment to say anything, Dora would need to come to the truth of what happened in her own time.

'I thought I'd lost my key,' said Dora. 'But I think Barry came and took it from me when I was working.'

'The key to home?' Peony asked.

Dora nodded. 'He locked me out.'

Izzy looked at Anthea, whose eyes were furious.

'I was going to sleep in the back room, if that's OK, I will speak to him tomorrow and see how I can fix this.'

Izzy felt rage well up in her chest and throat and was about to jump up and scream that Barry needed to fix this, but she felt Rob's hand on her shoulder, gently pushing her down into the chair.

Peony reached out and took Dora's hands in hers.

'What else does he do like this, Dora?' she asked.

Izzy noticed the whites of Dora's knuckles showing as she squeezed Peony's hand.

'He gets very angry,' she paused. 'Throws things, you know, he can't seem to express his anger very well.'

'Does he put you down? Make fun of you?' she asked and Dora nodded.

'Does he manage the money in the house? Not let you make financial decisions for yourself?'

Another nod.

'Does he blame you when things go wrong even if they had nothing to do with you?' Peony continued steadily.

Tears fell again and Izzy clasped the hem of her jumper to stop herself from crying with Dora. She knew Barry was an idiot but she hadn't taken him for this level of abuse.

'Does he always need to know where you are?'

'Does he tell you that your feelings are irrelevant?'

'Yes and yes,' came her reply.

Peony stroked Dora's hands with her thumbs. 'Darling Dora, you're in an abusive marriage. You need to leave.'

Dora looked at Peony in what looked like shock. 'Abuse? No, he hasn't hit me.'

'Yet,' Peony spoke firmly. 'This is the first time he's locked you out but it won't be the last. What if it was the middle of winter? You would have to sleep in your car and freeze to death.'

Izzy noticed that Peony's tone was firm but also kind, and not at all judgemental. She must have been a very good social worker she thought.

'He wouldn't do that,' Dora protested.

'He already has,' Izzy couldn't help herself. 'He's a truly awful person, Dora, and you're not. Do you know how many people love you in the village, including the people in this room?'

Dora shook her head. 'No, that's not true, I'm not interesting, Barry is.'

Rob snorted. 'He's an idiot and you will see this when you start to spend time away from him.'

She shook her head. 'I have nowhere to go.'

'Yes, you do, I have so many spare rooms I could start a hotel,' said Anthea. 'You'll come and stay with me and rest for a bit, and we can become great friends.'

Dora started to cry again and now Peony joined in and then Izzy felt her eyes sting with tears.

'I can't afford it. I have to pay for the house and Barry and everything else.'

'You can afford it, because you work for me now, and I'm giving you a week's holiday away from the village at Spindle Hall and then we will sort it all out. But you and Barry, it's done. It's finished. And if he comes near you again, he will be facing charges,' Anthea said.

Dora looked up at Anthea. 'I don't have any friends, Barry didn't like the ones I had.'

'Well, he's going to hate the new ones even more,' she laughed and Peony and Izzy joined in and soon the three women were sitting at Dora's side, hugging her.

'Thy friendship makes us fresh. And doth beget new courage in our breasts,' said Rob in the background.

'OK Will Shakespeare, now go and make up another pot of tea, and grab that tin of lemon slice. We need sustenance for the plans we need to make,' Peony ordered and Rob, the good man that he is, did exactly as his daughter bid, including bringing out more wine and a plate of cheese and crackers because he had the feeling they were going to be talking all night.

IO

Peony

Peony dialled the number and waited. Listening to the phone ring out, she finally gave up. She had called Fergus repeatedly over the past three days and he wouldn't answer her call so she decided to be honest and brutal and texted him.

> Hi, I'm pregnant. I don't care if you don't want to be involved. I have no desire to get back with you as I am sure you don't with me. The baby is due in November. Not asking for anything, including money unless you feel you want to be a part of the baby's life. That's up to you. I will wait for your decision once you have processed this information.

She stared at the phone for a minute, wondering how many swear words were coming out of his mouth while he read the text and then slipped her phone into the pocket of her apron.

'Hello?' Peony turned to see Anthea standing by the kitchen door.

'Hey, come in, I'm about to make some fresh pasta.'

Anthea put down some large folders onto the end of the kitchen bench. 'These are the fabric samples I have from when I did Spindle. Lots of gorgeous things in these, and not everything is super expensive.'

Peony opened the closest book and touched the beautiful, embroidered jacquard. 'This is very fancy. Something for a fine dining establishment.'

Anthea opened another one and flipped the fabrics until she found a ticking stripe.

'This is lovely also. I don't think you need to be all Lady and Unicorn style wise, keep it simple and comfortable.'

'You're right,' said Peony. 'We will have to close for a few weeks to get it done but it will be worth it, although Dad is having a fit.'

Anthea laughed, 'Men don't like change. Women thrive on it, we're used to it. Our bodies, lives, children, everything changes with the seasons with us.'

Peony thought about it as she touched her stomach. 'That's very true.'

'How are you feeling?' Anthea asked.

'Fine, OK, I mean, tired but that's normal. I'm going for an ultrasound tomorrow, just because I have been quite sick and I feel a bit worried. I asked for one just to check.'

'Do you have anyone to go with you?' Anthea asked, concerned. 'I can come.'

'No, I'm fine, it's just to work out dates.' She smiled at her. 'But thank you. You here to see Dad?'

Peony had the feeling there was a frisson between her father and Anthea but neither had admitted as much to her, or probably to the other knowing her father.

'Is he around? I need to talk to him about Dora and coming back to the pub?'

'He's in the cellar. Hang on, I'll tell him to come up.'

Peony went to the trapdoor and called down.

178

'Anthea's here,' she yelled and soon enough, Rob was emerging from the hole in the floor.

'Hello you,' he said and Anthea beamed at him.

Peony stifled a giggle and turned to the bench, pretending to look at fabrics.

'How's Dora?' she asked Anthea.

'Upset, sleeping a lot, then not sleeping, I'm going to get the doctor to come to the house and see her this afternoon.'

'Any word from Barry?' Peony asked.

'No, she doesn't have a phone, another one of his tactics, so he has no idea where she is.'

'He's been calling here asking where she is,' said Rob. 'Came over yesterday but I told him to piss off.'

'Oh my God, Dad, you didn't tell me that. What did he say?'

'Wanted to speak to Dora, and I told him no and that we know he locked her out of the house and that he's an abuser and she will be going to the police.'

Anthea made a face. 'Is that wise? To antagonise him?'

'I don't care, he needs to leave Honeystone, not Dora.'

Peony smiled at Rob. 'You're a good egg, Dad.'

'You're right, he needs to go, but we are the only ones who know about Dora's situation right now, and I don't think she would want people talking about her behind her back,' said Anthea.

Peony thought for a moment. 'But what if people know and they saw it as protecting her, not gossip?'

Anthea sighed. 'Maybe but I have to get her to see the situation clearly. She's like a little bird, so scared and anxious, it's awful. I just want her to know she's safe here and we won't let Barry do anything and that includes trying to get her back. He can go and buy his own bread from now on.'

'Want to come upstairs for some tea?' Rob asked Anthea.

'No thanks, Dad, I need to make pasta,' Peony said with a wink at her dad.

'I didn't mean you, you have a lunch to cook.'

'I know, I was being cheeky. Don't kiss Anthea's lipstick off, it looks too nice.'

'Peony,' Rob exclaimed and Anthea blushed and left the kitchen for upstairs.

As Peony weighed the flour for the pasta and put it on the bench, she thought about Dora. She had consumed her thoughts since that night. How many times had she dismissed Dora as being an irrelevant part of the landscape of Honeystone? She knew everyone, she had minded every child at some stage, she had drawn pictures of their dogs and cottages, she had volunteered her time and energy to so many village events when Peony was growing up. She remembered her mum spoke fondly of Dora, saying she didn't know how she did it. At the time she thought she meant all the activities she did but now she wondered if her mother was actually talking about Dora's marriage.

Peony had worked in social work long enough to know that women went back to their abusers for many reasons. They went back because men promised to change but she doubted Barry would do that. They went back because they didn't have any money. Anthea had solved that for the moment. And they went back because they didn't want people to judge them, because the abuser had convinced people he was a good person and the victim was being dramatic and difficult. Peony had no doubt that Barry would be telling everyone about Dora having mental health issues, gaslighting her to anyone who would listen.

Leaving the pasta for a moment, she pulled her phone from her pocket.

No reply from Fergus, which was on brand for him she

thought and she went to the Honeystone WhatsApp group and found Jenn's number and sent a message.

> Hi Jenn, it's Peony from the pub. Do you have time to drop in? I'm planning a little renovation at the pub and thought it might be of interest for the paper.

She put the phone down on the bench and waited. Within moments there was a text back.

> I might pop in now, as I'm running a new edition next week.

Peony sent a thumbs up emoji and then mixed the eggs into the pasta, working the dough with her hands. This was what she knew she had to do to protect Dora from all angles, and for the first time since she had come back to Honeystone, Peony felt like a local again.

Joe

Joe sat in the kitchen of Anthea's house and wrote on his prescription pad.

'She's anxious but I don't want to give her Valium or the like. She's also very depressed, but not enough to have her hospitalised. She seems to like your cat, he was purring away on her lap before.'

'It's not my cat, it's Izzy's but he's decided to live here for the time being. He had remained hidden until Dora came to stay and now, he sleeps on her bed and follows her around.'

Joe nodded. 'Well at least she's finally safe for now and now she's feeling all the feelings.'

Anthea frowned. 'What do you mean, "safe for now"?'

Joe looked up at her and his eyes narrowed. 'Never underestimate a narcissistic personality like Barry Mundy's. He will be trying everything to bring her back, and the more she says no, the more he will try.'

'Is she safe here? Am I safe here?' asked Anthea.

Joe shook his head. 'Barry doesn't know she's here so she's safe now, but let anyone who knows where she is know that it needs to remain private until she is stronger.'

Anthea rubbed her temples. She seemed to be getting headaches lately, which worried her more than she would admit.

'I wish she would go to the police and get an injunction. She's never going back to him, I can assure you of that,' she said firmly.

'She still can get one if he tries anything again.' Joe tore the script off the pad and put it in front of Anthea.

'He wouldn't dare,' Anthea snapped.

'This is a low dose anti-anxiety and anti-depressant. Will take a few weeks to kick in but she will feel better and clearer when they start to work. I have an interest in mental health, and I feel she will need something like this to give her a boost.'

Anthea took the script and looked at it and then at the doctor. 'Can I ask you something?'

'Go ahead,' he smiled at her. Yes, Izzy was right, he was handsome.

'I lost my sense of smell a while ago, after having Covid. I was very sick, in ICU for a few weeks and after I became better, it's never come back. I've had all the tests, seen all the specialists and so on, tried the sprays and had cameras up my nose and so on and they have no answers. Do you know much about that sort of thing?'

Joe frowned. 'Any loss of taste?'

'Nope, it's duller but I can still taste things.'

'It could be a response to something happening, not physically but mentally. Like you turned a sense off. Did something traumatic happen besides being in the ICU?'

Anthea paused. 'I mean, I was sick, yes, and ICU was terrible, but I'm not sure. I would have to think about it.'

'Have you spoken to anyone about the time in ICU?'

'Like a psychologist?' she asked.

'Yes, you might have post-traumatic stress disorder.'

Anthea shook her head. 'No, I've never spoken about it in that way to anyone, I've never seen anyone for talk therapy.'

Joe smiled at her. 'It might be worth considering. It sounded like a terrible time for you and that sort of experience can do all sorts of damage to us emotionally and physically.'

'You know, no one has ever asked me if it might be psychological. It's been two years and no one asked me anything about my feelings or what was happening around that time.'

Joe shrugged. 'People often think that successful people don't have these sorts of worries. You're a wealthy, successful entrepreneur who presents without a care in the world. So no, often people don't ask because they assume you have everything in hand.'

Anthea gasped. 'Yes, that's so true.' She made a growling noise. 'People never ask me how I am. They ask me what I'm up to, it's so odd.'

Joe laughed. 'It's the belief that if you have money then you don't have problems.'

'You're right,' she said. 'Do you have the details of someone you can recommend me to speak to?'

'Let me go back to the surgery and look some names up and ask a few other doctors in the area.'

'How is the surgery without Dora?' Anthea asked.

'It's fine, hasn't been so bad that I can't manage it myself for a bit.'

'Great, Izzy is helping at the pub at nights, which is fun.'

Joe looked up. 'Is she? I'll pop over for a drink.'

Anthea looked at him. 'You should, she's a fabulous girl.'

Joe nodded. Izzy was a fabulous girl but the last thing he wanted to do was get involved with someone when he wasn't staying forever. He wanted to travel still and was then thinking he might go back home and study psychiatry. There were so many options.

'I was telling Izzy she could travel and work anywhere, she's young, you should encourage her.'

Joe nodded. 'I did mention it when we had a drink together not long ago.'

'Good, keep pushing. I know she wants to go, but I think the ties with her niece are strong.'

'She's a cute kid. I can see why it would be hard to leave her.'

Anthea smiled. 'Indeed.'

'I'd better go,' said Joe and he stood up. 'I'll be in touch with you about the therapist.'

'Thanks,' said Anthea.

Joe went to his car and sat for a moment. He worried about Dora, not just her mental health but the husband. Men like Barry didn't like to be shamed and he would be doing everything to ensure she was back by his side.

And Dora was so fragile and lost. She had no confidence, years of being berated by Barry would do that to you. He could tell Barry was a powder keg the moment they met, with his grandiosity and yet no real attempt to connect to him.

He would keep an eye on Barry from afar, as he had the distinct feeling that Barry wasn't finished with Dora yet, no matter what Anthea thought.

Connor

The apple trees at Raspberry Hill Farm were a rare variety, brought over from America in the 1800s by a relative who was a descendant of pilgrims who seemingly didn't find God but apple seeds instead. Part of Connor had always been tickled that an ancestor chose to give up God and plant the fruit of Eve's downfall instead but now he wondered if the apples wouldn't be his own downfall.

Naturally, the apples were going to be wonderful this year, as the blossom had turned into fruit and now it was nearly the end of April it looked like it would be a bumper crop.

There wasn't much use for the Sheep's Nose apples that he grew, as it was a sharp, tart flavour that had a hint of spiciness. It worked when cooked but he wasn't sure he knew anyone who would need the supply of apples he had unless there was a national mandate to make apple pies in every household across the United Kingdom.

With Izzy working at the pub at night, he had been spending more time with Clover and he knew she was excited about school. He didn't know how he was going to solve the problem.

Plus, Clover wouldn't stop asking about Peony and could she come over again and when could she go to the pub and when would they make another cake.

Connor wanted to see her again too but Peony hadn't reached out and while he suspected she had other things going on, he wished they could sit and chat like they did when she came for dinner.

It was just so easy to be in her company again and he wondered if she had the same thoughts.

He needed to stop thinking about her, he told himself. He

needed to stay busy, perhaps he could do some paperwork, or maybe he could cook something for dinner.

What was he like? He laughed at himself. Peony wasn't interested in him, and while he was pleased they weren't fighting, he wondered if they could call themselves friends. Besides who would want to take him on again?

He was an orchardist with too many apples and not enough opportunities. Izzy was out with Clover, a note on the table telling him that they had gone to see the garden for the doctor's surgery in the village and might stop at Mabel's for a scone and lemonade.

Clover would be thrilled, he thought with a smile as the doorbell rang. A scone and the doctor she kept talking about in one day would be big news at dinner.

Yes, he would make them all something nice for dinner, he thought and he grabbed his keys to head to the shops to buy something to cook.

As he opened the door, he took as step back seeing Peony standing in front of him.

'Did Clover invite you again? Because she's not here.' He laughed and then he saw her face.

'What's wrong?' He ushered her into the house.

She was paler than usual and her eyes were filled with tears.

'What's happened?' He wanted to hold her but held back.

'I'm pregnant,' she said to him.

'I thought as much,' he said.

'And I have to go to Cheltenham now and have an ultrasound to see how far along I am.'

'Great,' said Connor, 'It will be fine.'

'But I thought I could go alone, like it didn't matter, I would be the chill single mum, you know because I told my ex about the baby and he still hasn't replied, so I guess we

186

know what the answer is there, and now I have to go and I'm terrified. I can't ask Dad because that's weird and Izzy and Anthea are great but they don't know me like you do. I know you would tell me to snap out of it and see the good stuff and just calm me down but if you can't come or don't want to, that's fine because asking you this is weird, I know.' She took a breath.

'OK the baby needs oxygen so slow down. And yes, I'll come. It's fine, thank you for asking me.'

Peony hugged him. 'Thank you, thank you, thank you.'

She let go of him. 'Sorry, I'm just so nervous.'

Connor laughed. 'It is a nervous time but we can do this together, OK? Let me get changed into something that isn't this and we will go together.' He gestured to his work clothes.

Peony nodded and he went and changed, wondering what the hell was happening.

'Want me to drive?' he asked as they walked outside after he was in jeans and a nice shirt.

'Yes please,' she said and threw the keys at him.

Soon they were on their way to Cheltenham, with Connor telling her about Clover and her obsession with Peony, to try and keep her mind off things.

'She's so social,' said Peony.

'Yes, she needs friends her own age, she's ready for them. She's spent too much time around adults and doctors. Medicalised children are super social which is good and bad,' he said. 'She needs to be a normal kid for a while.'

Peony wound the window down a little.

'Do you hear from Mel ever?'

He shook his head. 'Nope, not even a birthday card.'

'Gosh that's sad, I wonder where she is now.'

'No idea, I used to be angry but now I'm angry for

Clover. She deserves a mum but I have to assume Mel is somewhere living the life she wanted and not with us on an orchard. Mel always fancied herself as a burgeoning celebrity. I'm surprised I haven't seen her on *Love Island* or one of those shows yet.'

Peony laughed, 'You're not serious?'

'Sadly yes, let's just say the connection between Mel and I wasn't intellectual.'

Peony screamed laughing, 'Oh dear me, well at least you got Clover from it.'

'True,' he said as they came into the outskirts of Cheltenham.

'Do you think your ex will come around to the idea of a baby?'

Peony snorted. He had forgotten she did that when she laughed.

'No, he's a child. He should hook up with Mel, they sound perfect for each other.' He glanced at her and she smiled back at him.

'So, it's just us left then,' he said and she shrugged. 'Two rotten apples at the bottom of the barrel.'

'Speak for yourself. I am a fine apple, the sweetest fruit ready to ripen in November.'

'A November baby huh?'

'According to Dr Fisher, yes,' she said as she opened her phone to look at the address.

'Left here and then right, it's the building with the orange circle logo,' she said.

Connor parked the car and looked at the time. 'OK, you ready?' he asked.

'Nope,' she said and she touched her stomach.

'Come on, Mumma, let's go look at this kid,' he said and got out of the car. Peony reached for her handbag and jacket and when she looked up Connor was opening the door for her.

'That's very gentlemanly of you,' she said.

'I am nothing but manners once you get over the curmudgeonly exterior,' he said and she laughed as she got out of the car and waited as he locked it and they walked into the building together.

'Peony Grayling for 2 p.m.,' she said to the receptionist.

'Lovely, if you and Mr Grayling can wait for a moment, I will get you to fill in these forms and they'll call you for your scan.'

Peony took the clipboard and pen and went to sit next to Connor.

'She called you Mr Grayling,' she giggled as she sat down.

'I've been called worse things,' he said.

'She thinks you're the father though,' she said, looking at him.

'Good,' he said with a smile and for a moment, he saw confusion on Peony's face and then she smiled. Her face moved closer to his, and he held his breath.

'Peony Grayling?' he heard and Peony looked up.

'We're ready for you now.'

11

Peony

Peony wasn't the sort of child who dreamed of getting married and having children and being a mother. She preferred reading books and cooking and hanging out in the pub with her father.

Her mum became sick when she was twelve and was dead a year later. There was nothing they could do, they told her and she told Peony that she had to leave sooner than she had expected and the only things she could give Peony was her recipes. For the first three months of her diagnosis, she had shown Peony the basics of everything she knew in the kitchen. How to make a roux without a floury taste. How to get a sponge to rise. How to bone a chicken. How to make a stock.

The next three months, she showed Peony how to work pastry in a way that it was buttery and flaky and never dry. How to make pasta with the well in the centre and to work it fast and confidently because the pasta can tell if you're not serious and will fall apart when you cook it, and no one wants sad pasta.

When Christina was getting treatment to try and stay alive to show Peony how to make a soufflé and a baked Alaska, Peony was trying recipes alone in the kitchen using her mother's book, *The Joy of Cooking*, as a guide along with an old textbook of her father's of medicinal herbs through the ages. It had very fine line drawings of the herbs throughout, along with their uses and supposed magical properties. It was his grandmother's he told her and sometimes, when she opened the pages, an old dried and pressed leaf of tansy, sorrel or germander would flutter to the floor.

Peony lay on the bed as the technician squeezed gel onto her lower stomach and then pressed the transducers hard onto her. Peony winced and closed her eyes, anxiety coursed through her body and she put her hand out for Connor to take, grabbing his rough hand in hers. At the touch of his hand, the anxiety dissipated and she opened her eyes and looked at him and saw him smiling at her and she felt like she had relaxed for the first time since she arrived in Honeystone.

The technician moved the transducer around and typed on the keyboard a few times, and then moved it again and then paused and zoomed in on the screen and then turned it to Peony and Connor.

'There it is, all looking very healthy,' the technician said and then turned on a switch. Just like that, the heartbeat came through the tinny speaker, sounding full of life.

'Oh, is it OK?' she asked.

'It's fine, only one, and a strong heartbeat.'

'Thank goodness, I don't think I could cope with two,' Peony said to Connor who was staring at the screen with a smile.

'It's just a blob,' said Peony to Connor.

'But a cute blob,' he said and she smiled.

The technician continued the scan and typed as they went until he finally handed Peony some tissues.

'All done, I'll send the report to your GP or midwife but

everything is good. You can wipe the gel off and I'll give you some pictures.'

Peony smiled at Connor. 'A portrait of a blob, I will need to get a frame.'

'Yes, you will.'

After Peony was cleaned up, the technician handed her the images.

'Sweet blob, I already love you so,' Peony said as she slipped them into her handbag.

She turned to Connor. 'You all right to go?'

'Yep,' he said and they walked outside and towards the car. Peony felt sobs coming up from deep inside her and she grabbed Connor's arms.

'I'm about to wail,' she managed to get out and then she felt the cry come from somewhere she didn't know existed inside her.

Connor said nothing. He just held her tightly and then when her knees went beneath her, he picked her up and carried her to the car and managed to open the door with one hand and put her in the passenger seat and sat on the kerb and held her hands until the sobbing subsided.

Finally, she caught her breath and wiped her eyes on the corner of her shirt.

'I need some tissues,' she managed to croak and Connor was up.

'Be back in a minute,' he said but she thought it was probably only thirty seconds and he had a packet of tissues, a bottle of water and a packet of wine gums.

'I love wine gums,' she said as she took them from him.

'I know,' he said and he opened the water for her and handed it over.

She took a sip and then another and one more and let out a big sigh.

Then she blew her nose and handed him the wine gums to open.

She took the first one, blackcurrant, she noticed. Her favourite.

'Can we go home?' she asked him.

'Absolutely,' was the answer and he was in the driver's seat, driving back to Honeystone.

They sat in silence, Peony processing everything she had just felt. She hadn't cried like that since her mother had died and never since, not even for Fergus.

But everything was fine with the baby, she didn't understand.

Her phone pinged with a text message and she took it out of her bag and read the message and put it back into her bag.

'Everything OK?' asked Connor.

'Fergus,' she said.

'OK?'

'He doesn't want the baby.'

Connor sniffed as he drove them home. 'Bit late mate,' he said.

'He doesn't have to be involved, I'll let Little Blobby know who his father is and keep the door open. Children are curious, it's normal for them to want to know who the missing piece of the puzzle is.'

'Are you really calling your baby Little Blobby?' he laughed.

'I am, until it forms some sort of shape. I suspect as it gets a shape, I will lose mine.'

'I don't know, Mel didn't really lose her shape, she just had a bump poking out.'

Peony nodded and looked out of the window. The mention of Mel jarred her somehow yet she didn't have a right to feel any jealousy towards someone who wasn't around anymore.

'I'm sad that my mum isn't here,' she said. 'I thought if I ever had children, and it isn't like I've thought about it a lot but I assumed I would have my partner with me, not my boyfriend from my teenage years.'

'Fair enough,' he said and she glanced at him and noticed he wasn't slightly miffed which pleased her.

'I thought my mum would be a great grandmother, you know? She can cook and knit and knows all the old stories and had all these funny sayings and superstitions. And now she's gone, I wish I had learned them all, but I didn't. I mean she taught me how to cook, which she loved and I loved but there was so much wisdom in her that's gone now.'

Connor nodded. 'I understand.'

'I know you do, all that knowledge gone from your parents and them not knowing Clover. What a huge loss that is. I reckon your mum would have loved her.'

Connor laughed. 'Because they're the same, both up to no good and trying to bend the world to their benefit.'

Peony laughed. 'She's special,' she said.

They drove into Honeystone.

'She is, or maybe I'm just biased,' he laughed.

'Do you like being a dad?' she asked. 'Did it come easily?'

He turned to her and smiled. 'It's the best thing in the world being a parent, it's also terrifying and overwhelming and exhausting but I wouldn't change anything.'

'What about Mel going? Would you change that?' She hoped she wasn't crossing the line with the question.

He paused, 'No, I wouldn't, because I couldn't. People do what they have to do. I would change it for Clover though, she finds it hard not to have a mum, and while Izzy is amazing, she's more like an older sister than an aunt.'

Peony sighed. 'That's what I think about for Blobby, I mean he has a father but one who doesn't want to know about him. That's not a nice legacy to grow up with. I've seen it many times when I was in social work.'

Connor turned to her laughing. 'You cannot call the baby Blobby.'

'I won't call it Blobby when it's born but it stays until it gets some more pronounced limbs.'

'Am I taking you to the pub?' he asked.

She paused, 'Maybe not? I'm not cooking tonight and I don't want to have to deal with Dad and his bon mots and trivia about the *Canterbury Tales* or whatever he's reading.'

'Come and hang out with Clover and me for a while. I will make you some tea and we can hear her tell us about the latest episode of Ottolenghi that she's watched. I swear that child loves food as much as I love...'

As they turned the corner, Peony could see an ambulance at the farm.

'Jesus, what's happened?' she said as Connor sped to the farm and nearly skidded to a stop in the driveway.

He slammed on the car brakes and jumped from the car, with Peony following.

'Clover? Clover?' he called as he ran into the house. Peony chased after him and looked around and then saw a paramedic come from around the side of the house.

'They're outside,' she called to Connor and in the direction where the paramedic came from.

Izzy was sitting on the ambulance trolley, her arm in a sling while Clover sat on the end of the trolley, sorting through plasters with a chicken under one arm.

Connor came running up beside Peony and looked at Izzy.

'What's happened? Is Clover, OK?' He picked up his daughter and checked her over.

A paramedic came to Izzy's side. 'We're going to have to take you over to Cheltenham to pop that shoulder back in.'

Izzy made a face. 'I dislocated my shoulder,' she said to them.

'How?' Connor looked around and saw his ladder lying on the ground.

'The chickens were out and Eggmerelda, the one-winged chicken, got on the shed roof. I have no idea how she got up there but I said to Clo I'd get her down because Clo was worried and so was I. Anyway, I got up on the shed roof and there must have been something slippery, I don't know how but I was near the top, about to climb on and the ladder slipped and down I went.'

Izzy hissed at the bird under Clover's arm. 'That's the one. Eggmerelda is looking good for Sunday roast next week.'

Clover gasped. 'You can't, she's not an eating chicken, she's a laying chicken.'

Izzy rolled her eyes. 'She's lucky I'm on morphine because it would be over for her.'

The paramedic strapped Izzy into the trolley.

'This might be a bit bumpy,' he said to her and started to push the trolley towards the ambulance.

Peony noticed Izzy squeezing her eyes tightly together and biting her lip.

'Oh you poor thing,' she said.

'Clover called the ambulance,' said Izzy as they came to the back of the ambulance. 'She tried to call you but you left your phone at home, you goose. Where were you anyway?'

Connor looked at Peony who gave him a nod.

'I went with Peony as moral support for her ultrasound.'

'Oh wow,' Izzy said.

'I'm just going to give you a little more pain relief for the trip to the hospital,' said the paramedic as he injected her cannula in her hand with the drugs.

Izzy closed her eyes and smiled. 'That's nice,' she murmured. 'What are you having, Peony?'

Peony smiled. 'A little blob.'

'Oh wonderful, I love blobs,' said Izzy and she was pushed into the back of the ambulance.

Connor turned to Peony. 'Is it too much to ask if you can stay with Clover? I'll follow Izzy in the ambulance.'

Peony put her hand on his arm. 'I was planning to anyway, you don't need to ask. Go.'

The doors of the ambulance closed and Connor ran to Peony's car. 'Can I take this?' he asked.

'Yes, go,' she smiled and Connor opened the door and then paused as the ambulance started to drive out onto the road.

He ran back to Peony and Clover who were standing side by side, Clover's hand in Peony's. He leaned down and kissed Clover on the head. 'You are the cleverest girl for calling the ambulance, I am so proud of you,' he said.

Clover smiled.

Connor looked up at Peony and kissed her on the forehead. 'And you? Mother of the Little Blob, you are the best thing that's ever happened to Honeystone and I am so glad you're back.'

And then he was gone, Peony wondering what the hell had just happened.

Anthea

The walls of the room were painted in soft, neutral tones, the colours probably chosen for a reason. Anthea thought as she looked around the room. This was her fourth appointment with the therapist that came recommended from a friend yet, she still felt ill at ease.

There were a few pieces of artwork adorning the walls,

that depicted serene landscapes and abstract designs, adding character to the room without overwhelming it but they certainly weren't inspiring.

Anthea sat in one of the pair of comfortable chairs that sat facing each other in the centre of the room. A small coffee table between the chairs held a box of tissues, a practical touch that acknowledged the often-emotional nature of the conversations. Anthea mentally scoffed at them every time she came into the office, as though they were taunting her yet she had decided she wouldn't ever cry in this office. She didn't need to cry, she needed to smell again.

The therapist's desk was situated to the side of the room and was impeccably organised, free of any clutter or distractions. Anthea admired her for the order. Didn't a person's desk reflect their mind? She was sure she had heard that somewhere.

The therapist picked up a notepad and pen and gave Anthea a quick smile and then spoke.

'Tell me about your mother?'

'Do I have to?' asked Anthea with a half laugh.

She didn't like to talk about her mother, or her father. They gave her the best of schooling and the best holidays and the best clothing and the best manners. But she did so because they believed it would serve them well. It made them look good in their middle-class circles where they were constantly trying to keep up with the more moneyed, the ones who married better and those who had made cannier financial decisions than them.

Anthea was an only child and she was sure she was an accident from a single sexual experiment between her parents.

They never shared a bedroom, she never saw a moment

of tenderness between them, and she never felt a moment of love from them to her.

But she couldn't complain, could she? She asked the therapist. There were children who had had it so much worse, the beatings and the starvation and the abuse and so on.

'It still affects you. It brings up intense feelings of inadequacy and loneliness,' the therapist said.

This was Anthea's first session and she wished she had a gin and tonic made by Robert in her hand.

Instead, there was a box of tissues, as though goading her to give in to them. She ignored the tissues. Not today, she told the box. Not ever. She would never cry in therapy. She never cried in her everyday life as an adult. Why would she start now?

'The emotionally neglected child often turns into an adult who never feels fulfilled even after they have achieved incredible success.' The therapist said and Anthea was silent.

'They can often feel they don't know what they like or know because they never had their feelings validated.'

Anthea swallowed and crossed her legs.

'You mentioned you became ill, eighteen months ago,' the therapist checked her notes.

Anthea nodded. 'Covid.'

'Did you know it was Covid?'

Anthea thought for a moment. 'I don't think so. I mean I didn't think I would get it. I did all the right things, precautions and so on. John was very lax about it, thought it was overreacting and he sort of flouted the rules now I remember.'

The therapist nodded. 'Did he have Covid?'

Anthea nodded, 'But he said he was fine, that it was like a cold.'

Anthea was quiet, trying to remember the details. 'I had

isolated and he told me I was overreacting, but then I went to work followed the rules and so on. I started to feel a little under the weather but thought I was getting a cold. I just took some paracetamol and vitamin C and pressed on. I was naive or in denial.' She looked down at her hands, embarrassed to remember the timeline.

'And then what happened?'

She tried to remember. 'I was at work, I was getting a temperature, so I took more paracetamol and stayed at work, because John had wanted me to go through the new presentation for the men's line we were creating. We had a board meeting the next day.'

'So you have a temperature, and you feel unwell, your husband had had Covid but you stay.'

She nodded.

'And then what happened?'

'I remember I was feeling nauseous and I thought I should book the doctor for the day after the next because of the presentation.'

The therapist nodded and wrote down on her notepad.

'Did John know you were feeling unwell?'

'I might have mentioned it but I didn't tell him how sick I was feeling. He needed me to approve everything.'

'Did he ask you to stay even though you were feeling ill?'

She shook her head. 'No.'

The therapist paused and looked at Anthea.

'What happened when you were sick as a child? How was your mother with illness?'

Anthea paused. 'My mother was a hypochondriac. When life became too hard at home, she put herself to bed.'

'And did you have to step up?' she asked.

Anthea thought about carrying trays of soup and toast to

the bedroom, opening the curtains, taking out wine bottles, leading her mother to the bath.

'A little,' she said and looked down at her hands again. She needed a manicure.

'And if you were sick when your mother was having an episode, what happened then?'

Anthea could feel the tissues mocking her.

'I didn't tell her. I just got on with it.' She said stoically.

'What age were you when you mother started this behaviour?'

Anthea couldn't remember a time when it wasn't happening.

'I remember it from early years,' she admitted.

'Were you allowed to be sick when you were a child?'

Anthea was silent and then she shook her head. 'No.'

'And what's happened now as an adult is that you continued to disallow yourself to be ill, so much so you nearly died.'

Anthea wanted to leave but also wanted to know more.

'Why did I do that?' she asked.

'Because you don't know what you feel.'

'What do you mean?' She sat forward. Now this was interesting.

'A child whose parent cared for them when they were sick teaches them to check in with their bodies. They learn how to care for a temperature, they know they need to rest and when to see a doctor from the way they are nurtured through illness.'

Anthea felt the pain of carrying the tray upstairs to her mother when she had fallen off her bicycle and had to pick the gravel out of her own hands and put iodine on them. The briny scent of the medicine, her synaesthesia responding and showing her the darkest parts of the ocean at the smell of the liquid.

She felt the temperature rise in her body as a child, but still pushed herself to go to school otherwise she would have to be with her mother at home all day.

The pain of being a teenager being pushed aside repeatedly for her mother and her needs.

'You put your mother's needs ahead of your own repeatedly and now you don't know what you need. You have no internal compass to what you want or need to be happy.'

Anthea pulled a tissue out of the box so forcefully that it fell from the table onto the floor.

'And how do I solve that?' she asked, feeling the tears fall. God, this wasn't what she wanted at all.

'You have to re-parent yourself,' said the therapist. 'But you're not alone, you have me, I will work through this with you.'

Anthea wiped her eyes and nodded. 'And I would suggest you spend time with anyone who you think is a great role model in self-care, who knows themselves and how to enjoy life. Someone who forgives themselves for the past and looks forward to the future while remaining present in the everyday. Do you have anyone in your life like that?'

Anthea nodded and started to cry.

Dammit, she felt like she was betraying herself.

'You seem to be angry, what's going on?' the therapist asked.

Anthea shrugged, feeling like a defiant child.

'I'm just angry that I didn't see this, the connection.'

The therapist smiled. 'That's why I'm here. I went to university for a long time to be able to tell you that this isn't your fault or your ex-husband's fault, it's just how the cards fell for you, but we can fix it. We need to help Little

Anthea to find a way to see what she needs. When you can do that, you will heal.'

Little Anthea? Anthea wanted to scream at the ridiculousness of it all but yet, it all made sense.

She had given herself up to her mother, and as a result she had nearly died.

If she couldn't take back her power at fifty-five, then what would the rest of her life be like?

No matter what happened now, Anthea knew that she was the only one who could heal herself, with a little help from a man she knew in Honeystone.

Izzy

Dora sat next to Izzy in the living room of Spindle Hall. It was a grand room but also comfortable with large sofas covered in pale blue linen with beautiful cushions in Japanese block prints. There was a collection of seashells in a wooden bowl on the coffee table with some posh-looking books about interiors and artists. The rug was a pale pink with white and green roses and was possibly the most beautiful thing Izzy had ever put her feet on, so much so she had made Clover take her shoes off when they came into the room, and she had put them next to her boots in the hallway. She was not about to be responsible for leaving mud on the work of art on the floor.

Connor had dropped them off after Anthea had texted her to come and sit with Dora while she went out and since she couldn't drive, or garden or even cook while her shoulder was healing, a trip anywhere was preferable to sitting at home.

'Are you supposed to be babysitting me?' Dora asked Izzy.

'I don't think so, I think you're supposed to be hand-feeding me soup and cutting up my sausages.' Izzy laughed.

Dora looked the same, maybe a little more tired than usual but who would be getting any sleep after what she had been through.

It was a week and a day after the dislocation and Clover and Izzy were at Spindle Hall while Anthea was out at an appointment.

Dora was mostly silent, except when she was around Clover, who didn't ask for a moment why Dora was living at Spindle Hall.

Instead, they drew pictures, and Clover showed her the drawings of her dreams.

'This is the wind,' she said to Dora. 'I saw it before anyone else did.'

'I have no doubt,' Dora said to the child. 'Children are unsullied by the ideas of adults. It's when we try and make them see sense that they lose their senses.'

Izzy had no idea what Dora was talking about but Clover seemed more than happy with the answer.

Now Clover was lying on the plush rug, looking up at the ceiling. 'There are rabbits on the roof,' she said.

Izzy looked up. 'No, they're hares, hares are bigger than rabbits,' she said.

'Can you show me how to draw a hare?' Clover asked but Dora had her eyes closed.

'I have a headache,' she said and whispered to Izzy. 'Barry will be furious, I've never been away from him for this long.'

Izzy leaned forward and looked at Dora's face. 'You're not thinking of going back, are you?'

Dora shook her head. 'I don't want to but I don't know what else I will do, I can't stay here forever.'

'You can, actually,' Izzy heard Anthea say as she came into the room.

Dora looked at Anthea and smiled as Joe walked in behind her.

'Hello,' Joe said to Izzy and Dora. 'I'm here to see how you are Dora but I should check on you also,' he said to Izzy.

'I'm fine, I promise,' she said. 'Just a silly accident.'

The last thing she wanted was to be examined by Joe – unless it was under other circumstances – but he hadn't made a single move on her nor had he even followed up for another drink.

Izzy stood up and gave Clover a gentle nudge with her foot. 'Come on hare spotter, let's leave Dora and Joe alone.'

Clover got to her feet, somewhat slowly but independently.

'Let's go and raid Anthea's biscuit tin,' she said to her niece as she closed the door behind her.

Anthea was looking outside at the empty garden.

'No workmen today?' Izzy asked.

'Not today,' Anthea said. 'I'm meditating on something I've been thinking about.'

'What's meditating?' asked Clover.

'Something to make you find inner peace,' said Anthea. Izzy looked out at the large expanse of fields, a few of them fenced and dug but not much more had happened.

'It's a lot of land, isn't it?' Izzy said.

'I know, that's why I'm meditating on it, trying to tune into the land and see what else it needs.'

'That sounds very hippy, I like it.' Izzy laughed but not unkindly.

'What's hippy?' asked Clover.

'Someone who loves in peace, love and freedom, baby,' Izzy laughed.

'Then I'm a hippy,' announced Clover.

'Excellent, I can't wait to tell your dad.'

Izzy picked up the kettle with one hand. 'Tea?' she asked.

'I should be making that, sit down,' Anthea demanded.

Joe's head popped around the door. 'Can I have a word, Anthea?'

Izzy put on the kettle and went to the pantry, looked for the biscuit tin and took it back to the table.

'All yours, hippy chick.'

Clover smiled and lifted the lid of the tin and looked inside. 'Yuck,' she said and put the lid back on.

'What?' Izzy opened the tin and saw a few garibaldi biscuits. 'Oh, yes. That's a bit grim.'

'We could make some biscuits,' said Clover.

'I don't think so,' said Izzy. 'We shall have to be brave and have tea without a biscuit.'

Clover moaned.

Anthea came back into the kitchen and looked at Izzy and sighed.

'Everything OK?' she asked her.

'I hope so,' she said and she smiled at Clover. 'Do you want to play with my jewellery? I have a lot of it.'

'Hippies love jewellery,' encouraged Izzy and Clover looked at them both.

'If you want me to go, so you can talk about grown up things, then just tell me.'

Izzy laughed. 'We will go outside, and then we can talk about things.'

Clover shook the tin. 'Do you have anything nice to eat?'

Anthea nodded and went to the large pantry and came back with a different tin.

'That's the tin for the guests I don't want to stay. This is the tin for the guests I don't want to leave.'

Clover opened it up and gasped.

'Hobnobs and Jaffa Cakes!'

'There might be a Viennese Whirl down there but they're my favourite so there won't be many.'

Clover was already nibbling on a Hobnob as Izzy followed Anthea outside.

'Dora wants to see Barry.'

'God, really?'

Anthea sighed.

'And if she sees him, he will say all the right things and then it will happen again and again until God knows what will happen.'

'You can't stop her,' Izzy said as Anthea's dogs wandered outside.

'I know.'

'Did she say why she wanted to see him?'

Anthea patted one of the dogs on the head as it leaned against her. 'She said she had something to tell him.'

'Maybe she's going to tell him goodbye.'

Anthea stared into the distance. 'I don't think so.'

'Ooh, got a biccie for me?' Joe came into the kitchen and Izzy turned around.

Clover pushed the tin to him.

'Which one should I have?' he asked.

'Jaffa Cakes are good.'

Joe picked one up and took a bite. 'You're right,' he said. 'Very good.'

Izzy smiled at him. 'You off then?'

'Yes, I have to go and water my garden, it seems my gardener was wounded in the field.'

'Oh gosh, I'm sorry. I'll come with you, I'll do it,' she said.

Joe shook his head. 'No, I've been doing it. It's nice to water things, watch them grow.'

'I know, gardening is a bit addictive.'

'Do you want to have dinner tonight?' he asked her.

She nodded.

'I'll pick you up,' he said. 'We can go somewhere else than the pub. I've eaten there every time it's been open since I've been here.' He patted his stomach. 'I'm becoming portly.'

Izzy looked at his lean physique and rolled her eyes. 'You're practically bursting at the seams. Carrot sticks for you tonight.'

He laughed as he walked past them. 'I'll see you at seven.' he said and he waved as he went to his car.

'Did he just ask you out on a date or dinner with a friend?' Anthea asked as they watched Joe's car drive away.

'I have no idea but I don't like not knowing so I will find out tonight. Whatever it takes,' Izzy said.

'Easy tiger, you don't want to dislocate the other shoulder,' teased Anthea but Izzy wasn't listening. She couldn't read Joe and she wanted to know, was she just a friend or something else?

12

Anthea

When Izzy had asked about what she would do with the land at Spindle Hall, Anthea had been non-committal, but the more she sat with the uncertainty, the clearer it became she had to wait for the inspiration to strike. The muse would find her, she thought, but she knew that chasing after a dream she had already fulfilled to try and prove something to John was ridiculous. What she was learning about herself and her former relationship with John was that she had recreated the same relationship she had had with her mother.

Nothing she ever did would be enough, she would be chasing her own tail until the day she died if she had stayed married to him.

She nearly did die, she reminded herself.

The flower farm was lovely but she wanted something more than just that. Something that would last for hundreds of years.

She sat at the kitchen table thinking, and pondering if another headache was rumbling in the back of her head when Cat wandered in and Dora followed.

'You all right?' asked Dora as Anthea was rubbing her temples.

'Just a headache coming, I think.'

Dora nodded, 'Do you have any feverfew tea?'

'Do I what?'

'Feverfew, you know it, the little daisy.'

'I know it. I've used it in perfumes but not in tea,' Anthea said.

'You have some growing by the walled garden. I'll get some and make some tea,' said Dora.

Anthea walked outside with Dora to the walled garden where she and Peony and Izzy had shared their secrets the night they became friends.

'You know, there is a lovely echo here. The night I became friends with Izzy and Peony, we all shouted our secrets to the echo, it was lots of fun.'

Dora looked at Anthea as though she was mad, and in hindsight, Anthea realised she did sound more than a little unhinged.

Dora went to a small plant and pulled off the daisy-like flowers and put them into a handkerchief that she pulled from her pocket.

Anthea realised Dora would never shout her secrets to a walled garden, they were far bigger and more painful than anything the three women had shouted that night and she felt silly for mentioning it.

She held it up for Anthea to smell. For a moment, she thought she might be smelling something, a bitterness, maybe camphor, and then it was gone. Or perhaps she was imagining it. She wasn't sure.

'Do you think planting a garden for people to visit and pick their own flowers and make their own perfumes and lotions is something that people would like?'

'Here?' asked Dora. 'At Spindle Hall?'

Anthea sighed, 'Yes, that's what I wanted to do when I bought the house but it feels like an idea that's sort of like what I used to do, as though I was trying to prove something to my ex-husband. Look what I can do without you.' She waved her hands in the air as though her ex-husband was in the room.

Dora nodded, 'I understand. But you have to be doing things for the right reasons.'

'Do you think that if I am trying to do something to prove something to someone, it's the wrong reason?'

'Perhaps,' said Dora thoughtfully. 'But you like flowers, you like gardens, perhaps to share that with people is enough of a reason to do what you planned but does it make you happy to think about having people wandering through your garden? Opening the grounds to everyone?'

Anthea thought for a moment. 'When I moved here it was to be alone but over time, that's changed. Somehow Honeystone has opened my heart in ways I didn't know it needed but I still want privacy.'

Dora plucked an old rose hip from a shrub and played with it in her hand.

'Maybe you don't need to open your garden all the time to everyone. Perhaps it's just a sometimes thing, then you're not beholden to it.'

Anthea watched Dora play with the rose hip. 'You know, you're right. I've always been an all or nothing sort of a person but being here has shown me that there can be grey areas in life, that we don't have to know everything all the time and we can have time with people and then have our own time.'

Dora started to walk away from the house, down towards the woods and Anthea followed.

'I don't think I've had my own time since I married.' Her voice was soft and if the cool breeze hadn't carried the words to Anthea, she wasn't sure she would have heard them.

'You know you can tell me anything, Dora, I would never

213

judge you. I was married to an awful man for a long time, I thought I had to stay but I didn't know I could have left at any time. It wasn't the same I know but I am here to talk to.'

They stood on the edge of the woods and Dora turned to look at Anthea, her eyes dark and tired. 'But I couldn't leave at any time.'

The implication was strong and Anthea understood that John was an arrogant bastard but Barry Mundy was dangerous.

'No, you're right, it's very different,' she said. The woods seemed dark and unwelcoming in the light of the conversation.

'Shall we go back to the house?' she asked Dora. 'Have a cup of this tea you're claiming to solve my ills?'

Dora laughed, 'Yes indeed.'

They turned and walked back towards Spindle Hall as a flock of birds flew over them.

'Flock of birds before my eyes, when will I get a nice surprise?' she said aloud.

Dora smiled, 'I've never heard that before.'

'It's one of Izzy's,' Anthea laughed.

'I like it, I might use it, I could do with a nice surprise instead of a terrible shock.'

Anthea put her arm around Dora. 'You will get a nice surprise I think when you least expect it. They're the best ones.'

Once they returned to Spindle Hall, Dora put on the kettle and put the flowers into a mug and then after it boiled, she poured hot water over the top of them.

'We just have to wait for ten minutes and then you can drink it and the headache will be gone,' she said.

'This is all very witchy and wonderful Dora, how do you know this?'

'Oh I know a lot about herbs and plants, it's just that

Barry didn't like me telling people. He said I would be called the local witch you know, on account of being older and not having children and all.'

Anthea laughed. 'Then I will be an old witch with you.'

When the tea was steeped, Dora bought it to her and put it down.

'It's a little bitter but it will keep the headache away.'

Anthea took a sip. It wasn't so bad, she thought as she took another.

Dora sat down at the table, while Cat came and purred next to her feet.

'You know, I do have secrets,' she said to Anthea in her small voice.

Anthea nodded, 'I'm sure you do, but you don't have to tell me anything unless you want to.'

The tea was helping she realised and the pressure in her head was easing.

'I will tell you one day,' Dora said. 'But I wanted to say thank you for letting me be here. I've always loved Spindle Hall, it's a very welcoming home and you are a lovely host.'

Anthea smiled at the woman. 'You're welcome, Dora, I just want you to be safe and well.'

'I'm trying,' said Dora and she pushed her seat out and stood up. 'I might have a nap.'

'Lovely, and thank you for the tea, my headache is gone.'

Dora smiled and left the kitchen with Cat following her.

Rob

Rob was deciding if he would do a Wordle or the crossword in *The Times* or take a nap when his phone sounded with a text message.

He saw a text from Anthea.

Feel like taking a road trip with me?

Absolutely he typed back.

Pick you up in fifteen her message came back almost instantly.

Rob changed into some clean clothes and took Baggins out for a run and then was back downstairs, waiting for Anthea at the front of the pub.

He watched a few tourists wandering through the village, no doubt looking for something to do but the pub was closed and so was Mabel's, and unless they felt like a visit to the doctor, there wasn't much else they could do. He could have opened the pub today but Peony wasn't working and he honestly couldn't be bothered. Time spent with Anthea was much better.

Anthea's car came up the road and he waved at her and pretended to direct the non-existent traffic so she could park in front of the pub.

He opened the car door and got into the passenger seat. 'Goodness, Honeystone is busy today.'

She laughed.

'What are you laughing about?' he asked.

'You, you looked about eighteen and so goofy when you were waving all the invisible traffic around you.'

'I feel eighteen and goofy around you,' he said and she blushed.

'Flattery will get you everywhere,' she said.

They still hadn't done anything more than kiss but Rob wouldn't push her. He loved being around her and if that's all she wanted to do then he would take her lead.

'Where are we going?' he asked as he put on his seatbelt.

'The wineries; you said we should go and look at a few,' she said as she punched an address onto the screen in her car and the directions came up.

'Wineries? OK then,' he said.

'You OK with that?'

'I will do whatever you want if I can be here in your presence,' he said and she smiled at him waiting for the joke but it never came.

He was serious and she gave a little smile at him, seemingly pleased but perhaps a little shy.

'You're so sweet,' she said.

'I'm a sucker,' he said as he put his coat onto the back seat.

'Oh? For what?' She glanced at the map and drove on.

'Love,' he said and then he turned up the music playing on the stereo and the sound of Stevie Nicks came playing through the speakers and he started to sing 'Dreams' at the top of his voice.

Anthea joined in and as they drove along the roads, singing and putting on silly voices, he had a feeling of completeness that he hadn't had since his Christina had died so many years before.

He had always been at peace with his lot in life, but now he felt as though he had been wearing black and white glasses until this moment and now as Anthea drove him, Peony was more present in his life and a grandchild on the way, he felt as though he could finally see the world in all its vibrant colours. The lush green fields stretched out as far as his eyes could see, while on the side of the road he could see buttercups and wildflowers.

The trees were coming into their full bloom, boasting rich shades of emerald and lime and the hedgerows, burst alive with bright foliage, adding to the kaleidoscope that travelled beside them.

They drove through villages that Rob had seen for fifty years and counting, now they seemed even more picturesque, each one offering a unique blend of limestone buildings and thatched-roof cottages, each one sweeter than the last, while the limestone glowed in the warm honeyed spring light.

Is this happiness? He wondered as Anthea turned off at a sign for the first winery.

'This is a lovely place,' said Rob as they parked. 'I know the owners here, I buy their whites for the pub, lovely drop.'

Anthea stopped the car and opened the door and stood in the silence.

She took a deep breath and then gasped and started to cry.

'What? What's happened?' he asked rushing to her side.

She closed her eyes and inhaled deeply. 'I can smell everything,' she said.

'OK?' He was confused.

She opened her eyes again and looked at him, tears falling.

'When I had Covid, I lost my sense of smell. I never thought it would come back and I was ashamed. Who wants a perfumier who can't smell anything?'

Rob frowned. 'You didn't tell me. I don't care if you can smell or not.'

'But I do,' she cried. 'It's more than scent, I can see the colours, it's hard to explain but I can see them.'

'Synaesthesia,' he said.

'How did you know what it is?'

'I know a lot of random things and it seems since I met you, I finally have a use for them. It's as though I've been collecting knowledge in preparation for you, to come into my life.'

She kissed him and then walked towards the vines.

'I can finally smell the fresh air and that wonderful earthy aroma,' she said perhaps to him, or perhaps to the world around her, he wasn't sure, it didn't matter.

She turned to him. 'Can you smell the dampness from the recent shower?' she asked.

'I swear I can smell the new buds on the vines, and the scent of the soil as the worms turn it over beneath us, weaving through the roots, doing Bacchus's work below the surface.'

Her hands were over her face now and she openly sobbed as Rob came to her side and pulled her into him and held her as she wept.

'I can smell it all,' she said to Rob who nodded at her and smiled.

'That's amazing Anthea, what a gift to have had and lost for a while, I'm glad you're whole again, not that you ever weren't to me,' he said.

She smiled at him. 'I think you've helped heal me,' she said. 'My life is so much better with you in it.'

He laughed and moved a lock of grey hair from her face. 'This is you healing yourself, my love.'

They looked out over the vines. The once bare vines were now adorned with tender green leaves and tiny grape clusters forming, promising new yields and blends. The patchwork of green rows, so orderly and even, it pleased her sense of discipline.

Anthea turned to Rob. 'I want to have this, at Spindle Hall. I want to make some wine,' she said, feeling tears form. Ever since she had started crying, she couldn't seem to stop.

'What about the flowers?' he asked her.

'I want that also. I will have both. We can have the flowers in the summer, wine in the winter and what a life we will have. I want to open Spindle Hall a few months of the year, just to share it with everyone, it's not mine but the people of Honeystone's and whoever else wants to visit. I can see it all now. The flowers, the café, strawberries and cream, Peony's blackberry roulade and raspberry galette, big grazing boards. People wandering about picking bouquets of flowers to press into oils and perfumes. I think we might even have a little perfume bar, instead of tastings we can have smelling sessions. And then in winter we can have wine tastings on special occasions.'

Rob pulled her in tight. 'I think that's a wonderful idea, the ground is perfect and you're in a little valley there, so you could grow a Sauvignon Blanc grape, they're perfect for that area. I have often thought what a great little vineyard Spindle Hall would be.'

Anthea gasped, 'Why didn't you say so? I've been wondering what to do and you knew all along?'

Rob laughed, 'It's not my place to decide Anthea, this is all yours, but of course I will support you anyway I can. I would never presume to tell you what to do, you're incredibly independent.'

Anthea put her hand in his, 'I think I'm ready to be a little dependent on someone.'

He pulled her close. 'You know I'm falling in love with you Anthea.'

She smiled at him. 'So, this isn't just a country affair?'

'I hope it will be more but I'm OK if you're not ready, you've been through so much.'

Anthea smiled, 'I like that you never rush me, like this, us being together, the winery idea, having sex.'

Rob gave a deep laugh, 'Oh I would like to rush that last one very much but not until you're ready and things are sorted with Dora at the house.'

She leaned up and kissed him. 'You know, I don't think I've ever been in love before, until now,' she said. 'I am falling for you, Robert Grayling, the only man I know who seems to collect facts like conkers and quotes like pennies and who I think about every morning and every night.'

And as they kissed, the sun came out over the vineyard and Rob wondered if life could get any better than this moment.

Peony

'You're just in time for some croque-monsieur, or madame. You choose,' announced Peony to Rob and Anthea as they came upstairs to where Baggins was sitting patiently at the kitchen bench waiting for a morsel of ham or cheese or whatever Peony deemed suitable for him.

Peony began to cook as Anthea and Rob took off their coats and Rob took a reluctant Baggins downstairs for a quick run. The kitchen was alive with the tantalising aroma of melting butter and bubbling cheese, and Peony felt herself relax as she worked. The croque-monsieur might be simple but it was easy to mess up, not that Peony ever did.

'Where have you two been?' she asked Anthea. 'There's wine in the fridge and glasses up there,' she nodded at the cupboard to her left.

Anthea poured herself a glass, 'We went to a winery, I'm thinking of planting some grapes. God that butter melting smells incredible,' she leaned into the pot and inhaled deeply. 'Madame please.'

Peony started the alchemical process of creating a silky béchamel sauce. Butter, flour, and warm milk melded into a velvety texture that would soon blanket the sandwich in luscious decadence. As she added Gruyère cheese, she marvelled at the creamy magic that unfurled before her eyes.

'I never get tired of making these,' she admitted to Anthea.

'You are such a brilliant cook,' said Anthea. 'It's wonderful to watch you work.'

'Growing grapes? That's interesting,' said Peony. 'They take a while though, don't they?'

Anthea nodded and took a little piece of grated cheese and popped it into her mouth.

'I'd love to have my own label, I can get Dora to draw Spindle Hall for it, gorgeous,' said Anthea excitedly. 'But yes, it takes time, which is both annoying because I am impatient, and good, because I have to learn patience.'

Peony selected slices of the bread she had bought from Ajay at Mabel's. She could have made her own but Ajay's sourdough was perfect and why reinvent the wheel as it were, she thought.

'If you want to do something faster, you could buy the cidery in the Cotswolds that's going to go under, and use Connor's apples,' she laughed. 'Then you could have a Spindle Hall cider.' She half joked.

With artistic precision, she layered the ham and cheese on one slice of bread, ensuring an even distribution of smoky, savoury ham and the slightly sweet, nutty Gruyère cheese. The other slice was lovingly coated with the velvety béchamel sauce, transforming it into a work of art.

The toasting ritual was what Peony loved the most about the process, where the bread transformed into a golden masterpiece. It was vital that the outer layers achieved the perfect crunch while the interior retained its creamy, luscious core. Peony watched carefully as she toasted the bread and assembled the sandwich and then placed it on an oven tray and popped it inside the preheated oven.

'I like to add an egg, do you want an egg?' Peony asked Anthea.

'You know, that's not a silly idea,' said Anthea.

'The egg?' Peony said. 'The egg is the *pièce de résistance*.'

The perfectly fried egg was her secret weapon when she made these sandwiches. As she prepared it to her preferred level of doneness, she envisioned the moment when its runny yolk would cascade down, creating the perfect light dinner.

'No, the cidery,' said Anthea.

'Really?' Peony stood with an egg in her hand.

'Really,' Anthea said as Rob came upstairs with Baggins who went back to his place to wait for a tidbit.

'Monsieur or Madame?' she asked her father.

'Monsieur, merci,' he answered.

'Peony said I should buy the cidery, and buy Connor's apples and make a cider,' Anthea poured Rob a very large glass of wine and handed him a glass.

He held it up to the light, 'Does it come with a goldfish?'

Anthea ignored his joke but Peony laughed. 'Classic dad joke, Dad.'

'Rob, I'm talking to you,' she said. 'The cidery, what do you think?'

Rob shrugged, 'I think you should do whatever you think will be fun to do. A cider could be fun, you could expand and add a distillery and make gin or absinthe, that's fun, real potion making stuff, wormwood, fennel, anise, it's the extra botanicals that give it its green colour. The green fairy, some call it.'

Anthea gasped, 'I love that, yes, let's do it,' she said to Rob and turned to Peony.

'Let's have these and then we might head over to talk to Connor, what do you think?'

The sandwiches emerged from the oven, and Peony laughed.

'Gosh, you don't waste any time do you?'

Anthea shrugged, 'Never, life is far too short to sit and wait for it to happen to you, and as the French say,' she took the sandwich, took a sip of wine and kissed Rob. 'Mangez bien, riez souvent, aimez beaucoup!'

13

Dora

Dora knew more than she let on, which is what had kept her alive while being married to a man like Barry.

She knew she had to survive any way she could and while some might have thought her weak and powerless, she was doing what she could where she could.

But she needed to get back into the house when Barry wasn't there and that wasn't proving to be easy since Anthea had always made sure that someone was with Dora in the house. Izzy or Jenn Carruthers, even Clary had come over and sat with her, knitting and telling Dora that the tighter the curls on the sheep the finer the wool and that Ed's sheep had the tightest curls in the area and that's why his wool was best for knitting baby clothes. Clary had already knitted two cardigans, three hats and mittens and booties, and was now working on a pram blanket in rainbow colours as Clover told Clary that Peony's baby liked rainbows and Clary wouldn't argue with Clover about such things because everyone knew Clover had the gift.

Dora couldn't disagree with Clary, and not just because she couldn't get a word in but also because she understood what Clary meant about Clover. Sometimes Clover looked at her in a way that made Dora wonder if she saw everything that had happened in her life and everything that was yet to happen or perhaps Dora was being melodramatic. Barry always said she was hysterical.

But today, Dora was alone. Izzy had popped in earlier with some early strawberries in a little basket and some fresh eggs but said she had to go to see Joe and rushed out of the door.

Dora walked around the house, unsure what to do without a list of tasks that would make other people's lives easier. Barry, Joe, Rob and whoever else had asked for something using Dora's time. Her whole married life she had given her time away to other people and now she had it for herself, she didn't know what to do with it. Perhaps she would give Anthea's house a once over, she thought, as a thank you but even Dora could see there wasn't a speck of dust to clean.

Dora had walked a full circle of the bottom floor of the house, arriving back to the living room where she had started from and still she was restless. Perhaps a lie down might take away this feeling?

Dora hadn't taken a nap since she was a child, but the thought of having one now wasn't a choice, it was a need.

She climbed the stairs to the guest room Anthea had given her to stay in and went to the bed and lay on top, not bothering to even lower the blinds. She closed her eyes and felt her body sigh with relief she couldn't remember ever having felt before and drifted into a dreamless sleep.

Hours later, when Dora woke from her nap, she realised she had slept through lunch and went downstairs, where the dogs were sleeping in their baskets in the warm kitchen. Anthea must not be home, she thought, as the dogs usually followed their beloved owner around when she was at Spindle Hall.

On the kitchen table, Dora noticed a note from Anthea telling Dora she was out and wasn't sure when she would be back but to make herself something for dinner as there was plenty of food in the freezer. Dora stared at the note but was no longer reading the words. Instead, she was thinking about what to do next. The plan she had from the beginning.

Perhaps now, she could go home but she had to make sure Barry was out.

Dora picked up her new mobile phone that Anthea had given her. She hadn't texted or called anyone because she didn't have anyone to call but now she knew what to do.

She opened the phone and carefully typed out a message and then pressed send.

A message came back almost instantly.

She had a window to get to the village, the house and back to Spindle Hall.

Dora looked outside and saw the small farm runabout that presumably was for the gardeners when they came back.

She needed the keys and she looked around and then opened the drawer by the kitchen door.

'Spindle Truck' was written on the plastic tag and she put it into her pocket.

She opened the drawer more and saw a hammer and picked it up. That would do, she thought and she looked around, trying to think what else she needed and at the last minute, picked up a shopping bag from the counter that Anthea had bought items from Mabel's home in for tomorrow's breakfast.

Dora grabbed the bag, made sure the dogs were safe and left the house.

The farm runabout was easy enough to start and she was soon puttering up the driveway and out on to the road. She wasn't even sure it was registered to be on the roads but this wouldn't take long.

Taking the back way around the village to her house, she felt sick as every car passed her in case it was Barry. Finally, she arrived at her street, and drove past the house, hoping his car wasn't in the driveway. It wasn't; her plan had worked.

Parking across the road, Dora walked around the back of the house. She pulled the hammer from the shopping bag and carefully broke the small window next to the back door. Then, covering her hand with her coat, she put her arm inside and turned the lock.

The door opened and she stepped inside the house.

It was neat as a pin, and she wondered if Barry was doing anything else but cleaning in her absence.

Dora went upstairs to their bedroom and stood in the doorway. God she hated sharing a bed with him. Never again, she thought and she went to her dressing table and took out the blue velvet box that had the jewellery that her mother had left her.

It wasn't anything expensive but there was a small diamond ring, a pair of topaz earrings and a few gold chains.

Leaving her clothes, because they could wait, she went to Barry's study, where he pretended to work during the day when in fact all he did was send angry letters to the council and the papers.

She went through the small filing cabinet under the desk and found the papers she wanted and pulled out the shopping bag and shook it, putting the folder inside.

And then she opened Barry's computer. He thought she had no idea about computers but she knew more than he thought. She had used the computer at the pub and doctor's surgery for years but it served Barry to believe he was better at things than she was so she had just pretended to be ignorant about them all these years.

She sat down and typed in his password, Honeystone1. What an unoriginal man he was. She searched through the files and there it was.

'Termination of Barry Mundy.' She read.

He wasn't made redundant, he had been taking money from the firm, to buy the Audi, resurface the tennis court, and God knows what else. It wasn't as though Dora was seeing any of it but she had proof of it now and she could use the information as leverage. She always wondered why he hadn't been charged by the company but knowing Barry, he probably had some information about someone in power whose secrets he threatened to reveal. That's how Barry worked, blackmail and threats.

She emailed the documents to Anthea, and then deleted the sent email and logged out of the computer and closed it again.

Dora looked around the house and wondered if there was anything else she needed for the time being and then decided against it and opened the back door and left.

He would know it was her, but he wouldn't know what she had taken until it was too late, and for the first time in her married life, Dora felt what it was like to hold the power in a relationship.

Connor

The knock at the door came as Connor was thinking about what to make for dinner. He didn't have a wide repertoire of recipes but he did make an excellent shepherd's pie. Clover was watching television and Izzy was out with Joe for the second time that week.

Connor went to the door and saw Peony, Rob and the woman who owned Spindle Hall.

'Hi,' he said, confused as Peony smiled at him. 'Hi,' she said.

'Hello Connor, this is Anthea McGregor,' Rob said to him.

He looked at the woman and nodded. 'Izzy speaks highly of you,' he said.

'And she of you, and Clover also,' she said. 'You should come in for a cup of tea when you drop them off next.'

Connor nodded. 'I'm not really into social calls,' he said, watching them both.

Connor gestured for them to enter. 'Come into the kitchen,' he said and they walked through the house.

'Where's Clover?' asked Peony.

'In the living room,' said Connor.

'I'll go and sit with her,' Peony said and left the room.

They sat at the kitchen table, and Connor lifted the kettle.

'Tea?' he asked.

'No thank you,' said Anthea.

'I'm fine,' said Rob.

Connor sat down opposite them and waited for why they were in his house.

'If you don't do social calls, will you do a business meeting?' Anthea asked.

'What sort of business?' he asked warily. 'If you're here to buy the farm,' he said to Anthea, 'I could be interested.'

'Oh I don't want your farm,' said Anthea. 'I mean it's lovely but I have a home.'

Connor felt more confused than ever.

'I want your apples,' she said. 'I want to buy all your apples.'

Connor pulled out a chair and sat down. 'What? Why?'

Anthea looked at Rob and then back to Connor.

'I have decided to buy the cidery and add a small distillery. I want to make gorgeous local spirits and cider, I want to start a Spindle Hall label. I might even make wine if my plans go ahead but it will take time to get the grapes to

230

maturity to be able to get a yield and I thought, why not create a cider? We could do our own cider, a Spindle Hall brand but you can name each blend. You would also have a cut of the profits, because we should make this a real business for you and Clover, so I was thinking, would you like twenty per cent, then you know I'm serious and you can have some security.'

Connor shook his head, as though trying to fit the pieces together in his brain. 'Why would you do that? You could have all the money?'

Anthea laughed. 'Why would I want all the money? I have more than enough for five generations to come. Why not share it? And you know what happened when the captain's wife didn't share her chestnuts in *Macbeth*? Let's just say it wasn't good.'

Connor leaned forward and looked at Rob.

'I feel like I'm having one of those weird dreams where you know it's a dream but you can't get out of it,' he said as Rob smiled at him warmly.

He turned his attention to Anthea.

'I don't know anything about Macbeth or the witches, but chestnuts, I do know. You could make a liquor out of the chestnuts. It's called Châtaigne in France. I have a few recipes I've made with the chestnuts from your place. We could try a few.'

Anthea looked at Rob. 'I love this, all of it. This is a good idea, isn't it?'

Rob smiled at them both. 'I think it's all bloody wonderful.'

'I love this idea, I love it all, and I am so grateful. You will be changing mine and Clover's life,' he said to her, feeling emotion wash over him.

Anthea put her hand out for him to shake and he took it and held on and looked into her eyes.

'Izzy said you were magic, I guess she was right.'

Anthea smiled. 'We create our own magic, when we're ready. I'll call you tomorrow and we can work out the details and get moving. I will need your advice and knowledge, so let's catch up tomorrow at midday at Spindle?'

Connor nodded and as he walked them out, Clover was sitting on the sofa, and Peony sitting next to her reading her a book.

Connor moved Clover's drawing book that was open on the floor out of Anthea's path.

'Is that Spindle Hall?' Anthea asked as she looked down at the drawing in Connor's hand.

Clover looked up from the book that Peony was holding.

'Yes, I had a scary dream about it.'

'Oh dear there is nothing scary about Spindle Hall,' said Anthea with a smile. As she looked at the picture again.

'Why is it a scary story?' Anthea asked and she smiled at Peony.

Clover looked up at her, and then at Peony. 'Because the bad man is inside the house. You can't see him from where you are outside but he's waiting for Dora.'

Connor saw Anthea swallow and she looked at Rob.

'We should check on Dora,' she said. 'I'll call her in the car.'

'Do you want to come now?' Rob asked Peony. 'Or I can come back for you once we check on Dora.'

'I'll stay here a while,' said Peony and Clover snuggled in close.

'I'm sure it's fine,' said Connor as he showed Anthea and Rob out. 'I'll come and see you tomorrow.'

Anthea waved and jumped into the car and sped off with Rob next to her.

Connor stood for a moment, breathing in the crisp night air.

It was funny how life's direction could change in a minute, he thought and he had the strong feeling that there was a certain person who was responsible for it, and it wasn't one Anthea McGregor.

Dora

The time at Spindle Hall was healing for Dora: waking up each day without running through the list of things she had to do to not get Barry angry freed up her mind and she began to think of the slow descent into Barry's control.

She was both terrified of him and terrified of not being with him, because she didn't know how to exist for herself.

She drove back to Spindle Hall, her nerves on high alert until she parked the runabout and went inside and put the bag down on the table.

'Hello puppies,' she said to the dogs and she opened the back door to let them out for a run.

The sun was shining, and the dogs were happily galloping in the gardens and Dora let out a big sigh of relief.

It was done.

If anyone had said to Dora that at sixty years old she would have to start her life again, she would have wondered why bother but there was a feeling of something exciting in the distance coming towards her. It came the day the wind blew through the village and her shameful secret stash of bottles was spilled across the main street.

For years she had drunk and thought Barry didn't notice, but when he showed her the footage from his dashcam, he had laughed.

'Perhaps I'll tell everyone in the village this is where my drunk wife hides her bottles.'

And she knew he would, if he was displeased enough.

Living with the threat of his explosion was like living with a suicide bomber, she often thought, but not being able to do anything in case he pressed the button.

But she had her checkmate in the shopping bag and in an email to Anthea. As long as that was safe, there was nothing he could do.

But she reminded herself that he would have no idea where she was and the thought comforted her.

She wandered about the house, with the dogs following her, trying to find something to do. She wasn't used to not being busy, and she saw the sketchbook and pencils and charcoals Anthea had bought her lying on the dining room table.

The inspiration to do any art had been missing for a long time but now, without any tasks or demands, she wondered what she could create.

At this point in her artistic journey, she had stuck to drawing the village and the occasional landscape. Barry had been cruel about her attempts to draw people, making fun of the imperfections on the page and how poorly she had done in her work but now, without him, she wondered.

The dogs lay on the rug, with Cat sitting on the window-sill, looking out over his kingdom. Dora had always wanted a cat and it seems Izzy wasn't fussed about Cat returning home to Raspberry Hill Farm any time soon. As the sunshine poured into the room, Dora took the sketchpad and opened it. She found a pencil she liked and she started to sketch the two lurchers in all their lazy glory.

Taggie, was facing Dora, her face between her paws, eyes half open while Rupert, the show-off, was lying on his back, legs in the air, paws softened and his head to one side. The regal pose of Cat was at odds with the clumsy poses of the dogs, and Dora smiled as she drew them.

She could see the light shining through their coats and the little specks of dust in the air that floated like sun seeds.

The peace she felt as she drew was unfamiliar but she sat with it as the drawing came to life and the dogs and even Cat cooperated with her, as though also enjoying the silence and creativity that buzzed through Dora.

She drew easily and lightly, as through the weights on her wrists and hands were lifted. She turned the page as the dogs moved and drew Taggie's face with her melancholy eyes asking for love and possibly a little treat.

The detail in Rupert's paws and the underside of the pads, showing the patterning of the cushion like an old leather armchair, roughened from the weeks in the forests at Spindle Hall.

The defiant curl of Cat's tail against his straight back was perfect, she thought as her hands flew across the pages. She filled in the details of the room around the animals. The beautiful marble fireplace, the tall blue and white tulipiere that held thirteen white tulips, creating a magnificent shadow that Dora tried to recreate. If she could have drawn the quiet, she would have, the sense of safety that came in the moment, the feeling of existing just in this moment, not having to think about what she had to do next, the bread for Barry, the dinner, the cleaning, the jobs she had to do. Everything in Dora's married life had been for other people and now she had nothing to do but things for her own benefit.

As she drew, she felt like she could finally see everything and everything was art. Everything was art, she thought as she moved to another room to try and capture it all.

There was a cup left on the table in the snug, and Dora

drew it, next to the shoes Anthea had left on the floor. The crumpled blanket on the chair, the slightly drooping houseplant in the corner of the room, wanting water.

The hours passed and Dora's hand was aching but she couldn't stop. Is this what the girl in the red shoes felt like? She wondered as she finally finished and washed her hands in the kitchen sink.

It was becoming dark and she wondered if she should make something for dinner. Her appetite was back and she even thought she might heat up some of the lovely fish pie that Peony had dropped off for her and Anthea the day before. It would be nice with a little iceberg lettuce and some tomatoes, she thought.

Opening the refrigerator, she took out the pie and turned on the oven as she heard Cat hiss.

'What is it? You've had dinner,' she said, turning, expecting to see Cat behind her.

'Hello Dora,' she heard and she turned to see Barry standing in the kitchen doorway. Cat sat on the kitchen table, his hackles raised.

'It's time to come home,' Barry said.

Izzy

'Where are we going?' Izzy asked Joe as they drove towards Cirencester.

'There's a nice little Thai place I think we should try,' he said and he glanced at her and smiled.

She gave a weak smile in return and looked out of the window at the coming darkness outside.

'You OK?' Joe asked her and she nodded.

'Yes, fine.'

'Are you in pain?' he asked her.

Izzy touched her shoulder. 'No, not really.'

Taking her phone out of her bag, she checked it and saw nothing on the screen.

She texted Connor. **Clover OK?** She typed and pressed send.

'Sorry, just checking in on Clover,' she said to Joe.

'Is she OK?'

'I think so, I just have a weird feeling, I can't explain it.' She brushed down her jeans and checked her phone again.

'Do you want to head home and check on her?' he asked.

'No, it's fine, I'm just being a hovering aunt,' she tried to laugh but it seemed to get caught in her throat and she coughed instead.

A text came through on her phone.

Clover's fine. But call me

Izzy looked at Joe. 'I have to call Connor, do you mind?'

'Of course not,' he said with a smile.

Izzy pressed Connor's number and waited for him to answer.

'Hey, what's going on?' she asked.

The uneasiness was still sitting with her as she listened to Connor.

'Anthea and Rob came over … she's buying the apples, all of them,' he said.

'No way? Why? What for?'

'Well she's also buying the cidery, she's asked me to go in with her on the deal. She's going to turn Spindle Hall into a winery but is starting with cider while the vines grow.'

'Oh my God Connor, that's amazing.'

'It gets better, she's offering me twenty per cent on the cider as a co-owner.'

'Seriously? That's incredible, it's going to be so good. Finally you can have your own drink, how incredible. Is she there, can I talk to her?'

'No, she left really suddenly, not sure what was going on, but she seemed to panic and ran outside telling Rob to drive to Spindle Hall,' he said.

'What's happened?' She felt her stomach twist as he spoke.

'Nothing, I mean she was leaving anyway but she spoke to Clover who showed her a picture she drew, just one of Clo's scary dream pictures, nothing real.'

The chill draped over Izzy's body. 'What was the drawing of?' she asked.

There was a pause. 'Dora's at Spindle Hall isn't she?' he asked.

'Yes.'

'Does Barry know?'

'No, why?'

'Because Clover said she saw a man in the house waiting for Dora.'

Izzy turned to Joe. 'Turn around, we need to go to Spindle Hall, I think Dora's in danger.'

'Call the police,' she said to Connor. 'We're on our way.'

She ended the call and looked at Joe. 'Clover drew a picture of a man inside Spindle, waiting for Dora.'

'OK?' Is she psychic?' he half joked.

'I don't know, I just know she knows things. It's hard to explain.'

Joe sped up. 'Medicalised children often are observers, perhaps she sees the small stuff that we don't.'

'Maybe,' said Izzy. 'But she's been right about things before, it's hard to explain.'

He turned his lights on high beam as a huge hare ran into the middle of the road and then jumped into the darkness.

'Call Anthea,' he said.

Izzy dialled the number but Anthea didn't answer.

The car was flying through the roads now, and as they got towards Honeystone, Izzy felt faint as they came closer to the house.

'If he hurts her, I'll kill him,' she said to Joe as he turned onto the road and made his way to Spindle Hall.

In the distance they could see Spindle in the little valley and the lights were on, looking unassuming and quiet.

'Do we wait for the police?' Joe asked at the start of the driveway.

'Let's just go up to the house and see what's happening,' she said and Joe turned down his lights and drove slowly and quietly up to the house.

Anthea's car was there but she wasn't inside it and Izzy and Joe got out of the car and looked around. 'Use the torch on your phone,' he said to her and they then walked around the side of the house.

Anthea and Rob were standing in the kitchen.

'Where is she?' asked Joe, looking around.

Anthea looked at Joe.

'He's in the hall,' she said, her face ashen and drawn. Rob went to speak but Izzy and Joe pushed past them and walked into the hallway and there was Barry, on the floor, his neck at a terrible angle, clearly dead.

'Jesus,' said Izzy, as Joe bent down to check his pulse but it was a fruitless exercise.

'Where's Dora?' he said, standing up and looking around.

Anthea came out into the hall, saw Barry and turned away and went back into the kitchen. 'I don't know, I have no idea,' she said.

Joe grabbed Rob. 'We need to find her. She has to be around here, she can't have got very far.'

Izzy grabbed a throw from the sofa in the living room and laid it over Barry.

'Dora?' Joe called with Rob following. They went upstairs and through the house and checked every room but there was nothing.

'She can't have gone far,' said Izzy. 'She's on foot.'

'No, I think she's taken the runabout,' said Anthea. 'It's missing.'

Joe grabbed his keys and turned to Izzy. 'You stay here for the police. I'm going to find Dora.' He raced from the house and into his car.

Izzy went back inside and looked at the shape of Barry under the blanket as Rob came to her side.

'Do you think she killed him?' she whispered.

Rob shook his head. 'I have no idea, I mean I wouldn't have thought so but we don't know what happened.' He looked up at the top of the stairs. 'Maybe he fell?'

'Or maybe she pushed him,' Izzy said and turned to see Anthea behind them, her arms around an ashen faced Dora.

Peony

Connor sat in his chair and looked at Peony.

'Did you set that up?' he asked her.

Peony shook her head, 'Nope, I mean I mentioned the cidery was for sale, and she seemed keen.' She smiled at him sweetly. And he laughed.

'Well I'm not mad, because it really does fix everything, so thank you,' he said.

'Oh Connor, you so deserve this, it's perfect for you, like

all this knowledge and hard work have finally come to fruition, excuse the pun.'

He smiled, and she wondered if his shining eyes had tears of relief in them.

'Can I have a hot chocolate?' asked Clover to Peony.

She looked down at the little girl and adjusted her glasses so they were straight on her little nose.

'That's a question for your daddy, my love.'

Clover looked at her father, 'Daddy?'

'Fine,' Connor sighed and he looked at Peony curiously. 'Would you like a hot chocolate?'

Peony nodded, 'Absolutely, why don't I come and help make them, and Clover you keep my seat free in case anyone tries to steal it.'

Peony followed him into the kitchen, and as they walked inside he turned to her and stood close.

'Peony Grayling,' he said and he saw her eyes widen. 'You changed my life tonight.'

She said nothing, her eyes blinking quickly.

'You changed my life when I was seventeen and then I fucked it up because I thought I didn't need anyone, I was trying to be everything for Izzy and I pushed you away and I am so deeply sorry that we are both here now with all those wasted years in between.'

Still, she said nothing but he wasn't needing her to speak. He had more than ten years of things to say to her.

'But instead, we went on different paths, me with Clover and you with your little one.' He looked down at her stomach and she put her hand on it.

He put his hand on top of hers.

'And I think that what happened was meant to be, like Clover and this one, this one that I want to be a part of.'

She leaned forward and before he could continue, she had kissed him, a gentle kiss, a suggestion or a hint almost.

'What was that for?' he asked.

'You just kept talking and I wanted you to kiss me,' she said.

'You always said I didn't talk enough about my feelings and now I'm talking too much?' he laughed.

'Yes, well I know, but I have wanted to kiss you for so long and I have been pretending I didn't, it's very tiring pretending you don't want things when you want everything,' she said.

Connor laughed and pulled her closer. 'I have wanted to kiss you since you came screaming into my driveway about how we broke up.'

She laughed, 'That was Izzy's doing, up to no good as usual.'

'And yet, here we are,' he said and his hands ran up her back and hers around his neck.

Connor leaned forward now and they kissed again, and this time it was a hungry promise of a kiss that they both felt.

'Here we are,' said Connor touching her face. 'I've loved you since I was a teenager, Peony, and I haven't loved any woman since. Though I have Clover, and I am grateful to Mel for that, both of us knew it wasn't forever. But you, you're my forever.'

'What about the baby?' she asked.

'I will love that child the same way you love Clover, which I see when you look at her. All encompassing, big, crazy love.'

The sound of Peony's phone ringing interrupted them and she grabbed it and showed Connor that it was Izzy calling.

Peony answered the phone and put it on speaker. 'You OK?' she asked. 'I'm here with Connor.'

'No, Barry's dead, we're at Spindle Hall.' Izzy's voice was shaking and they could hear police sirens in the background.

'Is Dora, OK?' Peony asked.

'She won't say what happened. The police are here.' Izzy's voice broke.

Peony looked at Connor. 'You go, I'll stay with Clover.'

'I'm on my way,' he said to Izzy and Peony ended the call.

'You sure?' he asked her.

'Yes, I'm not able to handle that, not in this state,' she said. 'Go and see what's happening and let me know.'

Connor stood up. 'OK, back soon. You sure you're OK with Clo?'

'Go, we're fine, I promise and look after Dora for me.'

Peony sat at the table, thinking about Barry and Dora. Life was so short and you can't waste time. She picked up her phone and dialled a number and waited for the beep to leave a message.

'Fergus, let me know what you want to do about the baby. I will tell your mother about it because she deserves to know she has a grandchild, even if you don't want to be a father. I don't expect anything from you but know, one day, that child will come looking for you, and you will have to be prepared for that moment. Your choice is yours to make but I won't be asking for anything in return but a decision. Are you in or out?'

She put down the phone as Clover came into the kitchen and looked at her decidedly displeased.

'Daddy left,' she said.

'Yes, he had to check on something at Anthea's house,' she smiled at the little girl.

'And we don't have hot chocolate.' Clover said.

'I know, terrible of me. Now you sit here and I'll make it for us, with extra marshmallows.'

She set about making the hot chocolate when her phone rang and she saw it was Fergus. Nothing like threatening to tell his formidable mother to get a man moving.

'I just have to take this darling,' she said to Clover and she took the phone and went into the living room.

'Fergus, nice of you to check in on us.' She couldn't help the acidic words forming in her mouth.

'Peony, I've made a huge mistake,' he said, his voice strained.

Was he crying? What on earth was happening? The only time Peony had seen Fergus cry was when Scotland had bowed out of the Rugby World Cup early in 2019.

'What mistake?' she asked, feeling incredibly calm, looking at Clover's drawing book on the table and leafing through the sweet images of the child's imagination.

'Us, I shouldn't have let us go, I want to be with you, Peony, let's get married and have our little bairns.'

Peony turned the page and saw the drawing of the wedding cake. She noticed the big roses around and on it, the little naively drawn apples, and there were the chickens around the edge. On top was a man and a woman who had a baby in her arms. Peony felt as though the air was being pulled out of her, but where was Clover?

She looked over the very crowded drawing and finally she saw her. Clover was in the corner, a wooden spoon in one hand and wearing a chef's hat. Clover had baked the cake for them.

Peony felt tears forming and she bit her lip to stop herself from sobbing.

'I'm sorry Fergus, I'm getting married to someone else,' she said. 'I'll send you some information on the baby and when it's due but us, we're done. Completely finished.'

And she ended the call and wiped her eyes on her sleeve and took a deep breath.

'OK, two marshmallows or three?' she called out down the hallway.

'Three!' Came the reply from the little girl who could see it all before anyone else in Honeystone.

There was change in the air yet again but this time, Peony was ready for whatever was coming because it felt like everything good was waiting around the corner.

Dora

'I didn't kill him,' Dora said to the faces as the sound of police sirens became louder in the distance.

'What happened? Where were you?' Izzy asked her.

Dora looked at her feet where Cat was circling them in a figure of eight.

'I went to my house today, I took your farm car, Anthea, I'm sorry.'

'Why did you go to the house? Barry would have been there,' Izzy asked.

'I texted him from my new phone and told him there was a job interview at the council in Cirencester.' She looked down, ashamed.

Izzy raised her eyebrows at her. 'Sneaky move, and he believed it?'

'Barry would always believe what he thought he was owed. He thought the council should give him a job, so he wanted to believe it. Then he got there and I assume they said he was deluded so he drove home again but I was gone by then.'

Anthea shook her head, 'So how did he know you were here?'

Dora swallowed. 'I took a shopping bag that was on the bench here and a hammer to break the glass to get inside.'

'What was so important?' Joe asked.

'The deeds to the house. You see, it belongs to me. I was given the house when we married and we never changed it over. I mean Barry wanted to but then he became worse over the years and I told him I had gone to the bank and changed the title but I hadn't, I forged it. The house is still mine at the title's office.'

'God, that's a lot of work,' said Izzy.

Dora glanced at Barry's body. 'Being married to him was a lot of work.'

'And then what?' Rob asked her.

'When I opened the shopping bag, it was sort of crinkled and I shook it, there was an order in it from Anthea from Mabel's. It fell out at the house and I didn't realise,' she said. 'I went to his study and I got all the paperwork and then I sent some emails to you, Anthea, to show I wasn't about to be pushed around.' She glanced again at the body.

'And then I came here and I had a lovely time with the dogs, I even started drawing,' she said, hearing her voice shake. 'And then I turned around in the kitchen and he was there.'

She saw Izzy's hand fly up to her mouth.

'He told me it was time to go home and I said no. It was the first time I've ever said no to him and he was furious.'

Dora tried to remember clearly but it all felt jumbled up in her head.

'And then I told him about how I knew he was fired for taking money from his clients and they decided not to press charges if he paid it back, which he was doing, through me working two jobs.'

Anthea looked at Rob and back to Dora. 'That's terrible, and so unfair, Dora.'

'Yes, and then I said the house was still in my name and he would have to leave and if he didn't I would go to the police and report all the abusive things he's done to me, because Anthea, I read those articles you printed out for me, and Joe, I called those women's safety lines and he was abusive, and I didn't know. It's called coercive control.'

Joe nodded. 'Yes, that's right. It is.'

Dora turned and walked into the kitchen, away from Barry's body and sat at the table as everyone joined her.

'Then he lashed out at me and tried to grab my hair so I ran. I know it was stupid but I ran upstairs, I should have run outside, but I thought I could lock myself in my room, which is where I left my phone, and call Anthea.

'But he grabbed me by my leg as I ran up the stairs and I tried to kick him but Cat,' She paused. 'Cat came from nowhere and lashed at him so viciously, his claw was in Barry's eye and then went down the side of his face, and he screamed and then lost his footing.'

It felt like she wanted and needed to cry but the tears wouldn't come.

'And he went down the stairs and landed like that. I knew as soon as I looked at him that he'd broken his neck.'

The kitchen was silent and Anthea left the room. The guilt wept through Dora, knowing how kind Anthea had been to her and she'd paid her back by killing a man in her house.

'And I panicked. I thought everyone would think I killed him. So, I took the car and I drove, but I didn't know where I was going and the car didn't have much petrol and I didn't have any money. I came back and I suppose I will wait for the police. They will charge me and I will go to jail for murder. And I deserve it, because perhaps I did kill him in my own way. Abandoning him and then threatening him.'

Joe left the room and came back with another throw rug and put it around Dora's shoulders. 'You're in shock.'

'You didn't abandon him,' said Izzy. 'He forced you to leave and you told him the truth about the house and why he left his job. That was on him, not on you.'

'Police,' Dora heard and she looked up and saw several police walking into the kitchen.

'Arrest me. I killed my husband,' Dora said to them.

Anthea's voice came through the kitchen. 'No, she didn't and I have the evidence.' She held up a USB stick and handed it to the first policewoman closest to her.

'Everything you need to see is on here.'

Dora looked at Anthea. 'What do you mean?'

'I mean everything you said is true about what happened and the reason I know that is because I have a security system throughout the house that films when I'm not home. I assumed I had turned it off but you were here and it recorded it all. It's exactly as you said it was, and I am so deeply sorry that it ended like this for you and for Barry, but you didn't kill anyone, OK?'

Anthea was next to her, bent down and rubbing her back and Dora felt the tears coming.

'You need to have a huge cry for as long as you need. It's good for you. I cry all the time now.' Anthea's words soothed Dora, and with the touch of Anthea's hands on her back, she felt herself soften into the hardest moment of her life.

'I'm so sorry,' she kept repeating to herself, like a mantra but she wasn't even sure who she was apologising to. Anthea Barry, or most of all, herself.

Izzy leaned down and picked up Cat. 'I did always have

enormous respect for you, Cat, but you have surpassed my expectations.'

'Izzy,' said Joe. 'That's terrible.'

But she shrugged. 'Cat saved her life. Who knows what Barry would have done to her? And for that, I thank you.' And she kissed the top of Cat's head.

Everyone looked at the cat who purred in his moment of glory.

There was a reason he had come to Spindle Hall and now everyone finally knew why.

14

Izzy

Tragedy has a way of pushing people towards life and to direct them towards possibilities that they might have previously thought were out of reach.

For Izzy, being in the presence of a dead body was her defining moment to move towards everything she was frightened of in life.

After she and Joe had left Spindle Hall it was close to four in the morning. Dora had been to the police station and left after giving a statement. Barry's body had been taken by the coroner after the police had taken photos and the video Anthea had supplied. Rob had accompanied Dora to the police station and then returned hours later with Dora and put her to bed.

Finally, Anthea said she needed sleep and she and Rob went upstairs. Connor had already left so Izzy and Joe set off together.

'Can we go back to yours?' she asked him.

Joe glanced at her. 'OK,' he said but he sounded uncertain.

Izzy was silent as they drove towards Honeystone, trying to put the memory of Barry out of her mind but he seemed to be stuck on pause.

Joe parked at the front of the surgery and looked at Izzy.

'I'm really tired, Izz, so if you want to sleep then that's all I can offer you.'

Izzy shook her head. 'I don't want to stay for any other reason than I need to be with someone and you're the one here right now.'

Joe opened the car door and they walked up to the front door and he turned to her.

'Izzy, I know you like me and I like you but I don't want to have a relationship while I'm here.'

Izzy went to speak but he held up his hand. 'I don't want a relationship with you because I will fall in love, I know it. You're fierce and funny and you're a joy to be around and if I was here to stay, I would never want to let you go ... but I'm going to leave in a year and you want to stay, and I can't get my heart tangled up with you, I'm sorry.'

Izzy smiled. 'You like to overcomplicate things. I just didn't want to sleep alone. I wasn't asking for marriage.'

Joe laughed as he opened the door. They went upstairs and Joe opened the bedroom door.

'I'm nine years older than you,' he continued. 'You need to see the world and travel and be crazy, not hang out with me. I mean, once I travel I will probably head back to Australia and settle down. And you'll get bored and then we will split up and it will be a big mess.'

Izzy shook her head. 'God, you've already written our story and ending and we haven't even kissed. Calm down.'

'But it's true, you need to go and live your life, not hang out with me because I'm here.'

Izzy snorted her disdain.

They went upstairs and Joe turned on a lamp.

'You can sleep in the bed, I'll sleep on the sofa.' Joe said.

★

As soon as Izzy's head landed on the pillow, she was asleep, her dreams turbulent and haunting. Visions of Dora's face, the police lights, Barry's body lying still, were intertwined with images of her parents, Clover in hospital, Anthea and Peony and Connor. In the twilight state between awake and asleep, she saw herself standing on the village's edge, her heart pounding, and her gaze fixed on a vast horizon as though everything she knew would fall away from her if she took a single step forward.

Honeystone was home but it was also time to go out into the unknown world beyond the comforting embrace of the village.

When she finally came to, the morning light filtering through Joe's bedroom window, Izzy found herself in a contemplative mood. Last night had stirred something within her. Dora's life, a tale of unfulfilled dreams and stifled ambitions, had struck a chord deep within Izzy. The fear of ending up like Dora, trapped by her own hesitations and insecurities, was a chilling thought.

But she realised that it was more than just her bond with Clover that held her back.

The truth was that Izzy was scared – scared of stepping out of Honeystone's protective boundaries, scared of venturing into the great unknown without Connor and Clover to look after. They were her anchor and reason but it wasn't until Anthea came to Honeystone that Izzy had started to have a life outside of Raspberry Hill Farm.

Izzy could hear Joe making tea in the kitchenette and she swung her feet over the edge of the bed, opened the door and walked out into the living area.

'Morning,' she said.

Joe turned to her and smiled.

'How are you feeling?' he asked.

'Pretty rotten, I had terrible dreams.' She said and sat on the sofa and tucked her feet underneath her.

'Just your mind trying to process everything,' he said.

She nodded and took the tea that he offered her.

'Can I ask a question?'

Joe looked at her, 'Of course.' He bought his own tea to the table and sat in an armchair.

'When you decided to travel, were you scared?'

'Of what?' he asked with a confused look.

'I don't know, not having family with you, not having everything familiar around you?'

Joe smiled at Izzy. 'You know, I think the fear of the unknown is something we all grapple with when we consider travelling. Will I be safe? Will I have enough money? What if I get sick or hurt or don't find work. It's a perfectly normal feeling, and I'd be lying if I said I didn't feel it when I first started to travel when I was younger.'

He took another sip of his tea. 'Leaving behind the safety of everything familiar, including Clover, is a big step, but it's precisely that step that can lead to some of the most profound experiences of your life.'

Joe leaned forward, and Izzy saw a glint of excitement in his eyes. 'Imagine waking up in a new place, with every day offering a chance for adventure, learning, and self-discovery. No one knows you, no one has opinions about you, what you should be doing or being, instead you get to define your own path, explore your own interests, find out who you are and what your values are.'

Izzy sighed. 'I have no idea who I am or what I want in life. All I am good at is gardening and looking after Clover.'

'That's not true, I think you just haven't had the opportunity to do anything else. So how do you know what else you can do?'

They sat in silence, drinking their tea for a while.

'There will be moments of fear and doubt, but it's all part of the journey. You'll discover strength within yourself that you never knew you had, and you'll find that you're never truly alone because the world is full of kind souls and potential friends. It's a leap of faith, but it's one that can lead to a life filled with beauty, connection, and self-growth if you let it.'

Izzy smiled at him, 'You sound like you're pushing me out of the nest. What if I fall?' she said, thinking of her dream of her standing on the edge of Honeystone village.

'But, Izzy Hinch, what if instead, you fly?'

Peony

Peony woke as Connor was lifting her from the sofa where she had been sleeping and he carried her to his bed and took off her shoes and lay her down and covered her up and slipped in beside her.

They slept heavily, not touching and yet she had never felt closer to him.

When she woke, she could hear Clover and Connor in the kitchen.

Reluctantly she climbed from the bed and looked at the time on the little wind-up travel clock on Connor's side. Of course, he would use a clock like this, she thought, noting it was nearly ten in the morning. His old-fashioned ways had once annoyed her but age meant she understood why he held onto things that worked perfectly well.

She was supposed to be cooking lunch at the pub but didn't know if she could manage it after last night. Besides, she didn't want to have to hear all the gossip from everyone when it was all so terribly sad.

She went to the bathroom and brushed her hair using Clover's little brush and cleaned her teeth with toothpaste and her finger. That would have to do, she told herself and she went into the kitchen, where Connor and Clover were sitting at the table looking at a magazine.

'Good morning,' she said to them both.

'You stayed the night,' Clover informed her.

'I did,' she smiled at her. 'Daddy said you were very tired and I wasn't to go into the room when you slept but I did anyway.'

'Clover,' Connor told her off but Clover ignored him.

'You were sleeping like this.' Clover opened her mouth halfway and closed her eyes. 'And you made this noise.' She took in some guttural breaths.

'Great, good to know.' Peony shook her head and laughed.

'It's OK, because sometimes Daddy does loud farts in his sleep.'

Connor rolled his eyes. 'Clover, is nothing sacred with you?'

'I don't know what that means,' she said and pushed the magazine towards Peony. 'This is my school uniform book, did you want to see? I can wear trousers, shorts or a skirt or a dress. I think I should get one of each in case I feel different on different days.'

Peony sat down and looked at the book of options. 'It's all very smart, isn't it? The red and blue will suit your dark chestnut hair. It's so shiny.'

Clover smiled at Peony. 'Is it nice?'

'Nice? It's the sort of hair that I would love to have, not this thin sad mop,' she said, touching her hair.

Clover seemed pleased with the compliment and she touched the hair on her shoulder.

'Daddy, did my mummy have hair like me?' she asked.

Connor nodded. 'She did.'

Peony glanced at him and he looked at her.

'Do you think about your mum often, Clover?' he asked.

Clover turned the page of the catalogue and looked at the various types of school bags. 'Not really,' she said. 'She's somewhere, she knows where I am.'

Peony watched Clover's face as she spoke and saw she was unencumbered by any sadness. She saw it as it was: her mother was somewhere else and maybe she would come back one day and maybe she wouldn't. For now, it was enough for Clover to process.

'I should go and check the apples, now that they've been sold to Anthea,' he said. 'Izzy isn't here, I assume she's with Joe.'

Clover's head shot up. 'She's with Dr Fisher? Why? Is she sick?'

Peony and Connor exchanged smiles. 'No, they're friends. Probably having breakfast together.'

'Like you and Daddy are friends.'

'Yes, that's right,' Connor said.

'You could get married and live here and Izzy could live with Joe,' Clover said.

'We could,' Connor said and he caught Peony's eye and she laughed.

'Look at you two, making plans as though you haven't got a thing else to do.' She stood up. 'I'm going to go back to the pub and see Dad and check on things and shower. Come for dinner later?' she asked Connor. 'With Clo?'

'What's for dinner?' asked Clover.

'I don't know yet, what do you feel like?'

Clover thought for a moment, her little face turned up to the ceiling, concentrating. 'Roast chicken please.'

'Done,' said Peony and she leaned down and kissed the child's head and walked to the front door, picking up her bag and the keys where Connor had left them.

'She's very insistent, I'm sorry,' Connor said with a smile and he pulled Peony to him. 'I don't know where she gets it from.'

Peony laughed. 'I have no idea.' And she kissed him, her arms wrapping around him and pressing into him, as though trying to absorb him into her.

'By the way, Fergus rang me last night,' she said in his ear.

Connor stepped back so he could see her face but his arms were around her waist.

'And what did that idiot have to say for himself?'

She sighed. 'He told me he'd made a huge mistake and he wants us to be together and get married.'

Connor's mouth dropped open and he gasped. 'And what did you say in return?'

Peony bopped his nose with her finger. 'I told him he's too late. I'm getting married to someone else but he's more than welcome to get to know his child when it's born.'

'Getting married? To whom?' Connor asked, his voice panicked.

'To you, you goose.' She paused. 'As soon as you ask me. I figured we've wasted enough time now.'

Connor nodded, relieved. 'You're right.'

'I know, I'm always right. Well, mostly. I'll see you tonight?'

'Yes, and every night afterwards,' he said.

15

The funeral took place in a dimly lit and sombre funeral parlour in town. There were large brass vases filled with fake lilies that needed dusting and the sound of hymns being played by an organ greeted the mourners as they arrived, except it was a recording of an organ.

Izzy was sitting alone, waiting for Joe who was parking the car when a man came up to her.

'Excuse me, I'm the new celebrant for the day as the one booked has had to beg off sick. I am not really very familiar with the man who we are celebrating today, I have the notes but not much else.'

Izzy raised her eyebrows at the word 'celebrating'. But she was here for Dora and that was all.

'OK,' she said to the man. 'I'm sure it will be fine, there isn't much to say about him really.' She was careful with her words, keeping her promise to Dora that she wouldn't reveal the secret to anyone about Barry's unfortunate death.

'One thing,' the celebrant said.

Izzy narrowed her eyes, hoping he wouldn't ask about how Barry died.

'His name is Barry, is Barry short for anything?'

Izzy thought for a moment and then smiled, 'Barold.' She said and the man wrote it down on his notes.

'Barold Mundy, yes?'

'It's pronounced Monday,' she said with a sombre nod.

'Right, thank you,' said the man and he scuttled off to a door behind the Gothic looking lectern.

Joe came in and sat next to her.

'Who was that?'

'Just the celebrant,' said Izzy. 'Just telling me we're going to start soon.'

And she crossed her legs and clasped her bag in her lap and thought, that one is for you Dora.

The atmosphere was heavy with an uncomfortable silence, as if the patterned wallpapered walls themselves bore the weight of the unspoken truths of the lies about Barry Mundy. Lies until the end, Izzy thought as she sat next to Joe on an uncomfortable banquet chair.

A handful of mourners, the ones who had known Barry during his life, were present. Anthea and Rob, Izzy and Joe, Peony and Connor, Jenn Carruthers, Ajay and Mala were there. They had come to support Dora, even though her presence was notably absent.

Dora had chosen not to attend the funeral. Instead, she stayed behind with Clover, who had become her new friend. Dora felt no obligation to be part of the farewell to a man who had brought her so much pain and heartache she had told Rob when he offered to organise the funeral.

The organ music faded and the celebrant stood up behind the lectern and leaned into the microphone.

'Today we celebrate the life of Barold Monday, may he rest in peace.' Izzy looked down at her hands, trying not to laugh.

She glanced around and saw everyone stifling a giggle and Anthea and Peony staring at her, their cheeks sucked in trying to keep their laughter inside them.

Thankfully the service was brief, lasting just twenty minutes, with a celebrant, stood at the front of the room talking about the noble character of Barold Monday and all he did for Honeystone village. For a moment, Izzy wondered if she was at the funeral of someone else, because Barold sounded like a terrific fellow.

Then the celebrant offered a small prayer, one that asked for forgiveness for Barold's sins and encouraged those present to be kind to each other, as if the mere act of being there was an act of mercy itself for those who had attended.

In the sterile and impersonal setting of the funeral parlour, there was no mention of how Barry had died or the abuse that Dora had endured during her marriage. The painful truths that had marked their life together remained shrouded in silence. It was as though the funeral sought to sweep those dark chapters under the rug, a final act of denial accompanied by dusty fake flowers and a pretend organ playing him off to his next destination.

Afterwards, Jenn, Ajay and Mala went back to Honeystone to open the tea rooms for the afternoon and the rest went to a local pub in Cheltenham and with a drink in hand, they sat in silence.

The group was quiet until Rob cleared his throat and lifted his glass. 'To Barold Monday, he sounded like a grand fellow whoever he was, because that certainly wasn't Barry Mundy he was talking about.'

The group fell about laughing in hysterics.

Izzy cried with laughter, wiping her eyes.

'When he asked me what Barry was short for, I couldn't help it. It was too easy and besides, it was easier to sit through the funeral of a made-up man than the real one.'

No one could disagree with this fact. Rob raised his

glass. 'To Barold Monday, wherever he is now,' he said and everyone joined in and raised their glasses.

'I'm starving,' said Izzy to Rob.

'You know the old saying,' Rob said.

Izzy shook her head, 'No? Do I?'

Rob took a sip of his wine. 'Sorrow is dry and sympathy is hungry. Time we got some food into us.'

'You're turning into Clary with your old sayings,' she laughed.

'Gosh I hope not, she told Anthea to wrap the skin of an eel around her leg to stop cramps, after she mentioned them in passing to Clary at the pub.' Rob said as Izzy noticed Peony hold Connor's hand.

'Actually, we have some good news,' Connor said as Peony tapped on her glass with the end of a knife. He seemed shy, nervous even and Izzy felt a deep prideful love for her annoying brother.

They all looked at him. 'Peony and I are getting married,' he said.

Izzy smiled as the cries of celebration and congratulations came to the couple and she saw Anthea wipe away a little tear.

'Oh, I love a wedding,' said Anthea and she looked at Rob. 'Don't get any ideas, I'm not planning on marrying again anytime soon.'

Rob laughed, 'I wasn't planning on asking,' he said.

'Rude,' Anthea poked her tongue out at him. 'When are you thinking?' she asked the couple.

Peony looked at Connor and then back to Anthea. 'Actually, we're going to do it sooner rather than later. I don't want to be a whale on my wedding day, and we figured, we've waited too long anyway,' Peony said.

Connor smiled at his bride to be. 'We were thinking a July afternoon at the farm.'

They sipped their drinks and chatted about the wedding and Peony's baby and Anthea buying the cidery.

'It's funny to think so many good things can be happening and yet we just went to a funeral for someone, an awful person. The good and the bad seem to be always close together,' Izzy said to Rob.

'That's the nature of a dualistic world,' said Rob and everyone looked at him.

'You know, it's like if we never go through those cold, dark winters, we might not fully appreciate the sunny, warm days of summer. The reason we can feel so much joy at this news we have is because of the tough times that came before that.' He looked at Peony. 'Like you, being so unhappy for so long and so scared to leave and yet, here you are, finally understanding what it's like to know the simple pleasures of life and when you feel love.'

Rob looked at Anthea. 'And you, you turned your lessons into ideas of wisdom and brilliance. You're remarkable and only get stronger and wiser with each moment. Being around you is truly a gift. We can be happy and sad at the same time, because that's life and isn't it all so wonderful? This being alive business?'

'It really is,' Anthea said. 'It really bloody is.'

16

Izzy

It had been two months since Barry's funeral and life in Honeystone was settling into a new normal. Peony was planning the wedding and her love with Connor was stronger than ever. What was rewarding for Izzy to witness was the bond between Clover and Peony that had been there since the first time they met. Izzy was a wonderful aunt but Peony, she was a mother. The way she made things fun for Clover that Izzy used to struggle with like getting Clover into the bath. Peony would fill the bath up with warm water and bubbles and then pretend she was looking for something to go into the bath. In the end Clover would be jumping up and down begging to be put into the bath. It was brilliant and hilarious to watch and at no point did Izzy feel as though she was being replaced. Instead, she saw Clover just had another person to love her, and someone who wanted to be there forever for the right reasons.

Now Izzy sat on Anthea's sofa, eating cheese from the elaborate grazing board Anthea had served for just the two of them. In the centre of the wooden board lay an array of artisanal cheeses – creamy brie, marbled blue cheese, aged Cheddar, and crumbly goat's cheese. Some roasted nuts provided a satisfying crunch that helped to ease the tension in Izzy's head, or maybe it was adding to it, she wasn't sure, while crackers and artisan bread were the perfect canvas for the cheese that were the stars of the platter. There were plump grapes, vibrant berries, and sweet figs, and some quince paste for good measure.

'This is insane, who else is coming?' asked Izzy as Anthea handed her a glass of Chablis.

'No one,' said Anthea, 'But I can't stop creating these boards. Peony helped me set it all up that's why it looks so good, but I've been sourcing all the goods, they're all local suppliers. I'm going to have these in the café when we open.'

Izzy smiled at Anthea's enthusiasm.

'How are the plans coming for the flower beds?' asked Izzy, sipping her wine.

'Wonderful, I've taken your advice on the direction of the sun for the roses, and I told the garden designers. They were a bit upset they hadn't thought of it to be honest but now I have room to plant some vines and one day, we will have a Spindle Hall vintage.' Anthea threw her head back and laughed. 'Gosh, how life has changed since I moved here, everyone is just really finding their way aren't they?'

Izzy was quiet. Holding her wine in one hand, she put down the cracker she was about to bite.

Anthea looked at Izzy, 'How is Joe?' she asked.

Izzy smiled and shook her head, 'Joe's fine but nothing is happening there.'

'Oh?' Anthea leaned forward. 'You seemed close at the pub the other night when I came to see Rob. Chatting away and looking at things on your phone.'

Izzy shrugged, 'We're friends, I mean there is an attraction, but we both said we didn't want to start anything we can't finish, because I think I like him too much to only spend a summer with him yet ...'

She paused.

'Yet you want to see the world.' Anthea finished for her.

Izzy frowned. 'How did you know? I'm actually looking for a job, because I want to travel. I need to save up some money, I have a little but not enough yet but I will if I can get some more work.'

Anthea put her wine down and came to sit next to Izzy on the sofa and took her hand in hers.

'I think everyone should travel if they can. I have travelled a lot and never regretted it, seeing great wonders of the world for the first time, or swimming in a new ocean, finding new food and friends, it's an amazing experience.'

Izzy nodded, 'Yes, I want to do it now. Joe said I might get some work as a nanny in Australia, which would be good because I could earn some money.'

Anthea shook her head. 'No, that won't do at all.'

Izzy laughed, 'Well it's not like I have a huge amount of work experience other than gardening, looking after children and occasionally slinging plates at the pub when Peony is busy.'

Anthea squeezed Izzy's hand. 'I am going to give you the money to travel now. I don't want it back so don't even pretend you are going to pay it, because I will just give it to charity.'

'What?' Izzy said. 'No, you can't.'

'I can do whatever I want. I have a lot of money, far too much to be honest and if I can't help you, support you, when you have been my first friend in Honeystone, the one who bought me to Rob and Peony and Clover and everyone else, then what can I do?'

'You met Rob outside of me and you would have met everyone anyway,' Izzy argued.

'Not true, the day you were mushrooming and we chatted and you told me about the flock of birds rhyme, I have said it every time I see a flock and surprises keep coming, and you, my little magic garden fairy, are my good luck charm.'

Izzy snorted in an unladylike fashion.

'So think of my travel fund like this, investment in you Miss Izzy Hinch so you can see the world through your particular lens and come back and tell me all the things you have learned and the people you have met, and all the foods you tasted and music you danced to.'

'I feel like I need to do something to earn it?' admitted Izzy. Taking anything from people had always been hard for her and money was near impossible.

'You can help me plan the garden before you go,' said Anthea. 'I need your knowledge of the land and soil and you can help me choose the roses and we can work with the gardening team. When did you want to leave?'

Izzy thought for a moment. 'After's Peony's baby comes. She's due at the end of November. Or maybe after Christmas? I don't know, there is always something I think I will miss out on.'

'Yes, but there's also things to experience in other places. And there will always be Honeystone and its particular goings on, don't worry about that.' She smiled at Izzy who nodded.

'I'm scared,' she admitted.

'I think it's less fear and more eustress,' said Anthea.

'What's eustress?' Izzy asked, picking up her wine again and eating the cracker she had put down earlier.

'It's a word my therapist told me, it's the feeling when you're anxious about something but you know it's going to make your life better, push you forward. It's positive stress in a way. You know that you have decided and there is no going back but gee the path ahead looks intimidating.'

'Then I have eustress,' said Izzy. 'I wonder if Joe has a cream for it?'

Anthea laughed.

'You make me laugh Izzy,' she paused. 'Do you think you could work for me up until Peony's baby is born? I'll pay you. Hell, I'll overpay you.'

Izzy thought for a moment and ate a very juicy grape. 'Yes, you know, I think I would like that very much.'

Anthea raised her glass. 'To eustress,' she said.

'To eustress – the goddess of good things to come even though you're absolutely terrified.'

17

The Wedding

While the idea of a lovely garden wedding in July seemed ideal for Peony and Connor, the weather was in charge on the day despite Clary throwing beetles over her shoulder the day before to ensure sunshine.

Which is why the dining room at The Hare and Thistle was covered in fresh pale pink roses and greenery and smelled of the flowers and roast duck and potatoes, with the distinct scent of fresh paint.

The renovations had finished a week before, and with a new sous chef, working under Peony's exacting eye and beautiful menu planning, the pub was already becoming popular with tourists. With the apples harvested for the cider and the new art gallery that Anthea was planning where Biddy's Bits and Bites used to be, it was as though Honeystone had finally come to life. Rob had managed to get the pub licenced to be a wedding venue and they had hired a celebrant from Cirencester named Sam, who had pink hair and a nose ring and the sort of joyous energy that Peony and Connor wanted for the day.

Peony had convinced her father to take down the old wall to the garden that had been put there in the 1960s and open up the garden to the customers.

Izzy did the landscaping of course and the pretty containers of daisies, herbs that Peony used in the cooking and several raised vegetable gardens with lovely lettuces and some tomatoes fruiting from Izzy's garden.

The wedding party was small, with Clover as the flower girl and official photographer on Peony's phone. Izzy was best woman, and Rob was giving Peony away on the way to the bar.

The guests included Dora, Joe, Clary and Old Ed, Jenn Carruthers, Ajay and Mala and a few friends from London and Connor and Izzy's aunt and uncle from Wales.

But it was enough to celebrate and while Peony had planned the menu, keeping things simple with roast duck, vegetables, salads and excellent wines chosen by her father, it was the cake that was the *pièce de résistance*.

Peony had taken Clover's drawing and had asked Ajay to replicate it as well as he could.

Peony knew Ajay was talented but this was extraordinary. A pale green iced three-tiered cake with her and Connor on top, although the baby was still inside thankfully.

Ajay had piped on the blousy big roses around the bottom and had made little fondant apples that dotted the cake. He had pressed on edible flowers and little clover leaves. There were small fluffy chickens from the craft shop that Dora had sourced for him from Cirencester, and finally, there was a little girl, in a chef's hat, holding a wooden spoon, as though conducting the entire moment.

The cake was layered vanilla and caramel sponge filled with pieces of broken butterscotch and meringue buttercream, and Peony knew Clover would be ecstatic.

And now all that needed to happen was to make the gravy for the duck and for Peony and Connor to get married.

'You ready?' asked Rob from outside Peony's bedroom above the pub.

'Yes, I think so,' she said and she opened the door to face her father.

The dress was a simple pale yellow silk slip dress, and her hair, thankfully thick and healthier from prenatal vitamins and pregnancy hormones, was pulled up into a simple messy bun, with small roses tucked in it and a long tea-coloured silk veil, so fine it could be mistaken for mist.

Her make-up was beautiful, and she wore her mother's pearl earrings and a spritz of the new perfume Anthea was testing at Spindle Hall. She couldn't help herself, she said to Peony, now her sense of smell was back she wanted to create again, but only for special people in her life. This scent was called Peony and was a mix of peony rose scent, damask rose, apricot and peach. It was the most delicious scent Peony had ever inhaled.

'You look so beautiful,' said Rob.

'Is my bump showing too much?' she asked, her hand running over the front of her dress.

'I can't see a thing yet,' said Rob and Peony looked down at her body.

'Doesn't matter anyway, it's not like we're trying to pretend I'm not up the duff.'

Peony went to the table and opened the box on top and lifted her bouquet from it. An armful of Peony roses, courtesy of Izzy, who'd managed to get some late blooms for the special day.

'Is Connor here?' she asked Rob.

'Yes, he's been here for an hour.' Rob laughed.

'Good, is Clover with him?'

'Yes, she's ordering everyone around. Dora's meeting us at the bottom of the stairs.'

Peony smiled and then tipped her head back and looked at the ceiling. 'Trying to make my tears fall back inside my eyes,' she said.

'Why are you sad, Sweet pea?' Rob asked.

'I'm not sad, Dad,' Peony said, looking at her father, and holding his gaze. 'I'm so happy I could burst. And I'm so happy you let me come home. You changed my life by letting me stay here and take over.'

Rob laughed, 'Oh darling, why would I not ever want you back in Honeystone? Of course I did, but it's selfish to want your children to stay somewhere for your benefit. You came home because you had to and you stayed because you wanted to.'

Peony nodded. 'Perhaps Connor and I had to have that time away from each other to come back to the other.'

'I think so, and I tell you what, my life has never been more exciting since you came back. I met Anthea, I have this wonderful pub I can be proud of run by my daughter, and a beautiful grandchild in Clover and another on the way. As old Will Shakespeare said, "My crown is called content, a crown that seldom kings enjoy."'

Peony hugged her dad. 'I wish Mum was here too, but I'm glad you're here to support me.'

'I also wish your mum was here, but I have the distinct feeling she wouldn't be thrilled to meet Anthea under the circumstances.'

Peony burst out laughing. 'Dad, you're hilarious. OK, I'm going to go and get married.'

Clover was waiting for them downstairs, in a beautiful pink linen dress with embroidered clovers on the hem, gifted by Anthea for the flower girl. Clover carried a small basket of rose petals and she beamed as Peony came down the stairs.

'You look so beautiful,' she said, her eyes wide behind her glasses.

'So do you,' said Peony to the little girl. 'Are you ready?'

Peony saw Rob nod at someone and then the sounds of Neil Young singing 'Harvest Moon' came out across the stereo and Peony couldn't stop the tears as the lyrics resonated deeper than they ever had before.

Clover was carefully dropping rose petals in Peony's path and as she came to her father she smiled at him, while Izzy stood to his side in a beautiful black dress with a black ribbon headband in her gamine hair.

Peony kept eye contact with Connor as she clung to Rob's arm and finally she was in front of him.

'Hello,' he said.

'Hello,' she replied shyly.

'Feel like being with me for the rest of your life?'

Peony smiled at him, tears falling without her realising. 'I don't think we've ever not been together, even when we were apart.'

'Ready?' whispered the celebrant.

'Yes,' they said in unison.

After the ceremony the skies cleared and the sun came out, as though to remind the Honeystonians that while they might think they can bend the world to their desires, Mother Nature was still in charge. Anthea, more cognisant than ever of how special it was to be alive, stood out in the garden of the pub looking at the blue sky.

'What a gorgeous wedding,' she heard and saw Izzy next to her, a glass of champagne in hand. 'Makes me think that maybe marriage isn't so bad if it starts out like this.'

Anthea smiled. 'Maybe, you have to choose wisely though, Dora and I can tell you the red flags to look out for.'

Izzy smiled ruefully. 'Yes, hard-won lessons I guess.'

'Who's learning lessons?' asked Peony, holding a plate with a large slice of cake and three forks.

'All of us, all the time.' Anthea said, taking a fork that Peony offered her.

'Everything is perfect,' said Izzy to Peony. 'And we are finally sisters.'

Peony laughed. 'None of its perfect and it doesn't matter. As long as I'm with Connor and Clo then everything is fine. And I am thrilled to finally have a sister,' she said.

Anthea took a forkful of cake and ate it. 'Oh this is really good,' she said. 'Maybe I'll invest in Ajay's business, people need to be buying from him.'

'Calm down, Richard Branson. So far you have over-hauled Biddy's Bits and Bites to the new Honeystone Art Gallery and are now creating a vineyard and distillery at Spindle Hall.'

Anthea shrugged. 'I just want everyone to know how wonderful Honeystone is.'

Izzy laughed. 'Remember when you didn't want to know anyone or speak to anyone? I reckon if we had another vote, you'd be voted mayor now and Rob would be out of a job.'

'I reckon Dad would give you the job if you asked for it,' said Peony. 'He only ever did it to annoy Barry.'

Anthea shook her head. 'No, I don't want any of that but I wish I could bottle that feeling, when I'm outside at Spindle Hall, drinking my tea, looking at the world waking up in the morning, the dogs running, chasing hares and rabbits and I see someone walking through the woods, giving me a wave and I wave back. I think I could name fifty-five favourite things I can see, smell and hear in this moment right now. All my life I forgot to look at the perfect moments that are happiness. The cup of tea, the laughter, the bee's legs covered in pollen, your wedding cake,' she looked at Peony.

'The sound of rain when you're going to sleep,' said Izzy.

'Taking your bra off after a long day of wearing it,' laughed Peony.

'Yes!' The women agreed.

'Clean sheets.' Izzy said.

'The smell of people's dinner coming from their houses on an evening walk,' Anthea said.

'Peeling a boiled egg in one go,' Peony added.

'Turning on lamps in the evening, I call it lamp o'clock,' Anthea said excitedly.

'I love that,' said Izzy. 'Lamp o'clock.'

'And I love you both, so much. You've changed my life for the better,' Peony declared, and she pulled them both into a hug.

Peony wiped a tear from her eye.

'You know my mum used to say to me, "Don't overlook the magic of ordinary moments, the perfect cup of tea, the first hint of spring, laughing until you're crying, being really present in a moment and feeling as if time has stopped, because you can see everything that matters in that moment. That's the stuff that matters." This,' she looked around at the women, 'this moment matters.'

Anthea took some cake on her fork and lifted it in a toast.

'To my beautiful friends, the extraordinary, ordinary women of Honeystone.'

Peony and Izzy did the same.

'To us,' they said in unison. 'The extraordinary, ordinary women of Honeystone.'

Acknowledgements

Thank you to my agent Tara Wynne at Curtis Brown for brilliant advice and clever pivots.

To Rhea Kurien, how nice to be back with you again. Thank you for loving my work so much.

To Tansy Gorman for reading, proofing, cheering, and supporting my work any way she can.

Credits

Kate Forster and Orion Fiction would like to thank everyone at Orion who worked on the publication of *The Honeystone Village Diaries* in the UK.

Editorial
Rhea Kurien
Sanah Ahmed

Copyeditor
Laura Gerrard

Proofreader
Laetitia Grant

Audio
Paul Stark
Jake Alderson

Contracts
Dan Herron
Ellie Bowker

Marketing
Ellie Nightingale

Design
Tomás Almeida
Joanna Ridley

Sales
Jen Wilson
Esther Waters
Victoria Laws
Toluwalope Ayo-Ajala
Rachael Hum
Ellie Kyrke-Smith
Sinead White
Georgina Cutler

Production
Ruth Sharvell

Operations
Jo Jacobs
Dan Stevens